By Reason Of

Also by M.R. Henderson

IF I SHOULD DIE

By Reason Of

M.R. Henderson

Doubleday & Company, Inc.
Garden City, New York, 1986

Library of Congress Cataloging-in-Publication Data

Henderson, M. R.
  By reason of.

  I. Title.
PS3558.E487B9 1986   813′.54   85-25230
ISBN 0-385-23399-X

For Leonard and Kay St. Clair,
and, of course, for Morrice.

By Reason Of

1

He flexed his hands to ease the cramped muscles. The nicotine stains on the first two fingers of his right hand were muddy yellow over grime permanently imbedded in the pores and around his chipped nails. His knuckles, scarred from countless times wrenches had slipped and hot manifolds had burned them, were hatched with indelible black lines. One knuckle was swollen and raw, and there was a deep, fresh gouge along the back of his hand where blood had dried to a crusty scab. Above it was a dark stain on the cuff of his yellow sport shirt. He felt it and found it was stiff and hard. Blood—too much to be from the scratch on his hand. He stared at it curiously, then pressed his palm to his temple when he couldn't remember how he'd gotten it.

He fought the knife edge of panic that always hovered just beyond reason. Relax. It didn't matter. It was a temporary lapse. It happened sometimes, and he knew it would pass, but with it would come the empty feeling, like a balloon with the air let out.

How long had he been sitting here? He looked at the dashboard clock. Two-thirty. Afternoon. It was still raining, but it wasn't dark enough for night. The car smelled like a garage locker room. No, it was him. How long had he been wearing these clothes? He reached for a cigarette, but his shirt pocket was empty. He patted the pockets of his windbreaker, then

checked the seat around him and the floor. When he didn't find
a pack he opened the glove compartment and pawed through
the contents without any luck. Finally he dug in the ashtray and
found a butt long enough to light. He pinched it between the
tips of his fingers as he sucked smoke greedily. He got two drags
on it before it scorched his calloused skin and he had to drop it
back in the ashtray.

He sat back, then slouched automatically when his hair
brushed the headliner. Had he been the kind of man who wore
hats, there'd be no room for one. He studied the rain-shrouded,
gray world outside. He saw wavery outlines of other cars and
realized he was in a parking lot. A vague memory broke
through his clouded thoughts. Janine . . . the rain . . . cold
. . . He shivered. He had to get warm. Mexico. He was on his
way to Mexico.

The key was in the ignition. He turned it and listened to the
steady throb of the Camaro's engine. He was good with me-
chanical things. He enjoyed making them work smoothly and
effortlessly. When he was a child other kids brought him their
broken toys, scooters with scraping wheels, and balky bicycles.
Later it was cars. He knew what was wrong with an engine by
listening to it, and he could tune one as finely as a musician did a
violin. It was a talent, people said. Maybe it was, but he liked
things to run well. He didn't like discord.

He turned on the headlights and windshield wipers, scowling
when wet, oily lines appeared on the glass. The blade needed
replacing. It should have been done before the rainy season
started. Regular maintenance was important. Suppressing his
annoyance, he turned the defroster fan on high and opened the
window beside him a half inch to keep the windows from fog-
ging. Then he shifted into reverse and backed slowly out of the
parking spot, watching both directions for other cars.

It was a supermarket parking lot. He saw the haze of lights
behind the big plate-glass windows and the red and white sign,
RALPH'S, as he followed the yellow exit arrows on the puddle-
pocked asphalt. At the street he turned right and blended into

the flow of traffic, knowing instinctively where he was and the direction to head.

He drove slowly, staying in the left lane to avoid puddles that were hubcap deep at some corners. The Valley was a swamp. He hated the Valley. He never should have come back. It was a mistake, he realized that now. He especially hated the San Fernando Valley when the winter rainy season hit. Freeway access ramps flooded so only high-cabbed trucks could get through, and water ran in the streets like rivers. And everything was made worse by crazy drivers rushing around like they did on sunny days, doing thirty through the water without even thinking about what would happen if the distributor got wet.

The faulty wiper blade irritated him, but he couldn't stop for a new one now. Besides, in this kind of a storm filling-station jocks would try to unload their old stock. Blades that had been sitting on the shelf all summer would probably be as cracked and dried out as this one. Maybe he'd outrun the rain before he got to San Diego.

Traffic was backed up half a block at the freeway access. When he got closer he saw that a Volkswagen had stalled when the driver was making a left turn onto the ramp. A Chevie trying to get past was stuck in two feet of water the storm drains couldn't carry off fast enough. Stupid bastards, served them right.

He pulled the Camaro out into the turn lane and passed the snarl, sending up a wake of water when he had to twist the wheel sharply to avoid a blue pickup truck that tried to squeeze out in front of him. The Camaro slewed, and he cursed its light weight. He'd never buy anything this light for himself. He liked solid, heavy cars he could depend on. He realized he was clenching the wheel so hard the sore on his knuckle had broken open and was oozing blood. He wiped it across his green work pants and snapped on the radio, changing stations until he found a traffic report.

The San Diego Freeway was blocked by an accident at Valley Vista. Only one lane of the eastbound Ventura was open between Laurel and Tujunga because of flooding. He'd have to take one of the canyons. Laurel would be fastest, but it would be jammed. The hell with it. He'd take Coldwater. It was full of curves and switchbacks, but that didn't worry him. All he wanted was to be in San Diego before dark so he'd get to Mexico in plenty of time to have a couple of drinks before he found a place to sleep.

It took him twenty minutes to get to the foot of the canyon. When he finally turned off Ventura Boulevard it was a relief to start up the serpentine road. He kept the Camaro under twenty miles an hour and hunched over the wheel so he could see through the windshield. Even with the headlights, the rain obscured everything but a few feet of wet pavement and the shimmering outlines of the trees that lost themselves in the fog-shrouded hills. He'd driven this way plenty of times, but not for a while. He recognized the fancy private school and the church. Beyond them the climb became steep. He shifted into second gear. It was a peculiar area. There were big houses set back behind walls and fences or secluded by foliage. There were smaller ones, too, rustic and woodsy, perched at the top of steep driveways, invisible, so you couldn't see them until you got right up to them.

The higher he went, the slower he had to drive. Swirling water poured along the road, spouting from newly carved gullies in the hillside and stained with mud. A rushing stream along the inside shoulder overflowed onto the blacktop in places so it was hard to see the faded yellow line marking the center of the road. He didn't recognize landmarks anymore. It was a wet, gray alien world.

From time to time mailboxes sprouted in the path of the headlights like water birds perched on slender legs guarding the private drives to invisible aeries. It couldn't be much farther to the summit. Maybe the freeway would have been faster. Coldwater would dump him out in Beverly Hills, and he'd still have to drive across half the damned city to pick up a freeway going south. Cursing, he tapped the brakes and came to a stop as a burst of storm smothered the car in fog and rain. He couldn't see the damned road. The rain was pounding the car so hard, the windshield wipers couldn't keep up with the shimmering gray sheet. After a few minutes, as suddenly as it hit, the cloudburst eased to a steady downpour once more. He rubbed a spot clear of moisture on the window beside him and watched the river of muddy water splash and separate as it hit the front wheels. He put the car in gear again and crept on. The car slewed, veering to the shoulder before the tires gained purchase on the slick pavement. He concentrated, holding the wheel lightly so he could feel the car's response. It was sluggish. The carburetor needed cleaning.

He got about a hundred feet before the rain slashed viciously again. He stopped and waited for it to let up. It went that way for ten minutes. Move, wait. Move, wait. Was he near Mulholland? It couldn't be far.

He cocked his head, scowling as the engine missed. He shifted to neutral and pressed the gas pedal lightly. The engine missed again and sputtered. His gaze swept the dashboard gauges. The fuel needle was on empty. He swore and steered to the shoulder, getting the car as far off the pavement as possible before the engine died. In this goddamn downpour, there was nothing to do but wait.

2

Eve heard the phone as she unlocked the door. She hurried inside from the cold, damp garage, kicking off her wet shoes in the laundry room. She reached for the wall phone in the kitchen, but the answering machine in the office had already picked up the call and she lowered her hand when her sister-in-law's strident tone floated through the house. Eve padded through the living room and down the hall, monitoring the call to decide if she wanted to talk to Dorie right now.

". . . Cabot is fuming because I'm going to leave, but it's been more than half an hour since the school called. The poor lamb can't wait any longer. I'll take her home with me. You can pick her up—"

Eve snatched up the phone and snapped off the machine. "Dorie? I just walked in. What's the matter?"

"Where in the world have you been? The school's been trying to get you for an hour."

"Is something the matter with Cindy?"

"Honestly, Eve, you're never there when she needs you. I don't know what can be more important than your own child's well-being."

"Dorie, please!"

Dorie sighed irritably. "The school called me because they couldn't reach you. Cindy's got a stomachache and a fever. She has to see the doctor."

"I'll pick her up."

"Take her to Dr. Provel," Dorie insisted. "I'll call and make an appointment."

"I'll take care of it," Eve answered with all the control she could muster.

"It's no bother—"

"Dorie, I'd rather handle it myself."

Dorie sounded wounded and defensive. "All right, but promise you'll call the doctor?"

Eve didn't answer until the silence drew out painfully. "I'll see how she is. You know that sometimes these upsets don't amount to anything. She misses Paul." A lump thickened in Eve's throat. *She* missed Paul so much it was still a raw wound that threatened to split open at the mention of his name. It was so hard to accept that he was gone . . . gone so suddenly and awfully . . . leaving her and Cindy alone. . . .

Dorie's voice was laden with self-pity. "Paul would want you to—"

"Oh God, Dorie, not now!"

Her sister-in-law uttered an indignant gasp, then, regaining her composure, said, "Why don't you bring Cindy to my place instead of driving back up the canyon? You know where the spare key is. This rain isn't going to let up tonight. The parking lot here at the studio is already a swimming pool. Your road will be impossible."

"Thanks for the offer. I'll see. Now I've got to run."

"Call me when—"

Eve replaced the receiver, cutting off further admonitions. She rewound the tape on the answering machine and turned it to PLAYBACK. There was only one call other than the school's. She smiled when she heard Farley's voice.

"Hi. I was hoping you might be home early, but I guess I'll have to wait to hear how your day went. I have a feeling it was fantastic. We're going to break early this afternoon, so I should be back at the motel by four-thirty. I'll try you again, but if I miss you, I'll be waiting impatiently for your call at six. Give my love to Cindy."

Eve reset the machine, smiling. She stripped off her damp suit jacket and unbuttoned her skirt as she walked toward the bedroom. Farley's call pleased her as much as Dorie's annoyed her. For the thousandth time she tried to convince herself her sister-in-law meant well with her concern for Cindy, but it was a barbed hook Eve had trouble swallowing. Not that she doubted Dorie's love for her only niece. It was the *kind* of love. The same kind with which Dorie had smothered Paul as a child and into his adult life until he found the courage to escape. And even in his freedom he'd been reluctant to hurt his sister's feelings by telling her not to interfere in his life, or in his and Eve's after they got married. Pain tugged at Eve's heart. If she could have Paul back, she wouldn't complain about Dorie or anything else. She pushed away the impossible longing and sat on the edge of the bed to strip off her clammy panty hose.

She found a bulky white sweater and jeans and put them on quickly, then shoved her feet into heavy wool socks and an old pair of loafers. She'd gotten drenched crossing Sunset Boulevard from the studio to her car. Thank heaven she'd dressed Cindy warmly in waterproof rain clothes this morning. And thank heaven she'd gotten home in time to keep her sister-in-law from driving over to Peach School to pick up Cindy. Dorie's brand of solicitude was not what the doctor ordered.

It was eight months since the automobile accident that took Paul's life. Eight months of sorrow and pain that were etched on Eve's heart. Eight months of solitude, except for Cindy and frequent visits from Farley Cunningham, Paul's boyhood friend, who was a lawyer with Max, Barton, and Waterford, the firm that had handled Paul's estate. Farley specialized in entertainment law, but because he had advised Paul to set up a revocable living trust, the estate had been settled quickly, without fuss. Farley also located a buyer for Paul's thriving business and arranged the financing so Eve was assured a comfortable, steady income. When Paul's insurance was paid Farley set up another revocable living trust for the funds. He spared Eve all the trouble he could, and although he refused to let her cut herself off from everybody and everything, he willingly ran interference with Dorie and managed to keep her at bay when Eve wanted to avoid her.

Dorie was unwelcome company, too ready to draw on a lifetime of memories of her brother that were all the more painful for retelling. Eve avoided all her old friends, especially those to whom she'd always been part of a couple. Paul and Eve. Without him, she was an incomplete unit. It was Farley who finally helped her climb from the quagmire of self-pity by encouraging her to see her agent about getting back to work. Five days later she had an audition, and today she had done her first commercial since before Cindy was born. She'd been nervous, but it had gone well. They had a good take on the second shot. She felt reborn in a sense—reincarnated into a life that she had believed gone forever.

Farley was at a conference in Santa Barbara, and for the first time Eve admitted to herself that she missed him. She was sorry he wasn't here to share her triumph and joy. She wanted to thank him. He was right about work snapping her out of her depression. Now that she'd finally taken the first step, she felt more confident than she had for months. She was glad she'd promised to call him tonight to let him know how her day went. It had gone splendidly until now, despite the rain and her thorough drenching. She whispered a silent prayer that Cindy's stomachache was nothing serious.

In the laundry room she unearthed a white nylon raincoat and plastic boots that would take any downpour. As she opened the door to the garage the lights flickered ominously. Quickly she pressed the automatic door opener in case the power failed. When the lights glowed steadily again she let out a relieved breath and climbed into the Mercedes.

It was only two-thirty, but the driveway leading down to Coldwater Canyon was layered in gloom. The car headlights cut a murky path through the mist-shrouded pines and oleander that bordered the steep, switchback drive. She hated this kind of rain. There was something evil about it, deliberate and menacing. Before coming to Los Angeles, she'd thought rain like this was manufactured for movie sets.

She tapped the brakes as the car neared Coldwater Canyon and looked both ways before she pulled out. She doubted many people would be foolhardy enough to be out in this deluge, but she had become a careful, almost fearful, driver. She'd had the road to herself a half hour ago, but there would be plenty of traffic by late afternoon. She was already dreading the drive back up. Maybe she should take Cindy to Dorie's, at least until the storm let up a little. She'd never seen such a downpour. Dorie often worked until six. If Cindy felt better, they could be gone by the time Dorie got home from the studio. Eve sighed, knowing she wouldn't do it. It wasn't fair to use Dorie's condominium when she had no intention of letting her sister-in-law hover and cluck over Cindy, dispensing sympathy at every whimper and convincing Cindy she was truly ill.

With great difficulty, Eve had finally accepted the fact that many of Cindy's stomach upsets were psychosomatic. After the major surgery Cindy had as an infant, digestive problems were normal. Dr. Provel was certain the child would outgrow them in time, but he also warned that any infection that irritated the delicate lining of the stomach might cause more serious problems. Trying to determine when Cindy truly needed medical attention was like walking an emotional tightrope for Eve. The last eight months had been difficult, the stomachaches more frequent. Paul's death had been too baffling and heartbreaking for a three-year-old to understand. For weeks Cindy cried herself to sleep every night, demanding the bedtime story Paul always read after he tucked her in. Next she went through a stage of sullen withdrawal that frightened Eve badly enough to seek advice from the pediatrician. At his recommendation she took Cindy to a child psychologist who said Cindy was suffering from a feeling of being abandoned by her father and was afraid her mother might disappear as well. He advised Eve to treat her daughter's fears with gentle reassurances.

Eve peered through the arc the windshield wiper cleared as she started down the hill. She kept the car at a crawl, hearing, as she always did, Paul's admonition to "be careful of the sharp curves below the driveway." How long would it take until she no longer heard and saw Paul in everything she did? She chewed her lip and eased the Mercedes around the curve, hugging her own lane in case another car was coming up. Without warning, a dark shape loomed ahead of her on the road. She turned the wheel sharply to avoid hitting it before she realized it was a car parked on the opposite side of the narrow blacktop. The Mercedes skidded, and Eve panicked as her mind replayed the horrible crash that had taken her husband's life. No rain then . . . spilled oil on the freeway . . . tires screeching and Paul struggling to bring the car under control . . . and the look of horror on his face in that last instant when he knew he had failed . . . then the sickening crash and crunch of steel and concrete as they hit the abutment.

Shaking, Eve brought the car back under control. Her mouth was dry and her hands were trembling. The driver was crazy to park on a curve that way without warning lights. A car coming up the hill would have to swing out dangerously to pass. If there had been one now . . . Her trembling subsided as the moment of terror ebbed. The car had probably stalled because of the rain, and the poor driver was most likely trudging his way home through the mud. If he was on the road, she hoped he was wearing light-colored clothing so he wouldn't be as invisible as his abandoned vehicle.

"It's a shame you had to drive down in this storm, but I didn't think we should take a chance even with such a minor elevation of temperature." Miss Hollowell smiled professionally.

"You did the right thing," Eve assured the principal. "Tell Mrs. Whalen I'll call her in the morning and let her know if Cindy is well enough to come." The car pool was one of the advantages of the Peach School. Eve took her turn for a week once every month. She didn't envy Margaret Whalen this week in this weather.

"Okay, honey, let's go." She lifted Cindy from the cot where she sat decked out in a yellow slicker, hat, and boots like Paddington Bear. Eve nuzzled her cheek. "How's the tummy?"

"It hurts." Cindy's blue gaze was close to tears as she bowed her flaxen head and buried her face against her mother's shoulder.

"Well, we'll just get you home and into bed. I'll make cocoa. Would you like that?"

Cindy nodded without looking up. Eve thanked the school principal again and carried her daughter out to the car, pulling the rain hat close around the tiny flushed face for the sprint across the parking lot.

In the car, Cindy closed her eyes as Eve buckled the seat belt. Eve felt her brow, but it was cool. If there was a fever, it was no more than the tenth of a degree Miss Hollowell had noted. Dr. Provel said minor variations in a child's temperature were normal. As a guideline in Cindy's case, he said there was no cause for alarm unless it was up at least a full degree.

The streets of Sherman Oaks were as bad as those all over the city. Storm drains were inadequate to carry off the deluge of rainwater that poured down the hills. Many intersections were blocked by curb-deep puddles that Eve had to get around or inch through when there was no break in traffic coming the opposite way. Blaring horns evidenced flaring tempers. When Cindy whimpered restlessly Eve felt her face again, but her own icy hands were a poor thermometer.

Off and on the rain abated momentarily, but each time Eve was convinced the worst of the storm was over, the sky released another flood. By the time she reached Coldwater Canyon she was sorry she hadn't gone to Dorie's, but it was too late to turn around, and there was no place to do it safely. The canyon road was impossibly narrow with its twin rivers of muddy water and debris coursing down the sides. Even if she dared pull into someone's driveway, she'd never be able to see to back out. The blacktop was sheeted with water, and from time to time the tires sent up fender-high wakes as the wheels hit puddles.

It would be a relief to get home and get Cindy into bed. Eve wondered if she had inadvertently precipitated Cindy's stomachache by telling her about making the commercial today. It was possible Cindy equated her mother going back to work with losing her. But Cindy had heard the messages about wardrobe and the shooting schedule on the answering machine and had asked questions, which Eve answered truthfully. She explained as much as a three-year-old could understand, repeatedly emphasizing that she'd be home before Cindy came from school. Even so, there had been a worried, scared look in Cindy's eyes when Eve kissed her good-bye and put her in Margaret Whalen's station wagon this morning.

When they got home Cindy could take a nap. When she woke Eve would make cocoa and take some of those heart-shaped cookies from the freezer. She'd build a fire in the fireplace and spread a blanket. They'd have a party. Cindy would forget her stomachache and be smiling and running around in no time. She was going to be just fine. They had both come a long way in eight months, and for the first time Eve knew they were going to make it. There'd always be poignant memories, but they had a new life ahead of them. It would be a strange, different life without Paul. She would have to reshape the dreams and plans they had made and create new ones for herself and Cindy.

A startling slash of lightning crossed the sky and arrowed into the hillside above her. Eve winced as the clap of thunder made the car tremble. Leaning forward, she tried to pick out familiar landmarks. She saw a street sign and was dismayed to find she was only halfway up the canyon.

3

He listened to the relentless drumming of rain on the car roof. He'd be soaked in seconds if he got out. And where would he go? He rubbed the glass and peered into the gloom. There was no sign of house lights or even another car. He was better off where he was. At least he was dry. Anyhow, he'd never get to San Diego before dark now. San Diego. Mexico. He wondered if it was raining in Mexico.

He looked up at a sudden flash of light. Car headlights fanned the road ahead of him. He looked through the streaming windshield as a light-colored car came toward him out of nowhere. The car veered sharply as it passed and skidded on the wet pavement. He watched without emotion, his hands on the steering wheel miming what the other driver should do to bring the car out of the skid. He nodded when the car finally straightened and continued down the hill. When the taillights vanished he rolled down his window and tried to see where it had come from. If he hadn't seen it come out, he wouldn't have been able to pick out the faint break in the solid wall of trees and high shrubs. There were no lights showing, but a driveway meant a house. Maybe another car, or a can of gas. He rolled up the window.

On his knees, he searched the backseat for something to protect him from the rain, but there was nothing but a soiled satin pillow and a two-month-old issue of *Playgirl*. He tossed them aside. So he'd get wet. He'd been wet before. Opening the door, he stepped out into the pelting downpour and braced himself against the force of the wind. Clutching the collar of his windbreaker around his chin, he slammed the car door and headed uphill.

His shoes were soaked before he went three feet. Cold dampness penetrated his pants and jacket, and water dripping from his hair and face seeped under his collar. He hunched his shoulders and jammed his hands in his pockets as he sloshed to the spot where the car lights had appeared.

A driveway. Concrete, flanked by pines, live oaks, and a lush growth of oleander. It angled steeply up the hill before it made a sharp turn, so he couldn't see the end. The house could be a few yards or a mile, there was no way of telling. He started up. The noise of the rain slapping the trees and concrete was as loud as it had been in the car. He had to clench his teeth to keep from shivering. Water squished in his shoes with each step.

The drive made two switchbacks before it leveled off. The house stood in a clearing that backed up against the continuing rise of the hill. It was redwood and stone, a sprawling California ranch style, with lots of glass. It wasn't as big as the estates in Encino or the fancy places on the other side of the hill, but it wasn't any rustic cottage either. It took up most of the clearing and hugged the hill along one side and across the back. Through the blur of rain a light glowed at a window.

Ignoring the downpour, he studied it. At that distance he couldn't tell what room it was, but it seemed to be the only one with a light. He wiped his dripping face and squinted to look for any sign of life. When he was sure there was no movement he crossed the sodden lawn.

It was a kitchen window. He leaned close to the glass and looked inside. Clean, neat, and empty. A red kettle sat on one of the stove burners. The round glass table was empty except for a green vase with a single yellow daffodil. He smiled, knowing it was probably fake, but liking the touch of spring. On the far side of the room a door was open. Beyond it he could see a washing machine and dryer with a stack of neatly folded towels on top. A pair of women's blue, high-heeled shoes lay on the floor as if they'd been kicked off hurriedly. There was no sign of the woman or anyone else.

Standing back, he inspected the front of the house, determining the layout. There'd be a door from the garage to the laundry room. On the other end, closer to the ivy-covered hill, the front door and another window were dark. He made his way to the window, standing to one side as a precaution, and looked through the spattered glass. Enough light spilled from the kitchen to show pale carpet, gold and white furniture, glass and brass tables. The kind of living room they put in magazines. Homey. He wasn't sure why that word came to mind, except the room looked comfortably lived in. Only now it was empty.

The flagstone path that started at the driveway circled the house and was hemmed in by the ivy-covered hill. He followed it around the corner. The two windows on the side were dark. Through the first one he made out the dim outlines of office furniture. On the desk a small red light glowed on some kind of box. He couldn't make it out, but he studied it a long time before he moved away. At the second window there was a faint glow of light when he got right up to it. He rubbed the beaded water from the glass and peered inside. It was a night-light in the bottom of a lamp shaped like a teddy bear sitting on a drum. A kid's room. A little girl, judging from the pink ruffles and lace. There was a bed with high posts at the corners and a pink ruffle around the top that matched the pink and white lacy bedspread. Over a child-sized desk hung a white square of plastic with pockets that held crayons, scissors, a jar of paste, and some pencils. A teddy bear sat in a small rocking chair, and a little girl's bathrobe hung neatly on a hook of a peg rack that was low enough for a small child to reach easily. For a moment he was hypnotized. *Kristen* . . . It was the kind of room Kristen would like. His cheeks warmed, and he wiped his eyes. Kristen wasn't here. The room belonged to another little girl. He wondered what her name was. A trickle of cold water running down his neck finally roused him, and he moved on.

There was a fenced pool in back, tucked between a covered

patio and the steep incline of the hill where the clearing ended. Beyond the pool deck the ivied bank was black in the rain, its top invisible among the dripping trees bending in the wind. He ran his hand along the steel gatepost and slid up the latch. He shut the gate behind him before he crossed the patio and moved under the overhang of the roof. The sudden respite from the wind and pelting rain gave him a chance to wipe his dripping face.

The rear of the house was dark. Sliding glass doors faced a large family room. The drapes weren't closed, and he moved closer so he could see inside. Comfortable chairs, one of those big-screen TVs, stereo equipment, radio, a small desk, lots of bookshelves. A stuffed elephant lay on the tweed carpet by a child's rocking chair beside the fireplace. He tried the sliding glass doors but they were locked. He spotted the Charley Bar in place.

He stepped back out into the downpour so he could study the other end of the house. The master bedroom spanned the entire wing behind the garage. There were no curtains at the bay windows that faced a small rock garden surrounded by a thick wall of trees. It was the kind of seclusion that meant there wasn't a neighbor within miles. A bedside lamp was burning, but like the rest of the house, the room was empty. A woman's blue jacket and skirt were thrown over the back of a chair, and a rumpled pair of panty hose lay on the pale carpet. A dresser drawer wasn't closed all the way. The bay windows opened on cranks and were dead-bolted. He leaned against the wire-mesh fence and looked along the side of the house. He saw the faint indication of two draped windows and a smaller one that was probably a bathroom.

He retraced his steps, latching the pool gate after himself again and pausing at the front of the house to make sure nothing had changed and detouring to the soggy lawn as he passed the lighted kitchen window. Back on the driveway, he tested the overhead garage door. It was probably connected to an automatic system. He couldn't budge it. At the corner he stepped cautiously into the bed of ice plant. His shoe skidded on the slippery leaves, and he grabbed the wall to stay on his feet. He made his way along the garage to a small-paned window and tried to look inside, but there was a curtain over the glass. A curtain in the garage. He snorted, then looked around for a rock big enough to smash the glass. The noise of the wind and rain covered the sound. He knocked the jagged pieces out of the putty before he reached in to release the catch. Pushing the window up, he brushed away bits of glass before he boosted himself to the sill, swung his legs over, and climbed inside. For several minutes he stood listening to the rain and letting his eyes adjust to the thick shadows.

It was a two-car garage. In the stall near the window an oil stain showed where a car had dripped oil, but it wasn't fresh. There was no oil stain in the other space, but wet tracks in the center of the garage showed where a car had come and gone recently. Puddles had dripped from the bumpers and fenders. A faint impression of small footprints made a damp trail from the driver's side to the door leading to the house.

It was locked. He found a plastic strip in his pocket and pried it between the jamb and the door, wiggling it until the spring bolt clicked back. A moment later he was standing in the laundry room he'd seen through the kitchen window.

He hadn't realized how cold he was until the warmth of the house enveloped him. His clothes were dripping a puddle on the mat inside the door, and his shoes were outlined in mud. He bent to take them off, then his socks and the soggy jacket to wrap around them. He lifted the lid of the washing machine and dropped them inside. The rain had soaked the bloodstain on his shirt, and it was slimy against his skin. He folded the cuff back and wiped the watery red splotches on his wrist off on his shirtfront.

The linoleum was icy under his bare feet. Squatting, he turned the mat over so his muddy prints were hidden. Then he used one of the folded towels from the top of the dryer on his hair and face and to squeeze some of the moisture out of his pants so they wouldn't drip. He tossed the towel into the washing machine and closed the lid.

Walking softly in his bare feet, he went through the house to make sure it was empty. He didn't touch anything or leave any sign of his passing other than faint impressions of his steps on the thick carpeting.

Behind a swinging door in the kitchen there was a dining room. A sudden spate of noise made him tense until he realized the room had a huge Plexiglas skylight on which the rain was drumming steadily. He let the door swing shut and went through the picture-pretty living room and down the hall.

The office had an empty look: no papers or letters scattered around, no trace of cigarette smoke, although there was an onyx ashtray on the desk and another beside the leather armchair in the corner. The blinking red light was an answering machine for the telephone. He left the door open the way he'd found it.

He spent a long time in the child's room looking at everything a little girl needed to be happy. The size of the desk meant she was no more than two or three. He imagined her sitting there, concentrating as she drew a picture like the one tacked on the wall beside the white plastic catchall. He leaned down to study the picture, cocking his head to one side then the other until he decided it was a teddy bear like the one in the rocking chair. *Kristen had a teddy bear.* He turned away and pulled the door halfway shut the way it had been.

He glanced into the family room but continued down the hall to the master bedroom. It was as warm and pretty as the living room. The thick, cream-colored carpet was like summer grass under his bare feet. He glanced at the king-sized bed covered with a silky blue spread. On either side was a nightstand. The one with the lighted lamp had a box of tissues, a telephone, and a pad on it. The other was bare except for a lamp. Near the door a long dresser was big enough for three people's clothes. On it were two pictures in gold frames. He picked one up and held it toward the light. It was the little girl. She was cute, blond, with a pixie smile and laughing blue eyes. He touched the glass lovingly. After a long time he replaced the picture and studied the other one without picking it up. It was a wedding picture of a young couple. The woman was pretty. Darker hair than the

man and child but still blond. Her eyes were darker, too, and
they seemed to watch him from the photograph. The little girl
looked like her.

On the pad next to the phone on the nightstand someone had
written, "Tues—Shore Inn, Santa Barbara" with a phone number. In the big walk-in closet he ran his hand over the woman's
suits and dresses, enjoying the soft, sensual textures of silk and
wool. Her clothes took up most of the space. On one wall a
man's clothing was pushed into a corner. He went through the
things critically, then took a pair of navy slacks from a hanger
and a tan sweater from a shelf. He went back to the dresser and
opened drawers until he found one filled with men's socks and
underwear. In the blue and white bathroom he stripped off his
wet clothes and put on the dry ones, then rolled up the discards.
The underwear fit passably but the slacks came only to his
ankles. He pulled on the tan sweater. It covered the waistband
he couldn't get fastened. Back in the closet, he tried on a pair of
loafers from a rack, but he couldn't get his feet into them.
Carrying the wet bundle, he returned to the laundry room and
stuffed it in the washing machine.

He eyed the kettle on the stove, longing for a cup of coffee to
warm him up, but knowing the kitchen was visible from the
drive. The woman must have been driving the car he'd seen.
Where had she gone? She probably didn't expect to be gone
long, leaving lights on this way. But there was no telling what
time the guy came home from work. Los Angeles was a crazy
city where people came and went at all hours. Unless maybe the
Santa Barbara phone number meant he was away?

Soundlessly, he walked back to the living room and sat in a
gold armchair in a corner away from the window.

4

Cindy was so quiet, Eve studied the small heart-shaped face under the floppy-brimmed rain hat. Was the flush on her cheeks the excitement of escaping school or was she developing a fever? Since Paul's death Cindy hated nursery school, which previously she had loved. It was painful for Eve to make her go each morning, but the child psychologist had assured her it was the wisest course.

"Keep her in school, and be there when she comes home. Talk positively about her experiences and encourage her to share them with you. Eventually she'll accept school as part of her daily routine and it won't be a threat to her relationship with you."

Eve had done this, but it was not until a few weeks ago that she realized her own lingering grief and withdrawal were compounding Cindy's problem. Although Eve was always there physically, she was often emotionally on a distant planet. She missed Paul so terribly, she resented anyone or anything that intruded on the memory world she had been inhabiting since his death. Farley had been telling her that for some time. The trouble was, he couched the truth in such gentle ways that she'd been able to blind herself to it the same way she did the self-pity that was destroying her.

She thought of Farley fondly. She never would have made it

without his help and friendship. She'd come to depend on him in more ways than she believed possible since Paul's death.

She glanced again at Cindy. How like Paul she was with her dimples and wheat-gold curls. Several agencies in town wanted to sign her up for modeling, but Eve refused to consider it. Eve knew the reality of auditions, hot lights, and endless retakes. She wanted no part of it for her daughter. Cindy already had trouble coping with tension; the life-style of a model or actress would be her undoing.

Cindy's eyes were closed, and Eve realized she'd fallen asleep. When she didn't feel well Cindy tended to whine. Right now Eve was grateful for her silence. The pounding rain and the slick road were nerve-racking.

The storm was savage in the canyon, heightened rather than diminished by the overhang of trees that enfolded the road in dark, wet arms. The funnel effect that brought delightfully cool breezes in summer now channeled the wind so bursts of rain slashed viciously. Muddy water swirled down the road, sweeping along twigs and debris. Occasionally a heavy branch, torn loose by the force of the wind, blocked part of the road, and she had to edge around it carefully. Thank heaven there wasn't any traffic yet. Eve's hands ached from gripping the wheel as the car crept around the winding curves.

If she hadn't driven the canyon road so often, it would be impossible to tell where she was. The windshield wipers couldn't keep up with the deluge, and she could no longer see the yellow line that marked the center of the road. The hill above her was wrapped in fog, but she knew she was almost to the double curve below the driveway where she'd been startled by the parked car. Slowing, she studied the road ahead through the blurred windshield. The dark hump was still outlined under the trees. Nervously, she pulled out to pass it.

She came to a complete stop before making the sharp turn. Paul had insisted on having the driveway paved when he bought the house. He'd lived in Southern California all his life and knew the sloughs winter rain could make of the soft earth.

The car crept upward, slowing even more as it negotiated the double switchback and strained up the final grade.

Eve let out a relieved breath when she saw the cheerful glow of the kitchen window. Thank heaven the electricity hadn't gone off. Belatedly, she realized she should have left the garage door open in case it had. She quickly pressed the electronic opener and the door rolled up. When she pulled the Mercedes in and turned off the engine, Cindy opened her eyes sleepily.

"Are we home, Mommy?"

"We sure are. Come on, I'll give you a ride in." She picked up Cindy and hugged her close. "You'll be warm and cozy in no time, Teddy Bear." Eve slid out, hitching the child's weight to her hip as she dug in her voluminous purse for the fluffy ball that made her house keys easy to find. When the lock snapped open she pressed the button to close the garage door.

Eve perched Cindy on top of the washing machine. "First, let's get rid of these wet things." She undid the strings of Cindy's rain hat and the snaps of the coat. When Cindy whimpered and rubbed her eyes Eve kissed her cheek. "You'll be in bed in the wiggle of a teddy bear's tail. Now the boots. Hang on." She pretended to pull hard at the yellow plastic boots, but Cindy didn't giggle the way she usually did. Eve dropped the boots and took off her own coat and boots before lifting Cindy into her arms. "Okay, here we go."

Cindy felt warmer. Eve stroked her daughter's blond hair as she carried her through the kitchen and living room and down the hall to the pink and white bedroom. She snapped on the lamp and pulled back the ruffled bedspread before laying her down. Cindy's eyelids drooped. Worried, Eve got the thermometer from the medicine cabinet in Cindy's pink and white bathroom and slipped it under her daughter's tongue. Then she sat on the edge of the bed while she unbuttoned Cindy's pink cardigan with the row of brown teddy bears dancing around it. Dr. Provel insisted there was no cause for alarm unless Cindy's temperature rose sharply or her stomach pains became severe. Eve kept medication on hand to give Cindy at the onset of these upsets. If she didn't feel better in a few hours, Eve was to call him.

"Help me get your jammies on," Eve coaxed. Cindy raised an arm listlessly. Eve slipped off the sweater. "That's my big girl." She undressed her quickly and put on a pair of warm pajamas. "There. Now under the covers you go." Eve drew up the sheet and blanket before she took the thermometer. Bending close to the lamp, she read it. Three tenths of a degree. Higher but still no cause for alarm. She kissed Cindy's cheek.

"I'm going to get your medicine. Stay awake a few more minutes, okay?"

Cindy's eyelids fluttered. "Hurry, Mommy."

"Be right back."

In the kitchen, Eve got a teaspoon and the prescription bottle she kept on the top shelf of a cupboard. The elevation in Cindy's temperature could be from the ride home, dashing in and out of the rain, and getting overheated in her sweater and raincoat. She'd check it again in an hour, even if she had to wake Cindy up. With this storm she couldn't afford to take chances. If she had gone to Dorie's . . . She pushed away the thought. The last thing she needed was her sister-in-law's nagging criticism.

She put the spoon and bottle on the night table so she could prop pillows behind Cindy. Pouring the red liquid, Eve held out the spoon. "Open wide."

Cindy obeyed docilely. Thank heaven the medicine tasted good. Actually, Cindy was a very good patient. When she was in the hospital the nurses and doctors had been charmed by her and made sure she never lacked for attention. Eve gave her daughter an encouraging smile when she swallowed the syrup. Capping the bottle, Eve wiped Cindy's rosebud mouth with a tissue.

"Now it's sleepy time. Mommy will be right here. Call if you want anything, and when you wake up you'll feel lots better." She kissed the warm face. "I'll leave the light on, okay?"

Cindy nodded and popped her thumb in her mouth as her eyes closed. Eve switched the lamp back to the night-light and left the door open as she went out.

In spite of herself, she was worried. It wasn't like Cindy to be so quiet and tired. She wasn't as active and boisterous as a lot of other kids at Peach School, but she was usually excited about coming home, even on unscheduled sick leave. It was one of the barometers Eve used for evaluating her frequent ailments. If Cindy cheered up quickly when she escaped a stressful situation, the stomachache was apt to vanish. This listlessness could be a symptom of something more complicated.

In the kitchen, Eve put the kettle on to boil and glanced at the clock. Peach School was letting out for the day, but she could probably still catch Miss Hollowell. She lifted the wall phone and dialed. She was in luck.

"Miss Hollowell, this is Eve Foxx. I forgot to ask if anyone in Cindy's class is out sick? Is the flu going around or any of the childhood diseases?"

"Is she worse, Mrs. Foxx?" Miss Hollowell's voice was filled with concern.

"Her temperature is up a little, but she's sleeping. If I have to call the pediatrician, he'll want to know if she's been exposed to anything."

"Of course. We don't have anyone out with communicable diseases. I know that. Let me look at Miss Tilson's attendance record for today." She was gone a moment, then said, "Leo Monroe and Betsy Steinman were out today."

"Thanks. I'll call their mothers."

Eve hung up and turned off the burner under the kettle. Dropping a tea bag into a mug, she poured boiling water over it. While it steeped she found the Peach School parent list in a drawer and dialed the Monroes' number. She let it ring a long time, but there was no answer. She dialed the Steinmans'.

Mrs. Steinman told her Betsy had tonsilitis, then prattled on about the weather and about Betsy's predilection to severe sore throats and ear infections. She worried that if her daughter had another winter like last, the pediatrician might decide it was necessary to remove the tonsils. She was afraid such an experience would be terribly traumatic for Betsy. Uncomfortable, Eve finally managed to say good-bye and hang up.

She squeezed the tea bag and dropped it in the sink, then carried the mug to the living room and stood at the window looking out at the dark, wet world. The yard was a quagmire. The ground was saturated, and light reflected in puddles in every tiny depression of the lawn. Her flower beds, which were luxurious year-round with roses, camelias, and daisies, were mudholes, the plants beaten to the ground. She had never seen it rain harder. The city was caught in a series of storms that had been going on for five days now. There were occasional respites, an hour or two of clear skies when the city and valley shimmered in smogless clarity, but new fronts moved in rapidly, and the rain began again. She hadn't heard a forecast since early afternoon, but it didn't look promising. Restlessly, she pulled the drapes and went to check on Cindy.

5

Farley Cunningham caught himself doodling on the six-page handout the law professor from the University of California had distributed. Feeling guilty, he retracted the point of his pen and laid it aside as he focused his attention once more on the speaker. It wasn't lack of interest but lack of challenging new ideas and proposals that was depleting his energy as the afternoon wore one.

The Mental Health Law Seminar was in its third of four days. Psychiatrists, lawyers, legislators, and law-enforcement personnel from the entire state had presented papers, speeches, impassioned pleas, and a few outright arguments on the current status of California's NGI plea and the treatment and detention of offenders. John Hinckley's use of the insanity plea in his trial for the attempted assassination of President Reagan had raised nationwide debate over the validity of the defense. The fact that a "not guilty by reason of insanity" plea can be used only after conviction in California focused attention on the duration and type of treatment offenders should receive. Some argued that if insanity can be defined and recognized, the insane person could not be held accountable for his criminal act. If treatment relieved the symptoms of mental illness, the patient should be released without further punishment. Many law-enforcement personnel, however, saw this as a revolving door that put potentially dangerous people back on the streets. The argument had also, to a great extent, put mental-health people on one side of the issue and law enforcement on the other. Many lawyers and legislators still wandered in a desert of indecision in between.

Like half a dozen other conferences Farley had attended, this one was producing few definitive answers. His attendance was more a matter of conscience than responsibility. He was perfectly happy in the niche of entertainment law he'd chosen for his specialty. He had never aspired to trial law, especially criminal law, where a client's liberty or life hung on his skill and oratory. Two years ago Judge Samuel Howin had called Richard Max personally to ask if Max, Barton, and Waterford would accept the case assignment in a murder trial as a public service. Richard Max had, in turn, asked Farley to prepare the defense and try the case if it became necessary. Since Farley was well acquainted with the entertainment industry, he was the logical choice, Max said, and the best qualified for the task.

The defendant was a struggling actress named Stella Robain who shot and killed a prominent network casting director after he turned her down for a part. Judge Howin was reluctant to assign a public defender for fear the press might take the stand that a penniless actress was being railroaded by a giant corporation. Richard Max promised the firm's complete cooperation and put the legal staff at Farley's disposal. Farley recognized the honor being bestowed upon him. At thirty-three he was one of the youngest associates in the firm. Success in handling the Robain case would put him closer to the partnership he hoped to earn.

He tackled the assignment with vigor and dedication, which meant the young actress was entitled to the best defense he could provide. When his pretrial investigations showed the prosecution had evidence of Stella Robain's conviction that the producer was trying to destroy her career, as well as four eyewitnesses to the murder, Farley offered his distraught client the option of pleading guilty to second-degree murder, then using the insanity plea to obtain a mitigated sentence. Stella Robain was sentenced to Atascadero State Hospital for a minimum of

180 days and a maximum of fifteen years to life. After eighteen months she was out making the rounds of casting offices, trying to rebuild a career that had never been off the ground in the first place. Farley's handling of the case with minimal publicity had impressed Richard Max. Since then he was frequently asked to serve as the firm's representative to seminars such as this one.

Across the conference table, Deputy District Attorney Jess Mavella disguised a yawn. Farley winked and tapped his watch surreptitiously. Jess's answering smile said more than words. The law professor finally drew his remarks to a close, and there was a healthy spatter of applause. The seminar chairman adjourned the afternoon session, and chairs were pushed back and conversation erupted in pockets as the people milled about or headed for the door. Jess waited for Farley and they went out together.

"Another inconclusive battle stalemated," Jess said with a grin.

"There were some good points brought out," Farley argued. "I have the feeling supervision in outpatient programs is coming under enough heat that we'll see some new legislation."

"In the meantime we'll all go back to our corners and push papers around while we decide how far out on a limb we're willing to go. Then we'll schedule another conference. Come on, I'll buy you a drink," Jess said.

A general exodus moved toward the hotel bar. The planning committee had judiciously terminated the afternoon sessions early enough for people to relax a few hours before the banquet at seven. Farley had opted not to stay at the Miramar but at a small motel on the beach, closer to downtown. Now, looking at the rain-sodden grounds of the hotel, he wished he hadn't. He decided he could use a drink before driving the few blocks.

"You talked me into it." He brushed his hand across the smooth, sandy-colored hair that came almost to the collar of his tan suit and grinned at Jess. "You should be as convincing with our learned friends of the APA."

"Guilty, but mentally ill. 'I thought I was carving up a watermelon, your honor. Honest, Doc, if you let me out, I'll never cut up another watermelon, only cantaloupes.' Now you know why I stick with the D.A.'s office. I'd rather prosecute than defend these guys."

Farley had met Jess Mavella in law school and they had been friends since, despite the marked differences in their ambitions and choice of careers. Jess had become a public prosecutor because he excelled in and completely enjoyed the complexities of criminal trials. He juggled cases, preening when he won the difficult ones and able to shrug off the losses. He also had political ambitions. He had his sights set on a judge's bench by the time he was fifty-five. Farley was methodical and liked the intricacies of contracts and establishing congenial relationships with his clients. It helped that they weren't behind bars.

The two men paused in the doorway of the lounge and glanced around for seats. Many seminar attendees already occupied tables. Several people motioned to them, but Jess steered Farley to an empty spot at the end of the bar. Jess tossed down a bill and gave the bartender their orders.

"How's Eve?" he asked. When Farley met his gaze in the mirror behind the bar, Jess grinned. "I presume you were calling her when you slipped out during McConner's droning."

Farley smiled. "She wasn't home."

"I haven't seen this look in your eye since you were dating that little redheaded junior."

Farley took the kidding good-naturedly. Jess had met Eve and Paul at several parties, and he knew that Farley felt protective now about Eve and Cindy. But the rest was his creative imagination. Farley had never discussed his feelings for Eve with Jess or anyone else. More often than not he had trouble defining them for himself.

"Have you heard anything on Luke Miller?" Farley asked, changing the subject to one he knew would sidetrack Jess effectively.

"Christ—I wish to hell they'd round him up fast. The publicity he's getting is bringing enough heat on the department to melt the desks. I'm sure you noticed that no one on the podium today mentioned Miller. The mental-health contingent doesn't dare, and our people have been warned to keep our mouths shut until he's back in custody. The press would be all over us like a Santa Ana. Miller is the perfect argument for tighter restrictions on the 1229 program."

The recent news stories about the released mental patient had shaken Farley more than he cared to admit. Supposedly cured of the insanity that had led him to murder, Miller had been released from the state mental facility for the criminally insane to an outpatient program. Now, only a few months later, he was being sought for questioning in another murder, which, according to Jess, there was little doubt Miller had committed. His apparent return to violence made Farley wonder how he'd feel if Stella Robain killed again instead of slipping into obscurity.

"I take it they haven't caught him?"

"Hell, no. All's quiet on the North Hollywood front. I'll bet every cop in the division is lighting candles in church and praying that dude is five states away."

Farley finished his drink. "If he isn't, your office will get the case."

Jess shook his head. "He'll go straight to Department Ninety-five and be back in Atascadero before he knows what happened. He'll be counting his 180 days so he can start conning the board again. Hell, I'd like to throw away the key on his type. Miller may be insane, but he's also a killer. I say lock him up. Let the psychiatrists argue all they want about hypocrisy and a return to the Middle Ages."

Jess signaled the bartender for refills, but Farley shook his head. "I'm heading back to my motel. I'll see you at the banquet."

"Sure you won't have one for the road? It's mighty wet out there."

"The road's only a few blocks, and it's wet enough for both of us," Farley said.

Jess sighed. "Southern California monsoon season."

Farley slid from the barstool. "I hope we're at a back table tonight. I don't think I can stay awake for many more speeches."

"Only one more day to go," Jess offered.

Glancing at the flooded walkways beyond the wet windows, Farley said, "We'll need pontoons by tomorrow if the rain doesn't let up."

6

Ida Dawson muttered as the doorbell clamored insistently. She threw aside the crocheted afghan and poked her stockinged feet along the floor in search of her house slippers. When she found them she eased her bulk from the depths of the sofa. "I'm coming, I'm coming."

The apartment was gloomy. After five days of rain the damp chill was as much a part of it as the worn carpeting. The storm rattled the windows and drafts blew the curtains like waving palms. Ida hated being caretaker of the building. She hated being on call for tenants to pester her with their petty complaints. She hated the dingy ground-floor apartment. She hated the steady cross-flow of tenants coming and going at all hours, stomping on the stairs and shaking the walls of her bedroom. The only thing she liked about the Casa Risa was the cheap rent. It was practically nothing by North Hollywood standards, but it was meager compensation for having to listen to other people's woes. And being awakened from her nap.

The bell rang again as she reached the hall. "Keep your shirt on," she said, checking the safety chain before she unfastened the dead bolt and Yale lock. She opened the door the length of the chain. A woman in a red raincoat, high-heeled boots, and hat was dripping on Ida's mat. Not a tenant, but Ida had seen her before. She came to visit someone upstairs.

"I'm looking for Janine Peters," the woman said.

"It's 302." Ida started to close the door, but the girl pushed against it.

"She doesn't answer her bell."

"Then she's not home." For this her pleasant nap had been terminated? Ida glared at the woman. Too much makeup, and the pallor you got from bars and late hours. Ida sniffed disdainfully.

"She didn't come to work today."

Ida shrugged. "Maybe she's sick."

"Then why doesn't she answer the bell?" the woman insisted.

Ida really didn't care. "Maybe she went to the corner for cigarettes." Or maybe she picked up some guy last night and was too tired to get out of her nice warm bed, Ida thought. It was none of her business what Janine Peters did as long as she didn't traffic men in and out of here. She occasionally brought some guy home, but there was never any partying or loud noise. Most important, Janine Peters paid her rent on time.

"She doesn't smoke." The dark-haired woman's carefully penciled brows came together. "Can you let me into her apartment to wait? If she's just at the store or something, she'll be back soon."

"No," Ida said. "Try her again later."

"It's important!"

"You think I can just open apartments and let people in because they say it's important? I'd get in a lot of trouble doing that." Indignant, Ida started to close the door, but the girl jammed a red-booted foot in the opening. Ida bristled. "Now you cut that out, young lady, or *you're* going to be in big trouble. You have no right coming here and—"

"Please—"

"I'm calling the police." Ida stepped away from the door, then smiled as the red boot vanished. She slammed the door and slid the bolt. After a moment she heard the clack of high heels on the linoleum and the squeak of the outside door she'd been meaning to give a shot of WD-40. She hurried to the window and looked out at the street. The girl in red dashed across the wet sidewalk and climbed behind the wheel of a car at the curb and drove off. Now what do you suppose that was all about? Ida shook her head. Some people had nerve. Guess she'd told her.

Ida shuffled to the kitchen and put on the kettle. She wished the rain would stop. She hadn't been out of the building for days except to empty trash into the dumpster. She hugged her arms under the brown sweater. The sound of the rain whipping through the palm fronds always made her think of that lawyer rattling his papers when he told her that there was no property to be divided in her divorce from Fred. Somehow he'd managed to hide ownership so she couldn't touch it. At fifty-seven she found herself divorced, broke, and miserable.

She sighed as the kettle began to boil. She made tea in the chipped crockery pot and poured it through a strainer to fill her cup. Carrying it back to the living room, she switched on the TV before she sat on the green sofa again.

News. She was tired of hearing about the rain. She hit a button on the remote control. More news. She went through the stations until she found an old John Wayne movie, then settled back to drink her tea. When the phone rang some time later she picked it up irritably, lowering the sound on the television but not shutting it off. John Wayne led his men into battle silently.

"This is Stanley Morse in 304, Mrs. Dawson. That Peters woman has gone off and left her bedroom window open again. I've got a wet spot on my wall. If my stereo equipment gets ruined, somebody's going to pay for it. You'd think she'd have enough sense to close up before she goes out, for crissake."

A commercial interrupted the movie and Ida sighed. "I'll talk to her." Last week it had been Peters complaining about Morse's loud stereo when she was trying to sleep.

"In the meantime my place will be soaked! These walls are like blotting paper. I've already had to pull back my rug to keep it dry."

"What do you want me to do, Mr. Morse? I'll try to catch her as soon as she comes home."

"Go in there and shut the goddamn window!" Morse's voice

squeaked. "If it's soaking through to my apartment, you can bet the apartment below hers is getting it too!" He slammed down the phone.

Ida muttered and cast a wistful glance at John Wayne, who had reappeared on the screen. Morse could be right. And if three apartments suffered damage, the landlord wasn't going to like it. Sighing, she got up and went to the kitchen, where her set of duplicate keys hung on a nail beside the refrigerator. Janine Peters was determined to spoil her day. First the woman at the door, now this. Taking a heavier sweater from the hall closet, she pulled it on before she went out.

The hall was cold, and her knees were stiff. By the time Ida reached the third floor, she was puffing for breath. She could hear Morse's stereo playing some classical thing with lots of violins. She found the right key and opened the door of 302. The apartment wasn't any warmer than the hall. Ida couldn't understand why people opened windows in winter. She was always cold. She muttered at the thought of Fred basking in the sunshine in Miami.

The living-room windows were shut, but a cold draft swept through the apartment as Ida padded to the bedroom. The bedroom curtains were flapping like wet sails, and the room was icy. Ida shivered and hurried to close the window. She could feel the dampness of the wet carpet seeping through her felt slippers. Honestly! The wooden frame of the window was swollen and she had to bang it with the heel of her hand before it moved. When it did it slammed loudly. She hoped Stanley Morse heard it. With considerable effort she bent down and pulled a corner of the carpet back from the wall. The floor beneath it glistened wetly. Well, since it was Janine Peters's fault, it was only fair to use her towels to sop up the mess. Ida headed for the bathroom, noticing the unmade bed with its rumpled covers piled askew. It certainly looked as if Janine hadn't spent the night alone. It was no wonder she didn't have the energy to go to work after that romp, Ida thought. She snapped on the bathroom light.

She took a step onto the white tile floor before she saw the body. Janine Peters was naked under the pink satin robe that had spread open when she fell. Her eyes stared from the badly bruised, bloody face. A puddle of blood circled her head like a halo, and her brown hair was matted with it. Her swollen purple tongue protruded grotesquely. Ida blinked, then clapped a hand over her mouth as her stomach lurched. Turning, she stumbled from the apartment and downstairs faster than her limbs had moved for a very long time. Her hands were shaking so badly it took several tries before she got her door unlocked. She barely made it to the bathroom before she vomited. Wiping her face with a cold cloth, she staggered back to the living room and lifted the phone. She was blind to John Wayne's smile as she dialed the police.

7

The spicy aroma of tea made his stomach knot with hunger. He'd left this morning without breakfast. He wasn't used to going all day without food. He pressed back into the shadows until the woman passed the dining-room door that opened to the hall. Then he sidled across the room and watched her glance into the child's room before she continued toward the rear of the house.

Eve. It was a pretty name. It suited that dark-eyed, innocent appearance that was so full of promise. She looked young to be married and have a kid. Almost as young as Sharon, who was eighteen when they got married.

The little girl's name was Cindy. He liked that too. He was surprised by the mother's call to a school. Cindy wasn't old enough to be in kindergarten or nursery school. She belonged home with her mother. It was a mother's job to take care of children, not shove them off on someone else. The steady thrum of the rain pounding on the skylight covered the sound of his harsh breathing.

When the woman was out of sight he followed down the hall silently on stockinged feet. At Cindy's door he glanced toward the family room, and when there was no sign of the woman, he went in. The soft glow of the night-light bathed the room in pink dusk. He went to the bed and looked down at the sleeping child. She was even prettier than her picture. She had a cupid-bow mouth and deep dimples. Her cheeks were rosy, and her hair was like yellow sunlight on the pink pillowcase. She didn't look sick, but the mother seemed to think she was. He bent down to smooth the covers over the tiny form. Cindy's eyes moved restlessly under closed lids as if she were dreaming. He smiled and drew his hand reluctantly from the satiny quilt. Straightening, he walked around the room slowly, examining the silver-handled comb and hairbrush on the dresser, a collection of broken crayons on the desk, the soft, fluffy robe hanging on a peg. He picked up the teddy bear from the rocking chair and cradled it against his chest, lost for a moment in memories. With a pained grimace he dropped the stuffed animal. The jolt set the chair in motion, and a faint, tinkling music-box lullaby began to play. He aborted the movement of the chair with his foot and glanced at the sleeping child, but she hadn't stirred.

He slipped back into the hall and listened for something to tell him where the woman was, but he could hear only the rain and rumbling, distant thunder. He remembered the blue bedroom. Was she in there now? Undressing, maybe . . . ?

He walked to the end of the hall and stopped in the shadows. A lamp was on in the family room, but he didn't see her. There wasn't any light in the bedroom. He eased along the wall until he could see into the family room.

She was standing by the patio doors staring out at the rain. From time to time she moved her head, and he glimpsed her high cheekbones and delicate features. She was somber now, but he could still hear the soft, musical sound of her laughter as she talked to the child earlier. For a moment she'd sounded so much like Sharon, he almost started toward her. He'd caught himself just in time and stayed where he was. Her throaty voice was the kind meant for whispering in dark bedrooms.

She turned suddenly, and he blended back into the shadows. When she started toward the doorway he slipped quickly back to the dining room.

8

Eve stared at the rain-drenched gloom. It seemed more like midnight than afternoon, with the sun hidden behind a thick layer of clouds and marine air. Fog rolled up the canyon to enfold the summit, and the wind whipped trees and brush so the darkness of the woods surrounding the house seemed alive. Branches and leaves torn from limbs littered the deck. The rain hitting the water in the pool gave it the appearance of pebbled glass, and the water level had risen dangerously. If the storm didn't let up soon, it would overflow. She should go out and open the drain valve, but she wasn't sure she knew how to do it. Paul had always taken care of it. She bit her lip, not positive she even remembered where the instructions were.

So many things in her life had changed these past months. Each day she discovered some little thing, some detail she'd never worried about before because Paul had handled it. At first they had overwhelmed her, but gradually she was organizing her time and efforts so the tasks seemed less formidable. In time they would become routine, and life would settle comfortably.

The rain tapped steadily on the roof in a blur of sound. For a moment it took her back to her childhood when she used to play in the attic of the big, old three-story house in Minneapolis on rainy days. Unearthing clothes from dusty trunks, dressing up, pretending . . . So long ago. She'd enjoyed a happy childhood, secure in the love of two parents. Now she'd have to be more than a mother to Cindy. . . .

A shimmering reflection in the glass made Eve whirl, but there was nothing there. She chided herself for being jumpy. The constant howl of the wind was putting her nerves on edge. Shivering, she pulled the drapes to shut out the storm. She didn't like being alone in this kind of weather. The seclusion that gave the house charm in summer was stripped away by the keening wind and ominous dark sky. Dorie pestered her to sell the house and move down into the Valley, but Eve couldn't cut herself off from all the things that had been so dear to Paul. He'd always wanted to live in a canyon house and had bought this one soon after forming his own company as a consulting engineer. He admitted he was striking out from Dorie as well, establishing distance to escape her mothering and frequent well-intentioned visits. He was already living here when Eve met him, but together they had decorated and chosen furnishings to replace his stark bachelor pieces. They'd made the house warm and inviting, a place of love. And when she became pregnant she'd set aside her career joyously in anticipation of motherhood. Paul had gone to natural childbirth classes with her and rubbed her back and counted for her breathing during labor. Together they rejoiced over the magnificent infant they had brought into the world. And they cried together when they learned that their beautiful baby had a stomach problem that required surgery. They'd held hands and prayed here in this room and in the hospital. And Cindy had come through miraculously. Only now, Paul wasn't here to watch her grow up and fulfill their dreams.

Eve glanced wistfully around the room. Paul's chair . . . his shelf of books, one with a ragged strip of newspaper still marking his place . . . his pipes on the mantel beside the leather canister of tobacco. . . . She could never sell the house. It would be like denying everything she and Paul had shared. She'd told Farley that when he suggested she might want to put painful memories behind her by living elsewhere. He had understood. Dear Farley, so patient and empathetic. Dorie nagged and complained constantly, hurt because the person she loved more than life itself had been cruelly snatched away in his prime. Dorie would never understand. In her limited vision only she had the right to cling to Paul's memory.

Eve glanced toward the hall when she heard another sound. Cindy? She set down the empty mug and hurried to the bedroom. Cindy was still asleep, one arm flung restlessly over the quilt. Eve touched her forehead lightly. Was she warmer? She'd been sleeping only half an hour, barely long enough for the medicine to begin taking effect. Wait, Eve told herself. Wait.

She jerked around at another faint noise that seemed to come from Paul's office. Had she left a window open? No, she was positive she'd checked all the windows this morning before she went out. She tiptoed from the bedroom, closing the door partway to prevent any draft. She stopped with her hand on the doorknob of the office door. It was shut when she went by a few minutes ago. She always closed it when she was home so she wouldn't be haunted by seeing ghosts of Paul bent over the work he used to bring home from the office. She distinctly recalled pulling it shut when she went for Cindy's medicine, but the door was ajar now. Had it blown open? A draft when she'd come in from the garage? She pushed it gently. It swang inward.

The room was dark, the single window a gray rectangle of wavering, rain-soaked shadows. The window was tightly closed and locked, the way it always was. The red eye of the answering machine glowed unblinkingly. Relieved, she backed out and pulled the door shut. She was imagining things. It wasn't hard to do in a storm like this. There were always creaks and groans in a house as the wood swelled with dampness. She was nervous and on edge because she was worried about Cindy. That was all. She started back to the family room but stopped as the lights flickered. If the power went off . . . She reversed direction and hurried to the kitchen. She found candles and matches in a drawer and carried them to the dining room. She put the candles in silver and crystal holders on the buffet and laid the matches beside them. Lightning splashed an eerie pale blanket over the skylight, and the house shuddered as thunder rumbled. The lights flickered again, came on fitfully, then went out. She groped for the matches.

When she got one candle lit she used it to light three more. Leaving two on the table, she carried one to Cindy's room and put it on the dresser, then took the other one to the den. Grotesque shadows leaped along the carpet and walls. The heat would go off. She'd have to build a fire in the fireplace and bring Cindy in here if the house cooled. Was there wood? She lifted the lid of the woodbox and felt inside. Only a few pieces, but Paul had stacked a good supply in the garage where it was dry and close at hand. She left the candle on the mantel and felt her way along the dim hall. She carried one of the candles from the dining room to the kitchen and put it on the counter.

The lights came on, but she left the candle burning as she went through the laundry room and into the garage, propping the door open behind her. The canvas wood carrier wasn't hanging in its usual spot, but she found it beside the neatly stacked wood where she remembered leaving it a few days ago. Quickly she laid half a dozen small logs in it and carried it inside. The lights went out again as she closed the laundry-room door. She stood a moment until her eyes got accustomed to the eerie half-light of the candles before she made her way through the house.

As she passed the dining room she hesitated, sure she'd heard some faint, unidentifiable sound. Shadows played across the oak table and high-backed chairs, thrusting and reaching in the erratic light. The garage door had created a draft. Shadows. The rain on the skylight. Nothing else. Her mouth was dry, and she realized suddenly that she was afraid. Of what? The dark? The storm? Don't be a fool, she scolded herself.

She forced herself to walk down the hall, her teeth clenched in determination. The house felt cold, though she knew the temperature couldn't have dropped more than half a degree in so short a time. The dampness seemed to penetrate her bones, and she shivered as she dropped the wood in the box and knelt on the hearth. She crumbled newspaper, laid kindling, and stacked wood carefully in an open pyramid. Her hands trembled as she struck one of the long matches from a box beside the fireplace tools and touched it to the paper. Flames licked upward like hungry, yellow jaws. The kindling began to crackle, and a few of the smaller pieces caught. Eve got to her feet and held her hands close to the blaze. The room would be cozy in a few minutes. When it was, she'd bring Cindy in and take her temperature again. Then . . .

At the edge of her vision the shadows shifted perceptibly. She jerked around as a figure emerged from the dark hall. Even in the flickering light Eve knew she had never seen him before. Terror-stricken, she pressed a hand to her throat as he moved toward her.

9

Sergeant James Noble waited until the coroner's men carried out the body before knocking on the Casa Risa caretaker's door. He'd spoken to the Dawson woman when he and Rothman arrived. His suggestion of taking her to the station for questioning had produced near hysteria, so he told her to wait in her apartment until they finished upstairs. Noble heard the solid click of the door bolts being shot home before he was two feet from the door.

Now, after Noble knocked and identified himself in response to her query, Ida Dawson opened the door a crack and peered out. The door closed and he heard the chain being undone. As she led him down the hall to the living room, she kept looking over her shoulder as if the killer might be lurking in the shadows. Noble saw her apartment was laid out the same as the Peters woman's upstairs, but it was darker. Mrs. Dawson snapped off the television and turned on a lamp, but it didn't do much to improve the gloom. There wasn't enough light to read by, but it probably didn't bother her. There wasn't a magazine or book in sight.

Ida Dawson settled nervously on the sofa and clasped her hands in her lap. She was pale, but Noble wasn't sure how much of it was shock and how much was her mole-like existence in the dark ground-floor apartment. He settled his five-feet-ten, sparse frame on one of Ida's slipcovered chairs. He hadn't seen slipcovers since he was a kid, and he wondered where she got them. Making sure it wouldn't drip, he put his hat on the spindly-legged end table and gave Mrs. Dawson a reassuring smile.

"She's gone? I mean they took away the . . . ?" Ida's gaze couldn't settle.

"Yes, Mrs. Dawson. We have to seal the apartment until our investigation is completed. No one can go in until we remove the seal." His apologetic tone was designed to put her at ease.

Ida nodded, still nervous. "The rent is paid to the end of the month. Nothing like this has ever happened before. I'm not responsible for renting the apartments, you know. The landlord does that. I show the vacancies, but he picks the tenants."

Noble opened a notebook. "I'll need his address and phone number."

Relieved to be rid of the responsibility, Ida pulled a card she had waiting from the pocket of her brown sweater and gave it to him.

Noble glanced at it before he tucked it under a paper clip on the open page of the notebook. "Now, Mrs. Dawson, tell me how it happened that you found Miss Peters." He gave it just the right encouraging tone.

The caretaker hunched her body with a shuddering sigh. "I used my passkey to go in and shut the window. I don't usually go into tenants' apartments when they're not home, but the man next door complained his things were getting wet. She's done it before. Left the window open, I mean."

"What made you think she wasn't home?"

"Stanley Morse said so, and an hour before that, her friend said the same thing."

"What friend is that?" Noble asked, as if they were gossiping over the back fence.

Ida told him about the woman who wanted to go in and wait for Janine Peters, right down to a description of her eye makeup.

"Did she give you her name?"

Ida shook her head. "I didn't ask. They're friends, though. I've seen the dark-haired one here before."

"Do you have any idea where she lives?"

"No. She always drives."

"What kind of car?" The Dawson woman was the type who kept her curiosity fed on the lives of her tenants. Noble recognized the classic signs.

Ida frowned. "One of those little Japanese ones. It's red."

"Did the Peters woman have a car?"

She nodded. "A dark blue Camaro."

"Where does she keep it?"

"The parking lot out back."

"Is it there now?"

Ida looked surprised. "I suppose so."

Noble knew Ida had been too frightened after seeing Janine Peters's body to check, and she was regretting the lapse now. She'd probably correct it as soon as he left.

"Did the woman say why she wanted to see Miss Peters?"

Ida's head wagged. "No, but she said it was important. She seemed upset about something. Do you think she knew . . . ?"

Noble shook his head to dispel her morbid speculation. "Did you touch anything in the apartment?"

"The window. I shut the window in the bedroom."

"Nothing else?"

Ida frowned and looked afraid of leaving out any detail that might cause her trouble later. "The wall was wet, so I lifted the carpet to look at the floor. There was water all over. I was afraid it would leak down to the apartment below. I was going to wipe it up. I went into the bathroom to get a towel." She shuddered and pressed her pudgy hand against her chest. "That's when I saw her." She closed her eyes and breathed heavily.

Noble waited until she opened them, then looked sympathetic without encouraging her dramatics. "When was the last time you saw Miss Peters alive?"

Ida recovered quickly. "Last night about seven-thirty. She was going out."

"Did you talk to her?"

"No. I was just coming out of my apartment when she went out the back door."

It was more likely Ida checked when she heard steps in the hall. "Was it raining?"

"It was pouring, just like now. I remember thinking she must have a pretty important date to go back out in that weather."

"Was she alone?"

Ida nodded, her eyes bright. "But she didn't come home alone."

"ᴌou saw her come home?"

"No, I heard her."

"You heard her?" Noble furrowed his brow.

Ida explained that her bedroom was next to the stairwell and anyone going up the stairs usually woke her unless they were exceptionally quiet.

"How could you be sure it was Miss Peters and not one of the other tenants?"

"I heard her giggling and whispering. There was a man with her."

"You're sure it was a man?"

Ida nodded emphatically. "Men walk heavier than women."

"What time was this?" Noble asked.

"A little after midnight. I was tired and decided not to stay up for all of 'Johnny Carson.' "

"Did you see the man?"

She shook her head.

"Did you hear him leave?"

Again she shook her head. Apparently only people going up the stairs wakened her. Noble asked her a few more questions about the dead girl but didn't learn much except that she worked for a typing service and had no relatives the caretaker knew about. Noble got the name and address of the company that employed Janine Peters and, after cautioning Mrs. Dawson not to break the police seal on the door of the dead girl's apartment, left. Harry Rothman was waiting in the hall, comfortably slouched on the bottom step eating a granola bar. He got to his feet and folded the paper over the half-eaten bar before dropping it in his pocket. "Anything?" he asked, still chewing.

Noble and Rothman had been partners for almost a year, and

he'd gotten accustomed to the younger man's different approach to life and police work. If there was one thing Noble had learned in thirty-two years on the force, it was that police officers came in all shapes and forms. Harry was one of the higher species.

"There was a guy with her last night. How'd you make out with the other tenants?"

"Not much," Rothman said. "People pretty much mind their own business in a place like this, but I got the impression from the guy next door that it wasn't unusual for her to bring men home. He didn't call her a hooker, but I think he wanted to. Not much neighborly goodwill between them."

"That would be Stanley Morse?"

"Yeah. I guess the caretaker told you about the open window? I checked the floor and wall of Morse's living room, and like he said, water came right through from the next apartment. The walls are so thin neighbors could share pictures."

"Did Morse hear anything last night or this morning?"

"His bedroom is at the other end. He went out for his morning jog about seven. He says her newspaper was in front of the door, but it was gone when he got back a little after eight."

Noble remembered the crime scene. The morning *Herald* was lying on the floor beside the bed. "So she was alive this morning," he said, rubbing the wrist that ached arthritically with the fall of the barometer.

"Unless the killer picked it up," Rothman offered.

"After spending the night with the corpse?" It wasn't impossible, but over the years Noble had learned the simple answers were usually right. "We'll know when we get the coroner's report. Let's check out the parking lot in back. The Dawson woman says Peters drove a dark blue Camaro."

"Want me to bring the car up?" Rothman asked.

Noble eyed the gray veil of rain over the street. There was no use waiting for it to stop. The forecast was for two or three more days of it. His arthritis was already sending out a steady flow of pain signals.

"I'll go out the back way and have a look. You bring the car around."

Rothman hesitated, and Noble thought he was going to argue. Finally Harry shrugged. Turning up the collar of his London Fog raincoat, Rothman opened the door and sprinted down the sidewalk toward the place they'd parked the car. Noble sighed as he buttoned his plastic slicker and put on his hat.

10

Farley rescued his raincoat and hat from the checkroom and put them on as he crossed the lobby. From the doorway he studied the downpour. The windowless meeting room had shut out the storm, but now its fury was alarming. The big lobby windows, which usually afforded a magnificent view of the ocean, were opaque with rain. The palm trees bordering the walks and street were tortured shadows bent in the wind. A series of storms spawned by a hurricane off the coast of Mexico that had been hitting Southern California all week showed no sign of breaking. During the day the sky had gone from pewter to lead, and the rain from steady to savage. If it was worse in L.A., as Jess said, Farley couldn't help worrying about Eve and Cindy. He didn't like the idea of the two of them alone in the house. It didn't rain a lot in the Valley, but when it did, the sky opened up—roofs leaked and trees fell. The canyons were dangerous during severe storms like this.

He'd made numerous trips to Santa Barbara and always been fortunate to see it in good weather, when it lived up to the tourist association's brochure promises. Now, in the rain, its charm was dulled by a dreary, gray pall. Heavy fog rolled in from the ocean, where the sun usually glinted on the water in diamond sparkles. The streets were deserted except for an occasional car splashing by, windshield wipers slapping. Still there was an inviting magic about the storm. It created an atmosphere perfect for sitting by a fireplace and sipping wine. The kind of evening that called for a woman like Eve. Farley smiled, envisioning the two of them by firelight in that cozy Bed and Breakfast Inn he'd discovered last year.

He thought about Jess Mavella's teasing. It was more on tar-get than Farley was ready to admit. He realized a couple of months ago he was falling in love with Eve. A few times when he'd gone to the house on business, Eve had cooked dinner for the three of them. He was comfortable with her and Cindy, and he enjoyed their company. Cindy had grown to accept him openly and look forward to his visits. Eve was reserved, but he knew she was slowly separating herself from the painful memo-ries of Paul. Farley respected the friendly distance she kept between them, but he hoped it wouldn't be long until she was ready to begin a new phase of her life.

He was encouraged now that she was resuming her career, and he was especially pleased with her promise to call him tonight and let him know how the commercial had gone today. He always left a number when he went out of town, but it never occurred to her to call just so he could hear her voice. Her first day back before the cameras was cause for celebration. He'd ask her out to dinner as soon as he got back, and he wouldn't take no for an answer.

He dismissed the pleasant reverie as he hunched into his raincoat and made a dash for the car. His shoes and trouser legs were soaked by the time he crossed the crowded parking lot. Struggling with the sluicing rain and poor visibility, he pulled out and drove carefully along the oceanfront road toward town. He'd never told Eve about Paul's bitchy sister trying to make trouble. Paul left his sister a decent bequest, but everything else —his stock, the company, the house, and bank accounts—was undeniably Eve's and Cindy's. If Paul ever had a will giving Dorie part of the company, the way she claimed, it had been voided by the revocable living trust Paul set up. Farley seriously doubted such a will ever existed, considering Paul's long-stand-ing resentment of his sister's constant demands on his life. He'd paid off any debt he owed her long ago—the condominium in

Toluca Lake, an annuity. . . . Not that Dorie needed financial help. She had a damned good job with a top salary and benefits, and probably a sweet little nest egg tucked away. Dorie didn't need money. Dorie needed to be needed. She needed to control. And now that Paul was gone, she was setting her sights on Cindy. And the hell of it was, Eve was still too mired in grief over losing Paul to fight her effectively.

The rain was a drumroll on the car roof. If the storm was worse in L.A., he didn't like to think what kind of a beating the city was taking. With five days of steady rain, traffic would be snarled and roads blocked or maybe even closed. It made him nervous to think about Eve and Cindy in the house up near the summit of Coldwater Canyon. There had been some serious slides there during the record-breaking rains of 1980. Even though the house had come through without damage that time, this deluge made any canyon a catastrophe waiting to happen.

When he pulled up at the motel he made another sprint for his room. Inside, he hung his dripping raincoat over a corner of the bathroom door, then stripped and took a hot shower. Dressed in slacks and a comfortable velour shirt, he checked his watch, wondering if Eve was home. He probably should wait for her call, but he'd feel better knowing she was all right. There had been times after Paul died that she was depressed and wouldn't go out or even answer the phone. On several occasions he'd driven up to the house to make sure she was all right. He found her just sitting, sometimes with music playing softly, sometimes in silence. She'd left everything the way it was before the accident—Paul's office, his clothes in the closet, his magazines and the book he'd been halfway through, his tobacco and pipes. When Farley gently urged her to remove the painful reminders, even offered to do it for her, she smiled and said she'd take care of it when the time was right.

He picked up the phone and got an outside line. He dialed her number and listened to the phone ring, but she didn't pick it up and the answering machine didn't cut in. That was strange. Farley glanced at his watch again. It was a few minutes past four. Maybe she was waiting at the door for Cindy. It was

just about time for the car pool to drop her off. He hung up and
snapped on the television set and found a news station. The
storm was topping all other stories. With growing dismay he
listened to reports of damage throughout the Los Angeles area.
There wasn't any specific mention of Coldwater Canyon, but
several houses along Mulholland Drive had been evacuated
because the ground was washing away on the hillside.

He lowered the sound and picked up the phone again. As
long as he satisfied himself they were all right, he'd postpone
any lengthy chat with Eve until after she got Cindy settled.
While the phone rang he gazed at the silent picture on the TV
screen, where a reporter in a yellow slicker hunched under an
umbrella trying to shield his microphone. Behind him a dozen
people were filling and stacking sandbags in an attempt to con-
tain the erosion from a tide of water rushing down the street.

The distant sound of ringing wasn't answered. They both
should be there. It wasn't Eve's week to drive, and she reli-
giously made a point of being home when Cindy came from
nursery school. Maybe the car pool was late. Eve could be in the
garage or doing laundry. There were a dozen explanations for
her not answering, he told himself. Hanging up, he turned up
the volume on the television and listened to the news again, but
he couldn't keep himself from glancing at his watch every few
seconds. Finally, too impatient to sit still, he tried Eve's number
again. This time when she didn't answer, he dialed the operator
and asked her to place the call. While he waited he looked out
the window at the fog-shrouded city. Normally he could see the
ocean from here, but now he couldn't see across the street.

"Your party doesn't answer," the operator reported after a
minute.

"Will you check with the Los Angeles operator to see if the
lines are working, please? It's important." The girl put him on
hold, and he waited restlessly. Where in the world could Eve
be? She wouldn't go out in this kind of weather unless it was an
emergency.

When the motel operator came back on the line, she said,
"Your party's line hasn't been reported out of order, but the Los

Angeles operator says they're having a lot of problems because of the storm."

Farley thanked her and hung up. If she was right, it didn't relieve his anxiety. Nor did the television news coverage. He turned up the volume as the camera showed a house sagging dangerously, undermined by a torrent of mud that had come down the hill.

"The Walker residence at the top of Idle Lane in upper Mandeville Canyon was completely demolished as a mud slide ripped it from its foundation and swept it away. The slide picked up momentum as it moved downhill, where it slammed into the home of Mr. and Mrs. Thornton Peavey, a hundred yards down the canyon. The living room and bedroom were torn from the structure, which was left hanging precariously on the edge of the hillside, as you see behind me. Miraculously, no one was injured, since residents of lower Mandeville Canyon Road were evacuated earlier this afternoon.

"Widespread damage has also been reported in Topanga Canyon, Altadena, Monterey Park, and Malibu. The Los Angeles Fire Department is providing burlap bags for sandbagging free of charge to anyone who needs them. These can be picked up at local fire stations."

Farley sank onto a chair and leaned toward the set. The destruction had begun.

11

He stopped in the doorway, his eyes reflecting light like an animal's caught in the glare of headlights. Clutching the mantel, Eve tried to control her panic as she stared at the dark, menacing figure. She swayed as her legs trembled.

"Who are you?" she asked in a terrified whisper.

His voice was a low rumble, like distant thunder. "My car stalled. I saw your lights."

"How—how did you get in?" He was tall and muscular, with a thin face and square, heavy jaw. His eyes were glowing coals under his thick, dark brows. His gaze didn't waver.

He pointed toward the closed drapes. "You forgot to lock the patio door."

He was lying. She'd checked the Charley Bar and windows before she left this morning. In spite of her fear, she challenged him angrily. "Are you in the habit of walking into other people's houses?"

His indecipherable gaze pinned her, and his body tensed. "I was cold and wet," he said flatly.

She eyed his dry shirt and sweater. He was lying again—no, the clothes were Paul's! She recognized the alpaca sweater she'd bought him for Christmas a year ago, and the blue and gray argyle socks she'd knit so lovingly. She was struck dumb by rage.

He saw her glance, and his mouth curved in a peculiar smile

that infuriated her and snapped her from silence. "How dare you! That doesn't give you the right—" She broke off as his expression altered alarmingly. His eyes seemed to retreat deeper into his skull, and his jaw tightened. He blinked rapidly and breathed through his mouth, making air hiss between his teeth. Fear washed over Eve in a cold torrent. He didn't care about rights. He'd already claimed too many that weren't his. He'd come into the house while she was gone and been here all along, hiding, watching her. Panic knotted her chest. Who was he? What was he waiting for?

"What do you want?" She finally managed to push the question from her brassy tongue.

His glance slithered around the room, then lingered on the fire. "To be warm and dry. When the storm lets up, I'll go."

Eve clung to the mantel, wanting to believe him but knowing she didn't. She summoned her courage. "I'm afraid that's impossible. You'll have to go now." The words came out in tight, hard chips. In the fireplace a log shifted with a sizzle of sparks. Rain slashed against the house in a sudden spate. The man didn't move. "I'm telling you to leave!" Eve's voice climbed hysterically.

The man's gaze flickered. "You shouldn't be alone in a storm like this."

"I—I'm not. My husband will be home any minute," Eve said.

The intruder smiled as if he knew she was lying.

Confused, Eve faltered. "I—I don't care about the clothes. Take them. I'll find you a raincoat. Did you phone someone about your car? I know a very good mechanic—"

"No one's coming out in this rain."

"He will," she said desperately. She moved toward the phone on the desk, but the man blocked her way and grabbed her wrist. She winced under the pressure of his huge hand. For the first time she knew the meaning of true terror. She was no match for his strength. Or his cunning. He'd been in the house at least an hour, but she hadn't seen him until he decided to come out of hiding.

"I'll wait for the rain to stop," he said.

He let go abruptly and moved away. She rubbed the tender flesh where his fingers had dug. His brief flash of violence was over. He was remote again. Eve tried to make sense of his actions. He could have attacked her long before this if that's what he intended. If he was a thief, he could have taken everything of value and been gone. Had she surprised him in the act? No, there'd been plenty of time to escape while she was busy with Cindy. Good Lord—Cindy— She glanced nervously toward the hall.

"Go see if she's feeling better," he said.

Startled, she edged past him and ran toward her daughter's room. Her breath exploded in tiny bursts and her heartbeat thundered in her ears. He hadn't stopped her. Was he harmless? Was he only what he claimed—a person needing a port in a storm? She grasped at the thin hope, but the memory of his thick fingers circling her wrist, immobilizing her, was overpowering. She was afraid.

She breathed a faint sigh when she saw that Cindy was still asleep. She had turned on her side and lay curled like a caterpillar, her knees drawn up and her arms hugging her tummy. There were tiny lines etched between her brows, as though she were trying to squeeze away the pain. Eve sat on the edge of the bed and felt the child's forehead. It was hot against her icy fingers. She reached for the thermometer, shook it down, and coaxed it between Cindy's lips.

"Honey, let Mommy take your temperature," she whispered.

Cindy whimpered and opened her eyes. "My tummy hurts."

"I know, sweetheart. You'll feel better soon. Open your mouth. There, now keep it under your tongue like a good girl." She forced a smile, but Cindy's pinched expression didn't relax. For a moment Eve forgot her terror and the man in the other room. Cindy was ill. It was apparent now in her glazed eyes and flushed cheeks. Eve breathed deeply as the cow-shaped sweep-second hand on the nursery-rhyme clock ran its course around the moon face before she read the thermometer. Cindy's temperature had gone up half a degree.

When Cindy stirred restlessly Eve tried to comfort her.

"Would you like some cocoa?" It was a stopgap measure, a soothing panacea that might help until she could reach Dr. Provel.

Cindy nodded lethargically. Eve tucked the comforter around her. "I'll be right back."

"Turn the light on, Mommy."

"I can't, sweetheart. The electricity went off because of the storm. I'll bring another candle."

"I'm scared of the shadows. They're watching me," Cindy whimpered.

With shocking force, Eve remembered the man in the other room. She stroked Cindy's face and bent to kiss her. "There's nothing to be afraid of, sweetheart. I'm right here." The reassurance quavered on Eve's lips.

"I want Daddy," the child whined. A tear brimmed on her long lashes, then slid along her cheek.

Eve's throat tightened. She cradled Cindy in her arms. "Daddy's gone, honey, but you know he still loves you and is looking down from heaven right this minute. He wants you to get better." The tears overflowed Cindy's eyes. Eve rocked her, whispering, "Don't cry, darling. It will make your tummy hurt." Cindy sniffled and pouted. "I want my daddy."

Eve's chest burned with raw anguish. "Shh . . . Mommy's going to make you some nice warm cocoa to help you feel better." She kissed Cindy's damp, golden hair. "You close your eyes and think about the teddy bears' picnic." She lay Cindy back and adjusted the cover, smiling until Cindy played the game and closed her eyes. "I'll be right back," Eve whispered. Cindy nodded without opening her eyes.

As Eve rose the door whispered across the pink carpet. The man stood in the doorway, watching her. The sight of him in Cindy's room plummeted Eve back into terror. The sputtering candlelight made his face a distorted mask, and his body seemed to fill the doorway. Eve moved quickly, catching the door and pulling it shut behind her as she forced him back into the hall.

"She's worse," Eve said hoarsely. "I'm going to call the doctor." In the dark hall he loomed over her, so close she could smell wood smoke clinging to Paul's alpaca sweater.

"What's the matter with her?"

"She has a stomachache."

"Kids get them."

"She had surgery when she was a baby. We have to be careful about any kind of flu or—"

"What kind of surgery?"

The rational question frightened Eve as much as his violence had. She explained the delicate resectioning that had been necessary on Cindy's digestive system.

He scowled. "They say she's going to be all right?"

"They think so."

He snorted. "No guarantees, huh? That's doctors for you. You pay 'em and take your chances. I don't like doctors." His voice had an angry edge. He glanced at the closed door to Cindy's room. "It's getting cold in here. Is she warm enough?"

"I covered her," Eve said. She couldn't let him go in there. She watched him warily.

He was silent a moment, then said, "Go make her cocoa." It was an order.

Eve hesitated, startled by the realization that he'd listened to her talking to Cindy. Had he heard what she said about Paul? Would he go into Cindy's room? She folded her arms and tugged at her sweater nervously. "She's resting quietly. Please don't go in and wake—"

"You told her you'd be right back," he snapped. He put his hand on Eve's shoulder and pushed her toward the kitchen.

She flew down the hall. Make the cocoa and get back. Don't let him be alone with Cindy. He wouldn't harm her. He couldn't. He sounded genuinely interested in her health.

Reaching into a cupboard, she found the cocoa mix. Milk splashed on the counter as she filled a small saucepan and set it on the stove. She stopped with her hand in midair, then clamped it over her mouth as a sob escaped. She was so frightened, it hadn't occurred to her until now that the stove was electric. She whimpered and looked around the kitchen helplessly.

The phone. What was the matter with her? With a furtive glance toward the hall, she eased the receiver from the hook and hit 911. The line crackled and spat, then hummed. She broke the connection and dialed again. It began to ring like a distant buoy. Answer. Somebody answer!

"Mommy!" Cindy's shriek cut through the dark house like a bolt of lightning.

Eve dropped the phone and ran.

12

He was sitting on the bed beside Cindy, who was hunched against the pillows. She looked wan and feverish, but her gaze was wary and curious. She was watching the stranger the way she did when she encountered a new adventure that was potentially interesting. Eve heard the low murmur of the man's voice as she hurried to the bed.

"What happened? Cindy, are you all right?" Eve's gaze searched for reassurance. She turned on the man. "What did you do?" she demanded.

Tight lines knit across Cindy's brow as she looked at her mother. Her lower lip quivered. "You promised cocoa," she said sulkily. Her blue eyes clouded and she looked back to the man sitting close to her. "He said you were fixing it."

"If you left it on the stove, it'll boil over," he criticized sharply.

Eve's nerves snapped. "The stove is electric." She was close to tears, even though she was shaking with relief that Cindy was all right. He hadn't hurt her. Her reaction had been instinctive when Cindy cried out because she was terrified of this man. She patted Cindy's hand to hide her own nervousness and watched him covertly, trying vainly to convince herself he meant them no harm.

Abruptly he got to his feet and bent over Cindy. Before Eve

realized what was happening he scooped Cindy, quilt, and pillows into his arms. Eve jumped up, but he elbowed her aside.

"She'll be warmer by the fire," he said. Cindy snuggled
against him comfortably as he carried her out.

Eve stumbled after them, fighting her anger and fear. She
staggered down the deeply shadowed hall to the family room
and clutched the doorframe as she watched him settle Cindy on
the sofa. He plumped the pillows and tucked the quilt around
the child with a gentleness that elicited a wan smile from Cindy.
He touched her flushed cheek and smiled tenderly. Bending, he
pushed the sofa to face the fireplace, then sat beside Cindy
again.

His voice was a soft, comforting murmur as he coaxed her to
relax. Cindy's fear had vanished. Her eyes closed with complete
trust. Whatever had frightened her at first was gone now, but
Eve's heart was still pounding. When the man finally rose and
faced her, it skipped a beat erratically.

"Sit with her," he ordered.

Eve sank obediently to the sofa, watching him as he moved
away. He paused a moment in the doorway to glance back, as
though making sure she was still there, then walked out. Eve
listened to his footsteps retreat down the hall. She forced a
breath against the steel band squeezing her chest. This was
insane. A stranger, an intruder, capable of God knew what,
taking over her house and giving her orders. She had to do
something. She glanced at the telephone, then at Cindy, whose
eyes were closed. Her breathing was shallow and even. She had
drifted off to sleep again. Eve slid from the sofa, so she wouldn't
wake Cindy, and tiptoed to the phone. Glancing down the hall
to make sure the man was out of earshot, she lifted the receiver.
With a prayer of thanks for the silent push buttons, she dialed
911, then frowned when she realized there was still no sound on
the line. She jiggled the button, but nothing happened. Biting
her lip, she jabbed the emergency numbers again with desperate hope, but the phone was dead. She replaced the receiver.
Had the phone gone out because of the storm or had he disabled
it? The possibility made her shiver, and she looked around

quickly, wondering where he was and what he was doing. She
strained to listen for some sound that would pinpoint his movements, but the house was quiet except for the keening of the
wind and the steady beat of the rain. Eve paced nervously,
trying to think what to do next.

He moved so quietly he was in the room without a sound. She
felt his presence and whirled guiltily. His dark brows pinched
over his accusing eyes.

"I told you to sit with her." His voice rose on an angry note.
Eve sank to the cushion beside Cindy, her heart thudding as she
kept her gaze fixed on him. He was carrying the cocoa pan and a
long-handled wooden spoon. Hooked over one thick, blunt finger was Cindy's Care Bear mug. He glanced at Cindy with a
worried expression, then went to the fireplace. Kneeling, he set
down the mug and pan. From the pocket of Paul's slacks he
produced a pot holder, which he wrapped around the handle
before he held the pot over the fire.

For a moment Eve was hypnotized by the leaping yellow
flames and the slow, deliberate way he stirred the cocoa. It was
so *ordinary*. She and Paul had spent so many evenings like this.
But this wasn't Paul. It was a stranger she couldn't trust. She
glanced around the room covertly. If she could find a weapon
and knock him out while he was preoccupied with the cocoa,
she could grab Cindy and run for the car. She could—

He looked up as if she'd spoken aloud. Eve dropped her gaze
and busied her hands rearranging the quilt. She was aware of
his movements, but she didn't look directly at him again. When
the cocoa was ready he filled the mug and carried it to the sofa.
Eve reached for it, but he pushed aside her hand and motioned
for her to move so he could sit beside Cindy. Numbly, she slid
across to a chair, still watching him. Gently, he lifted Cindy's
shoulders and propped her in the crook of his arm. She opened
her eyes sleepily. He held the mug to her mouth.

"Drink your cocoa. It's not too hot. It's just right," he said
softly.

Cindy sipped obediently, her small face puckered. After one
swallow she tried to turn away, but he blocked the movement

deftly with his arm. He coaxed insistently, "A little more. That's a good girl." Before he laid her back on the pillows, the mug was empty. Cindy licked a chocolate mustache from her lip and gave him a hesitant smile. When he adjusted the quilt Cindy poked her arm out from under it and touched his hand. His blunt fingers closed around her tiny pink ones. Another wan smile touched Cindy's face as she closed her eyes.

Eve's breath strained. Cindy was accepting the stranger as someone who fit nicely into the order of her world. Why didn't Eve find it reassuring? There had been plenty of chances for him to do them harm, but he hadn't. He seemed filled with concern for Cindy. He'd quieted her, gotten her to drink the cocoa, and now to sleep. But somehow the domestic tranquility had an undercurrent of menace, a dark evil lurking beneath the surface. Being good to Cindy didn't change the fact that he was an unwelcome trespasser about whom she knew nothing.

After a few minutes Cindy's breathing fell into a soft, regular pattern of sleep. The man slid his hand free, tucked the quilt over her, and got up. He held out the empty mug. Eve took it automatically and put it on the table.

"She'll sleep now," he said.

"I still have to call the doctor," Eve said. She rose and started for the phone, but he stepped in front of her.

His eyes glinted in the firelight. "This doctor, is he a specialist?"

"A pediatrician." It seemed important to add, "He's very good. He's been Cindy's doctor since she was born. I'm supposed to call him if her fever goes up."

He digested her words for several moments, then said, "The phone's out."

She blinked. He knew about the phone. Had he picked up the kitchen extension while she was dialing? Or had he cut the wires? She thought of a hundred movies where killers had done it to isolate their intended victims. Terror crept along her flesh, and she suppressed a shudder. She had to get away from him and take Cindy to the doctor.

"He always wants to check her if her fever's up." She laced

her fingers to keep her hands from shaking. "I'll have to take her to his office."

A log snapped with a shower of sparks. Eve gave a nervous start. The room was suddenly still, the wind temporarily lulled as it gathered strength for another thrust. He was quiet so long she wondered if he'd heard her. He was studying her with an odd expression.

After a long interval he said, "You can't take her out in this rain."

"I have to—"

"I said you can't!" His voice rose sharply, and his eyes were glacial despite the pinpoints of fire gleaming in their black depths.

Eve wavered between fury and fear. His mood changed so abruptly it was hard to reconcile his anger with the tender concern he'd shown for Cindy a few minutes ago. He wasn't going to let them leave, not even for Cindy to go to the doctor. Yet he had comforted Cindy lovingly, the way a parent would. Did he have a child of his own? Cautiously she attempted to play on his soft spot.

"I'm sorry." She tried to sound contrite. "It's just that I'm so worried about her. I should have taken her to the doctor when I picked her up from school. I shouldn't have taken a chance in this weather." She watched for his reaction, but his face was expressionless. "She's getting worse!" It came out shrilly, and Eve struggled for control. "It's important to start her on medication before her digestive system gets inflamed."

His mouth compressed to a thin, white line. He turned to look at Cindy's flushed face. His voice was cold steel. "You said the cocoa would help."

"It helps, but it doesn't cure anything." Didn't he understand?

"She's sleeping quietly." He tilted his head for a better view of Cindy's face, nodding to confirm his statement.

"But her temperature is up. The doctor—"

"Damn doctors don't know everything! She's asleep. She's going to be okay, now shut up about it!" He turned away and walked down the hall, padding softly in Paul's hand-knit argyle socks.

Eve collapsed onto a chair and buried her face in her hands until her trembling subsided. She'd pushed him close to rage, and it was frightening. She could no longer delude herself that she was dealing with a rational man, but neither could she stand by helplessly and ignore Cindy's worsening condition because a stranger was giving her orders. Would he stop her physically if she tried to leave? She got up and moved around the room nervously, glancing down the hall and wondering how long he'd be gone. She tiptoed to the desk and lifted the phone again, but the line was still dead.

Cindy stirred restlessly. Eve went back to the sofa and sat beside her to smooth the damp, golden ringlets. Cindy's face was warmer, no question about it. Was she too close to the fire?

Eve tried to stay calm. If Cindy's temperature went any higher, she'd go to the doctor's office no matter what he said. Or did? Eve hugged her arms, remembering the man's vise-like grip and the smoldering rage in his eyes. He was capable of violence, but would he hurt Cindy?

She glanced at the dark hall, wondering again where he was. He moved so quietly he could be anywhere in the house. If she only knew what he wanted! There could be an element of truth in his story. She had seen a car down on the road. Maybe he had been looking for a telephone, but to break into a house and help himself to someone else's clothes, then hide—

A crackling sound made her jump. It came from the front of the house, and it took a moment for her to recognize the sound of the kitchen radio. Static shrilled and faded as he tried to bring a station in clearly, but the small set wasn't up to the task. She glanced at the expensive AM-FM transistor radio beside the television. Hadn't he seen it or was he afraid it would wake Cindy?

The radio in the kitchen went off. A sudden hail of rain on the roof created an echo as it swept through the canyon. Outside, something snapped with a loud noise, then crashed. Eve sprang up and pulled back the drapes. The storm was getting worse.

The patio and pool were shrouded in the pelting deluge. A branch had broken from a eucalyptus tree on the hillside and crashed onto the deck, its green, leafy fingers trailing in the pool. Daylight was rapidly giving way to darkness because of the thick clouds and fog. Even if she got Cindy into the car the drive down the canyon would be perilous. She'd have to be alert for fallen branches. She'd also have to bundle Cindy up and cover her face the way she did when she was a baby and had to be rushed to the doctor. Thank heaven Dr. Provel's office was in a building with inside parking so there'd be no danger of Cindy getting chilled.

Lightning painted the sky a murky yellow-green, and thunder crashed close enough to make the window rattle. Shivering, Eve realized that unless she managed to get away without his knowing it, there wouldn't be any trip to Dr. Provel's office. She and Cindy were prisoners in their own house. She shuddered and rubbed her arms. The room was getting cold. She saw that the fire was dying and hurried to throw on a log. Sparks fanned as she stabbed the charred wood in an effort to resuscitate the flames, but the fresh log smothered them before they could take hold.

There was no sound until she heard his mutter of annoyance behind her. He was standing so close she stumbled sideways to avoid touching him as he bent to lift the lid of the woodbox. He glanced inside.

"You got more kindling and newspaper?" he asked.

She nodded. "In the garage."

"Get it."

She hesitated, terrified of leaving Cindy alone with him.

"I said get it! We have to keep her warm. Move!"

Eve ran, trailing her hands along the walls of the hall to steady herself. She dashed through the kitchen and was at the garage door before she thought to go back for the flashlight she kept in a cupboard drawer. Snapping it on, she propped open the garage door. A cold, damp draft swept through the laundry room. She swept the light around and saw the curtain blowing over the broken window she hadn't noticed before. So that was how he'd gotten in—like a common burglar, not through any door she'd left unlocked. Shivering, she found a cardboard box and filled it with kindling. In the kitchen she found the morning paper on the counter where she'd left it because she didn't have time to read it. She dropped it on top of the wood, then froze as the beam of the flashlight hit a picture on the front page.

She bent to examine it more closely. It was *him.* There was no mistaking his heavy-boned face or the deep-set eyes and square jaw. With shaking hands, she picked up the paper and read the story under the unsmiling photograph.

"Lucas Miller is being sought by police for questioning in the murder of Merilee Hauptner, whose beaten and strangled body was discovered last Friday in a North Hollywood apartment. According to witnesses, Miller had been living with Hauptner for several months since his release from the state institution for the criminally insane. Miller, who spent eight years in the Atascadero State Hospital, was released last month after psychiatrists pronounced him cured of the violent mental illness which led to the strangulation of his wife and Miller's plea of not guilty by reason of insanity. In his original trial . . .

"Please see MILLER, page 9."

13

The blue Camaro wasn't in the parking lot. Noble got the license number from DMV and put it on the hot sheet, even though the chance of anyone spotting the car in this rain was remote. Every cop in the city had his hands full with rain-related accidents and the surge of crime that always came with sudden changes in the weather. And there was no guarantee the killer hadn't taken off; the car might already be a pile of parts after a quick trip through a south-of-the-border chop shop.

The coroner estimated that Janine Peters died between 7 and 9 A.M. She'd been strangled manually. Anything else would have to wait for the autopsy.

Noble started with the secretarial agency where Janine Peters worked. Stanton Secretarial had a storefront office in a strip mall on Victory Boulevard near Lankershim. Behind the tiny reception area, where a redheaded young woman manned a four-line intercom phone, three women and a lone male were tapping word processors behind glass dividers that partitioned the space into work areas and a manager's office. The manager was a handsome woman with gray hair and the straight posture of someone who'd never been allowed to slouch as a child. When the receptionist gave her Sergeant Noble's card she rose and came to meet him.

"Sergeant Noble? I'm Mrs. Lubell."

He displayed his identification, which she read quickly but

carefully before she said, "Come in, please." She waited until he was seated before she asked, "What can I do for you?"

"It's about Janine Peters, one of your employees," he said.

"She isn't in today, Sergeant. I can give you her home address."

"How long has she worked for you?"

"I would appreciate knowing what this is about before I answer any questions. I'm sure you understand my position, Sergeant."

He nodded. "Janine Peters is dead, Mrs. Lubell. She was murdered. We're trying to trace her activities."

She couldn't hide her shock, but she recovered quickly. "Of course, I'll do anything I can to help. What do you want to know?"

"How long has she been employed here?"

"Two years. She's very reliable and competent, an expert typist. Was," she amended.

"Did she call in this morning?"

"No. Which is—was very unusual. Janine has missed work only three times since she's been with us. Each time she called to say she was ill. Today was the first time she didn't. I had the receptionist call her apartment at nine-thirty, but there was no answer. I hoped it meant she was on her way after some temporary delay. Murdered . . . my word." For the first time some of her composure deserted her. It wasn't every day one of her employees was killed.

"Was she friendly with the other workers?" he asked, thinking about the young man in the typing pool.

"She was pleasant and got along well, but I don't know if she maintained any close friendship." She glanced toward the glass-partitioned work areas. "If she did, the most likely would be Nan. Nancy Wonderland."

Noble turned so he could see the typing cubicles. "Which one is she?"

"The girl in the red suit."

"Do your employees go out for lunch?"

Mrs. Lubell was surprised by the change of direction. "Why

yes, most of them do. I encourage it. I believe a break from one's work surroundings is beneficial. It gives new energy for the afternoon, provided, of course, the worker doesn't overeat or drink. There are a number of very pleasant restaurants close by where you can order and be served within an hour without being rushed."

Noble liked this woman. She was sensible and practical. "Did Nancy Wonderland go out to lunch today?" he asked. Mrs. Lubell frowned, and he knew she was concerned about invading the privacy of her other employees.

"Does this have anything to do with the murder, Sergeant?"

"It's part of our investigation." He gave her a reassuring smile.

Mrs. Lubell said, "Yes, she went out. She had to finish up a rush job and didn't get away until after two."

The Casa Risa was a ten-minute drive from the office. If Nancy Wonderland was the woman in red, she had plenty of time to get there and back on her lunch hour. "I'd like to talk to Miss Wonderland, if you don't mind."

"Of course not." Mrs. Lubell picked up the phone and spoke to the receptionist, who rose and went down the hall to the typing cubicles. She spoke to the girl in the red suit, who glanced quickly toward the manager's office, then rose and followed the receptionist. Mrs. Lubell got to her feet. "Use my office, please. I'm sure you want privacy." She went out, pausing to say something to Nancy Wonderland as they passed.

The girl was about twenty-five. She was pleasant-looking but not pretty enough to compete with the Hollywood hopefuls or the Southern California golden girls. Right now her face was pinched with a frightened look. She closed the door but stood just inside it.

"Please sit down, Miss Wonderland. This won't take long."

"You're a policeman? A detective?"

"Yes, ma'am. Sergeant Noble." He took out his ID and held it out for her to examine. She read it before she sat down in the other chair on the client's side of Mrs. Lubell's desk. Nancy Wonderland clasped her hands in her lap like a schoolgirl expecting to be reprimanded. Noble uncapped his pen and opened his notebook. "May I have your home address and phone number, Miss Wonderland?" When she'd given them he asked, "Did you go to the Casa Risa Apartments on your lunch hour today?"

She paled. "Yes, sir."

The way she said "sir" made him feel ancient. Maybe to her, fifty-two was. "Why did you go there?"

"To see a friend."

"Janine Peters?"

She nodded. "She—she wasn't home."

"Why did you want to see her?"

"I—I wondered why she hadn't come to work. She didn't call in and . . ." Her fingers unlaced, then clamped again.

Noble didn't rush her. There was more to it than that. Nancy Wonderland was jumpy as a cat. He changed course. "How long have you and Janine been friends?"

"A year. A little more. I started to work here last January."

"Did you meet her here?"

"Well, no. Jan told me they needed help here, so I applied and got the job."

"Where did you first meet her?"

She moistened her lips. "At the Rock. It's a bar."

Noble knew the place. It was a well-known singles' hangout on Victory Boulevard. Singles could find company for a drink or the night, or for a meaningful or not so meaningful relationship, if that's what they were looking for. "When was this?"

"Just after New Year's, a year ago. We happened to sit next to each other and started talking. I mentioned that my unemployment was running out and I needed a job. She told me about this place."

"And since then?"

"We've been friends," she said. "I mean, we see each other every day at work, and sometimes we have dinner together or a drink."

"At the Rock?"

"Sometimes. Is something wrong, Sergeant?"

"Were you there last night?" He was sure her nervousness stemmed from her trip to Janine's apartment. She had some reason to be worried about her friend before the police came around checking.

"Yes," she said very softly.

"Was Janine there too?"

She nodded.

"Did you leave together?"

She shook her head and stared at the hands in her lap. They were clenched so tightly now the knuckles were white. After a moment she looked up. "Jan left before I did. With a guy. Has something happened, Sergeant?" Her voice was so low it was barely audible. She looked like a scared kid.

"Janine Peters is dead, Miss Wonderland." She blanched and looked sick. She hadn't known, but she'd been afraid. "She was murdered," Noble said.

"Oh, my God . . ." Nancy buried her face in her hands, and moans escaped as her shoulders heaved.

"I'm sorry, Miss Wonderland. There's never any easy way to say these things." He hated this part of his job. It never got any easier to tell people someone they knew was a murder victim.

She looked up, wiping tears from her cheeks and streaking her mascara. She sniffled. "What happened?"

"We're trying to find out. Tell me about last night. Did you know the man she left with?"

Nancy dug in the pocket of her red jacket and pulled out a tissue. She wiped her cheeks and blew her nose before she answered. "No. She—we met him last night."

"At the Rock?"

She nodded. "He was sitting at the bar and we just talked to him." She twisted a corner of the tissue until it broke off in her fingers. "I didn't like him. He was—I don't know—strange. Sometimes you meet weirdos, you know?"

"This guy was a weirdo?"

"Well, not far-out like some, but he was different. He sat staring at the mirror as if his reflection wasn't there. Empty eyes. He never even heard Jan the first time she talked to him."

So it was Janine's pickup. Noble waited for Nancy to go on.

"She kind of laughed about it and tried again. She was feeling good and wanted to talk." She started twisting the tissue again. "He was the quiet type, but he seemed friendly enough once he got talking."

"Did he give his name?"

"Luke. No last name. He said it didn't matter."

"What time did he and Janine leave?"

She thought a minute. "It was after eleven. Maybe eleven-thirty or so. I was talking to some people at the other end of the bar. Jan yelled and waved as they went out."

"What did you think when she didn't come to work today or call?"

The direct question caught her off guard. "I—I don't know. I mean, I wondered what happened."

"Did you feel there was a reason to worry?"

Her breath caught and released in a tiny burst. "I don't know. I mean, I thought the guy was sort of a creep. I thought Jan was crazy to talk to him, no less take off with him. Then when she didn't come in or answer her phone, sure I was worried. Wouldn't you be?" Fresh tears spilled over and she wiped them with the shredded tissue.

Noble gave her a few seconds. Two single girls, a few drinks and laughs, a pickup if they hit it lucky. Or unlucky. "What can you tell me about the man?"

"Do you—do you think he killed her?" It was a frightened whisper.

"We'd like to talk to him."

"He was tall, wide shoulders, big frame. His face was long with a real square jaw. Stubborn. I had an uncle who had the same kind of jaw. Mean too. The guy's hair was straight and dark, and he had thick eyebrows. His eyes . . ." She shuddered. "They were what you'd call deep-set, I guess. He seemed to be looking right through you."

"What color?"

"Dark. Brown, probably."

"His clothes?"

"He had on a dark windbreaker and a yellow sport shirt. No tie. I didn't notice his pants but they may have been jeans. The Rock is pretty casual."

"Anything else?"

She thought a moment. "His hands. He had them on the bar. I figured he was a workingman—a mechanic or something like that. There were traces of grease around his nails. My uncle was a mechanic, and he had hands like that. No matter how much he scrubbed, you could always tell."

Noble smiled. "You're very observant."

Some of her tension eased, and she looked less frightened. Noble figured she didn't get a lot of compliments. Or a lot of dates. So she settled for places like the Rock. He reached for his leather case and handed her a card.

"You've been very helpful. Thank you, Miss Wonderland. If you think of anything else, please give me a call."

She read the card and nodded. When she looked up her pinched expression was back. "Can you tell me what happened? I mean, how—how she died?"

"She was beaten and strangled. The landlady found her an hour or so after you were there."

Nancy Wonderland looked sick. She was probably thinking what would have happened if Ida Dawson had let her into Janine Peters's apartment. Or maybe she was wondering what would have happened if she hadn't thought the guy was a creep, and she had talked to him instead of Janine.

14

Eve's breath pushed against her ribs painfully. A faint rustling sound startled her, and she realized the newspaper in her hands was shaking. She held the flashlight close and scrutinized the picture. The long face with its prominent jaw and sunken eyes stared back at her. Luke Miller. A murderer.

She fell against the cupboard, struggling for breath as she fought hysteria. She and Cindy were trapped in the house with an insane murderer! Cindy was alone with him now— The newspaper fell from her trembling fingers and she dashed for the hall. Sobbing with panic, she stopped and clung to the doorframe. If she went back without the paper and kindling, he might— No, don't think about it! She forced herself to go back and pick up the newspaper. Ripping off the front page, she stuffed it in the wastebasket under the sink, then dropped the rest on top of the kindling. Resisting the urge to run, she picked up the box and hurried back to the den.

He was tuning the transistor radio to a local news station. It crackled with static, and the newscaster's voice broke like a pubescent youth's.

"The latest storm front to hit Southern California has dumped more than an inch of rain on the Los Angeles Civic Center during the past hour and an estimated two or more inches in other parts of the city. Driven by forty-mile-an-hour winds, the storm that moved across the coastal mountains this morning is now blanketing the basin. It has left the city reeling as the season's total climbed to 17.89 inches, 8.46 inches above normal rainfall for this time of year and 5.76 inches more than had fallen at this time last year. And after our fifth day of rain the National Weather Service offers no relief in sight. Rain is predicted to continue through most of the night, with only a slight chance of slackening tomorrow. Satellite photographs show the present storm system is four hundred miles deep. A second, more intense system is only five hundred miles off the coast and moving steadily in this direction."

Sizzling static fragmented the announcer's voice. The man snapped off the radio and returned to the fireplace when Eve set down the box. She watched him crumble paper and lay kindling and logs. In minutes he had a fire blazing.

Eve cleared her throat nervously. "Maybe we should leave the radio on," she said. She could tune in one of the FM stations that came in well.

He glanced over his shoulder. His eyes were lost under the thick brows except for the firelight reflected like a night animal caught in the headlights of a car. "Why?" he asked in a suspicious tone.

"Sometimes—sometimes they evacuate the canyons. If there's any danger we should—"

"It's worse out there," he said flatly. "Flash floods, mud slides. Besides, we can't let her get cold or wet." He looked toward the sofa and some of his tension seemed to ease as he gazed at the sleeping child. "It's going to be a long night. You got any more candles?" When Eve nodded mutely he told her to get them.

She glanced nervously at Cindy before she fled down the hall. She was terrified of rousing his anger now that she knew he was a killer. In the kitchen she collected four partly burned candles she'd used for a dinner party the night before Paul's death. There were big, holiday candles in a box in the garage, but she couldn't take time to hunt for them. In the dining room she rummaged through the buffet until she found a box of new pink and gray, cellophane-wrapped tapers that matched her china. She rushed back to the family room and put them on the table.

He was listening to the radio again. He had pulled a bent-wood chair close to the set and sat hunched beside the speaker. The volume was too low for Eve to hear. Was he checking the weather or listening for news on the police hunt for him? She tried to remember exactly what the news story said: *Wanted for questioning.* It didn't say he'd killed anyone. Not this time. Eve swayed as the room seemed to spin. She sank into a chair beside Cindy.

It was a nightmare. Worse. For a long time after Paul's death she often woke crying from nightmares, but those seemed to pale by comparison now. A murderer. An *insane* murderer. The hospital had let him out. The psychiatrists said he was cured. But were they sure? Could they really tell? Breaking into a house and taking it over wasn't the act of a sane man. And the police were looking for him because they thought he murdered another woman. Eve swallowed convulsively as she glanced at the man by the radio. His face was turned away, but she couldn't forget his piercing, demonlike eyes. The eyes of a mad-man. She clenched her shaking hands and tried to think ratio-nally. So far he hadn't actually hurt her, only scared her badly. And he was concerned about Cindy. He carried her in here to make sure she was warm . . . made the cocoa when Eve had gone to pieces after the power went off . . . rebuilt the fire. . . . It was clear he intended to stay until the storm was over. And then?

The thought of spending the night in the house with a mur-derer sent a cold shiver through her. Maybe she was wrong. Newspaper pictures were often poor likenesses. And by flash-light—

Static hissed through the room and he snapped off the radio. Summoning every ounce of courage, Eve forced words from her dry throat. "I don't know your name."

He looked at her with a curious expression, and she thought he wasn't going to answer. Finally he said, "Luke Miller."

The room swam in a suffocating haze. Eve's fingernails dug into her palms, and the pain kept her in touch with reality. Somehow she managed to say, "I'm Eve Foxx."

He watched her as though he expected her to say more. She
tried to think of something, but her mind blanked except for
the newspaper words. *Luke Miller . . . wanted for questioning in the death of . . ."* She fought panic. *Talk to him . . .
say anything. . . .* The silence filled the room and sharpened
the plangency of the storm. When the telephone rang suddenly
the shrill sound made them both jump. Eve sprang up and
snatched the receiver before Miller could get to his feet.

"Hello—" Her breath exploded in panic. Miller came around
the sofa and stood close to her. His breath rasped faintly and his
eyes narrowed, but he didn't grab the phone away.

"Eve?"

"Dorie?" She was so relieved to hear her sister-in-law's voice,
she clutched the receiver with both hands. The phone was
working, and Dorie was on the line!

"How is Cindy? Why didn't you bring her here? I expected
you to be waiting when I got home. I stopped and got Italian
takeout and some chicken for Cindy. Really, Eve—" Static
chopped at her words. "Damned rain . . . lines down all over
. . . been trying to call for an hour . . . why didn't you . . .
Mark Stein's wife . . . perfectly well you should—" A loud
burst of static crackled so sharply that Eve yanked the receiver
away from her ear. Then there was only an erratic sizzle.

"Dorie? Can you hear me?" She had to be there! "Dorie!"

Luke Miller took the phone from Eve's hands, listened, then
replaced it in the cradle. "The line's out."

"But it was working. My sister-in-law—"

On the sofa, Cindy whimpered, "Mommy, is Aunt Dorie
here?" She sat up, disheveled and irritable. Her damp hair was
plastered to her head and her eyes were glassy. She began to
cry.

Eve darted to the sofa and scooped the child into her arms.
Hugging Cindy, she said, "Shh. It's all right, darling. Aunt Dorie
isn't here, but she called to find out how you're feeling. Are you
feeling better, honey?" She pressed her lips to Cindy's hair.

Cindy struggled to free herself. "No. My tummy hurts. I
wanna see Aunt Dorie," she whined.

"Shh—it's all right, it's all right, honey," Eve soothed. "Maybe we'll see Aunt Dorie later." If only they'd gone to Dorie's when they had the chance! She felt Miller's gaze on her. He was between her and the door, blocking any chance of escape. Eve closed her eyes. She had to find a way to get Cindy out of here, to get away from Luke Miller.

15

Dorie poured brandy and drank it in a swallow, silently damning the erratic phone connection, the storm, and Eve. Especially Eve. Why hadn't she brought Cindy here? It was plain pigheadedness driving up the canyon in this storm, staying in that isolated, lonely house when Cindy needed medical care. It was totally irresponsible, that's what it was. And absolutely typical of Eve.

Dorie poured another brandy and carried it to the sofa, where she kicked off her shoes and tucked her feet up under her soft, maroon wool skirt. Sipping brandy, she watched the leaping flames of the fire she'd lit when she got home. Usually it made the living room of the Toluca Lake condominium cozy, but tonight the fire's warmth wasn't enough to offset the cold anger Dorie felt. Eve wasn't a fit mother. Why in God's name had Paul ever married her? Angry, bitter tears stung Dorie's eyes. Her beloved Paul, to whom she'd been sister and mother, friend and adviser. For him to die in that car crash and Eve be unscathed was the greatest injustice of all. If Eve had been driving instead of him, Paul might be here now. And Cindy would be Dorie's to raise. Instead, Eve doled out miserly visits like a queen granting audience. It wasn't fair, not after the years Dorie had devoted to Paul, bringing him up because their mother loved her career more than her children. I deserve more than bittersweet memories, Dorie told herself. She had always made sure Paul was never neglected in any way. She was there for him to talk to, to give him guidance where their parents failed. After their untimely deaths she had been mother, father, and sister to Paul.

Jeremy Foxx and Diana Chartre killed in plane crash. Producer and leading lady die as private plane hits mountainside in rainstorm. The headlines were still imprinted starkly on Dorie's memory after twenty-five years. The story hadn't mentioned that Diana Chartre was Mrs. Jeremy Foxx until the third paragraph, and the existence of a fifteen-year-old daughter and a ten-year-old son, who were an embarrassment to a woman pretending to be twenty-six, barely made the final paragraph.

Dorie had stood beside the open grave in Forest Lawn with her arm around her brother's shoulder, apart from those of the film industry who had come to weep on camera. Paul wept, too, but Dorie understood that. After all, he was only ten. Dorie didn't waste any tears. She had struggled to hide a smile.

Instead of an estate, the Foxx children inherited their parents' debts. An executor was appointed guardian. When the big house on Sunset Plaza Drive was sold, there was barely enough money for both of them to finish high school. The rest had been lavished on high living and image-making, keeping Diana Chartre in her adoring public's eye. When Dorie graduated a friend of her father's offered her a job in a studio. The pay was good, and he let her arrange her hours to be home by the time Paul came from school, swimming, or football. As the years went by it was easier to stay where she was than to start over someplace else.

Dorie insisted on college for Paul. She didn't want him to have the remotest connection to the entertainment industry, which had warped their parents and shortchanged her and Paul's childhood. She sacrificed and saved so he could go to Stanford, and under her careful prodding he chose engineering and graduated with honors. He had his pick of a dozen job offers, and she was pleased when he accepted her suggestion of going with a Los Angeles firm. He insisted on his own apartment from the start, but she didn't mind since it was only a few minutes away in Studio City. He also insisted on repaying the money she'd spent on tuition, despite her protests. After eight years Paul decided to open his own consulting firm. At thirty he was well on the road to success. His company prospered from the start and built steadily. Dorie's happiness and pride were boundless. Until Paul met and married Eve.

Eve Lorand's face appeared in commercials touting everything from skin cream to vintage wine. Fresh from the Midwest, she had an innocent, youthful appeal that dripped with honesty and sincerity and sent viewers scurrying to the nearest markets. Pain wrenched Dorie's heart whenever she remembered she was responsible for Paul meeting Eve. It was one of those studio parties that breed like rabbits around Christmastime. Usually she refused all the invitations, but she'd accepted this one because she liked the producer who was giving it and because she was convinced that Paul needed to get out and meet people. He'd been in business for himself almost a year, and he was working too hard. Against her advice he'd bought a house near the top of Coldwater Canyon, and he spent what few free hours he had fixing things or puttering around the yard. He was a recluse as far as social life was concerned. Dorie coaxed and wheedled until he agreed to escort her to the affair. She bought a glittering silver lamé dress to celebrate. It set off her slim figure and deep, auburn hair to striking advantage, and heads turned as she entered on the arm of her blond, tuxedo-clad, handsome brother. She'd never been prouder or more aware of the striking picture the two of them made. She was enjoying herself tremendously. She planned for them to stay only long enough to have a few drinks and poke fun at the foibles of the industry they both hated. Dorie never dreamed Paul would tumble headlong for a snip of an actress with a pretty face.

The brandy glass was empty. Dorie uncurled and walked to the wet bar to refill it. For a moment she gazed out the window that ran with rivulets of water that made the patio lights ripple like reflections on a choppy sea. She'd never seen worse rain. By midnight the canyon would be impossible.

She glared at the phone. Damn Eve! Should she call again?

How could she convince her sister-in-law to bring Cindy here? She wondered if Eve had called the doctor. Probably not, Dorie thought. Eve's "wait and see" attitude was infuriating. She had no business taking risks with Cindy's health. The operation had been a serious one. Dorie remembered those terrible hours of waiting while Cindy was in surgery. She'd felt shut out when Paul and Eve comforted each other, but she refused to leave the hospital. When the surgeon finally came to say the operation had been successful, Dorie cried without shame.

Eve had no business putting Cindy in nursery school. Three was too young to be pushed out of the nest. With Paul gone, Cindy needed to be with her mother. And her Aunt Dorie.

She braced the phone on her shoulder and dialed Eve's number again. She sipped brandy while she listened to a faint ringing that broke off with a sizzling noise, as if the lines had gotten wet. Dorie slammed the phone down. L.A. phone service was lousy during storms. Often it went out completely. Once her phone had been out for two days. It was worse in the hills. If Eve's phone went out altogether . . .

The thought made her jumpy. She'd keep trying. She went to the window and rubbed a spot clear of condensation. If anything, it was raining harder. She could barely see the redwood fence that enclosed her private patio. An occasional flash of lightning blanketed the sky with a sickly green glow, but it was too distant to hear the thunder. Dorie went back to the phone and listened to the dial tone before trying Eve's number again. This time there was only an angry hum on the line. Disgusted, she snapped on the television and sank to the sofa as a newscaster's face filled the screen.

"The weather continues to make news tonight. Damage from the storm has been reported throughout the city as streets and freeways flood and the rain continues to weaken hillsides and undermine homes. A flash flood watch has been issued for the mountain and coastal areas. Pacific Coast Highway is closed from Topanga Canyon to Point Dume after a slide blocked the road this afternoon about four o'clock. A huge boulder thundered down the hillside and across the road, plunging through the kitchen of a house and narrowly missing the occupants, who were in the adjacent family room inspecting damage from a leaking roof. The boulder came to rest on the beach after tearing out a wooden stairway.

"Homeowners in Bluebird Canyon, which has been pounded by torrential rains since the storms began, face severe danger of mud slides as the sodden ground weakens. Deep crevices have been discovered in several places, and residents have been warned to evacuate.

"In other parts of the city, streets and freeways are at a standstill because of cars stalled in foot-deep water that's accumulated in low spots. Drivers are being advised to avoid areas which are prone to flooding or, better still, not to drive at all unless it is absolutely necessary."

The storm was hitting the hills hard. Damn Eve for not bringing Cindy here. Dorie listened for specific mention of Coldwater Canyon. If there was any sign of trouble, Dorie would drive up and *get* Paul's daughter.

The newscaster shifted to other stories and Dorie turned off the set irritably. She thought about the Italian takeout getting cold in the kitchen, but she wasn't hungry. She retrieved her shoes and walked back to the bar to pour a small shot of brandy. She had to keep her wits about her if she was going to drive. Picking up the phone, she dialed again. There was a hesitant ring, then crackling static. She depressed the button and dialed the operator, who came on the line after a long wait. When Dorie asked when service would be restored in Coldwater Canyon, the woman replied in a weary tone:

"We have crews out at most of the major breaks, ma'am. I have no information on specific areas."

"I have to get through to my party!" Dorie snapped.

"If you want to report a phone out of service, you'll have to call the service office. That number is 611."

Dorie cut the connection and dialed the service number. When it rang busy she slammed the phone down in exasperation.

Damn Eve! How could she be so inconsiderate!

16

The wind rattled the windows. Somewhere a branch was slapping against the house like a whip. Each slash laid open Eve's raw nerves. She pulled the quilt around Cindy, aware that Miller was watching her, but she dared not look up for fear of letting him see the terror she could no longer hide.

She rocked Cindy and struggled with her turbulent emotions. Miller hadn't changed. Her perception of him had. He was no longer only a frightening intruder, he was a killer. And she and Cindy were trapped—

She forced away the thought. She couldn't let herself think that way or she'd be reduced to quivering helplessness. There had to be a solution. No matter how frightened she was, she'd find a way to get Cindy out of here and away from Miller. If only she'd said something or screamed when Dorie was on the phone instead of letting her sister-in-law prattle.

One encouraging thing was that Dorie's call proved Miller hadn't disabled the phone. The line might work again soon. Would Dorie call back? Eve tried to recall the fragmented bits of her sister-in-law's chatter. Dorie was mad because Eve hadn't brought Cindy there instead of home. But there'd been something else too. A name . . . Mark Stein . . . no, Mark Stein's wife. What was that about? Stein worked with Dorie. Eve vaguely recalled the name, although she had never met him.

Luke Miller put another log on the fire and flames licked

around it voraciously, spreading warm air through the room.
Eve realized that Cindy had fallen asleep again. She laid her
down gently and spread the quilt over her. Restlessly, Cindy
flung it back.

"She's too warm."

Miller's voice startled Eve. "She'll get chilled without something over her," she said.

"Get her a lighter blanket."

So simple. So practical. Eve felt stupid for not thinking of it.
She got up unsteadily and started toward Cindy's room, then
turned abruptly and headed for her own bedroom instead, forcing herself to walk at a natural pace. The bedroom door was
open. Her heart raced as she slipped inside and eased the door
shut behind her. The warmth from the fire didn't penetrate this
far, and damp, chilly darkness engulfed her. She moved
through the familiar room without hesitation. Dresser . . .
chaise longue . . . hall to the bath . . . linen closet . . . She
opened the door and ran her hands along a high shelf until she
found the summer blankets. Lifting one down, she held it
against her body like a shield as she made her way to the bed.
Sitting with the blanket in her lap, she felt carefully for the
phone on the nightstand, praying that it would work. But there
wasn't even a faint hum to encourage her. She replaced the
receiver and made her way to the bathroom. Nervousness distorted her perception, and she bumped into the wall. The blanket she was carrying offset the force of the impact, but she was
stunned momentarily. She held her breath, panicked for fear
Miller had heard the noise, which sounded like thunder in her
ears. But the house was quiet except for the storm sounds. She
groped her way to the bathroom sink. Opening the medicine
cabinet, she tried to identify objects by touch. The bottles and
jars were useless unless she could see the labels. Besides, she
didn't keep any prescription drugs or potentially dangerous
medicines here where Cindy might take a notion to explore.
Anything like that was hidden on a high shelf in the kitchen.

Her hand touched cold metal. Fingering it, she identified a
small pair of scissors. She slipped them into her jeans pocket.

They weren't much of a weapon, but they made her feel a little less helpless. She completed her exploration of the shelves, but there was nothing else she could use. She made her way from the bedroom and back to the family room.

"Warm it first," Miller snapped when she began to unfold the blanket over Cindy.

Again Eve felt incompetent for having to be reminded of something so basic. When she manipulated the blanket awkwardly he took it from her and shook it out before he held it in front of the fire to warm. He tested it a few times with the palm of his big hand, and when he decided it was ready he covered Cindy deftly, pulling away the quilt at the same time in a smooth exchange.

"Thank you," Eve said honestly. "You're very good with sick children."

His jaw stiffened and his eyes glowed like embers falling through the grate. He looked so tense Eve bit her tongue and wondered if she had said something that upset him. She knew so little about him, she might easily be on dangerous ground. He was silent as he studied her. Did he suspect that she recognized him? Did he know about the news story and realize she'd torn it out of the paper? Outside, another tree branch broke with a rending crack. The sound made Miller whirl as if a shot had been fired.

Eve glanced at the windows nervously. "The storm is getting worse."

He crossed to the sliding glass doors and pulled the drapes open to look out. Water ran down the glass in wavering silver sheets. The patio and pool were invisible beyond the unrelenting gray shroud. Miller cupped his hand to his eyes and pressed close to the glass. Muttering, he left the window and turned on the radio again. When it blasted static he seemed to notice for the first time that it was set on AM. He switched it to FM and adjusted the dial to a station that came in clearly. He kept the volume low and sat close to the set.

Eve moved closer to the fire. Despite the heavy sweater, she was cold and her limbs were leaden. Fear. She was afraid of him, no matter how gentle he was with Cindy, how thoughtful and helpful. She was afraid of him because he was a killer.

". . . latest report from the National Weather Service. Flash flood watches have been issued for all canyons. Pacific Coast Highway is closed from Topanga Canyon to Point Dume because of a huge slide that dumped tons of mud and rock across the highway before destroying two beachfront homes. Many canyon roads in the city and as far north as Kanan-Dume Road are blocked by mud slides. A flash flood ripped down Laurel Canyon a half hour ago sweeping away two cars. The occupants of one miraculously escaped death and are in Cedars of Sinai Hospital with serious injuries. In other parts of the city, portions of Altadena, Monterey Park—" Miller snapped off the set.

"I told you it was dangerous out there," he said. Then with a frown, he asked, "Do you have trouble with slides around here?"

"Some." It was true. Frequently there were minor slides in the steep canyon, but Paul always boasted that the house had survived disastrous rains a few years ago with no more damage than a blocked driveway. The two of them had donned slickers and boots to shovel it out. They were like kids playing mud pies. The bittersweet memory stirred an ache under her breastbone. This storm was far worse, and Paul wasn't here to see her through.

"I don't know why people want to live in these canyons," Miller said, jutting his jaw. "You wear out your car just getting up and down. Transmission, brakes." He grunted and came over to her. It took all Eve's willpower not to cringe. "You got any food? I haven't eaten since . . ." The lines in his brow deepened. He didn't remember when he had eaten last. A long time. This morning? Yesterday? He had only drinks with Janine, no food. "I'm starved."

"I have some cheese and crackers."

"Get it. I'll bring in more wood." He picked up the flashlight, then turned to look at Cindy before he went out.

Scarcely breathing, Eve let him get a few feet down the hall before she followed. The wood was in the garage. He'd have to go out there to get it. She dared not let herself think about the plan that was forming in her mind. Just do it. He'd have to walk around the car to get to the woodpile. She'd have plenty of time.

The laundry-room door was open when she reached the kitchen. A wash of cold air swept through the house, and she quickly cupped the flame of the candle so it wouldn't go out. Miller had jammed one of Cindy's boots under the door to keep it from closing. Eve watched as the beam of light bobbed around the front of the Mercedes. It lowered and was steady when he set it down. A moment later she heard the dull thud of wood being stacked.

She darted past the washing machine and dryer and kicked aside the yellow boot as she shoved the door shut. Trembling violently, she slammed the dead bolt. In the garage logs clattered to the cement and a string of profanity exploded. Seconds later the doorknob rattled and Miller threw his weight against the door. Eve clamped her hand over her mouth as she backed away. Was he strong enough to break down the door? She huddled against the wall and listened. After a minute the noise stopped and the garage was quiet.

She backed into the kitchen and ran her hand along the wall in search of the phone without taking her eyes from the garage door. She fingered the push buttons as she visualized the layout of numbers. 911. Nothing happened. Desperately she tried again, even though there was no dial tone. *Please . . . please . . .* Nothing.

Tears surged in her eyes, and she wiped them furiously as she ran back to the den. Without much hope, she tried that phone. When it didn't work her panic began to mushroom again.

Miller could stay dry and warm if he got in the car. Would he drive off? She prayed he would. He could have the car as long as he went away and left her and Cindy alone. Would he know the valet key was in the glove compartment? She wrung her hands. If he took the car, she and Cindy would be trapped here with no way to get down the hill, but it didn't matter as long as he went.

She strained to listen for the car engine. Would she be able to hear it above the howling wind driving rain against the house?

Why didn't he go? No matter how hard she listened, there was only the wind and rain.

Why didn't he go?

17

―――――

"Did you find the lady in red?" Harry Rothman asked, dropping the empty carrot-juice container in the wastebasket. The detective squad room was hot and stuffy and smelled of wet wool. Noble avoided the soggy newspapers someone had spread under the coat rack as he hung his dripping raincoat.

He sat down and rubbed his wrist where pain clamped it like a handcuff. "Her name's Nancy Wonderland. She and the Peters woman were together last night at the Rock. Peters picked up some guy and left with him about eleven-thirty."

"Our murderer?"

"I'd make book on it. Nancy gave me a first name. Luke."

Rothman whistled softly. "Are you thinking Luke Miller?"

"It's his M.O., and both women lived in North Hollywood. This is his turf, and Nancy Wonderland's description of the man her girlfriend went off with last night could have come right off our rap sheet. Do we have a copy of this morning's *Herald* around?"

Rothman pushed his chair back. "O'Corley in Vice has one. I'll get it." He went out and returned a minute later to toss the newspaper on Noble's desk.

Noble sorted sections until he found the main news. He folded the paper and pushed it back to Rothman. Luke Miller's photograph stared out from the front page.

Noble verbalized his thoughts. "Janine Peters picks him up in a singles' bar and they leave together sometime after eleven, maybe eleven-thirty. Ida Dawson says a man was with Peters when she got home at midnight. It has to be the same guy. She didn't have time to pick up someone else. So she and Luke have their fun, and he stays the night. Seven A.M. when Stanley Morse goes out, her newspaper is at the door, but when we get there, it's on the floor by the bed. The landlady says she didn't touch anything."

Rothman looked skeptical. "Peters took the paper in when she got up, saw Miller's picture, and . . . ?"

Noble shrugged. "She's just spent the night with a pickup, a guy she doesn't know a hell of a lot about. My guess is she'd be pretty shaken up, maybe even hysterical, when she sees his picture and reads he's a murderer. What does she do? Try to call the police or try to throw him out? Either way, he has to shut her up."

"Fast," Rothman agreed. "He doesn't even have to look for a weapon. He's got his hands." He was out of the chair. "I'll pull Miller's jacket. Let's see if Nancy Wonderland and the bartender at the Rock can give us a positive ID."

Miller's file dated from his first arrest when his wife was killed. Miller had walked into St. Joseph's Hospital carrying his two-year-old daughter, Kristen. The child had been dead several hours. A woman intern in the emergency room told Miller there was nothing that could be done. Miller refused to believe it. He went berserk, attacking the doctor and almost strangling her before he was subdued by several orderlies. When the police went to Miller's apartment to contact his wife, they found her beaten and strangled body next to the child's crib. There was an empty vodka bottle on a table.

The psychiatrists had a field day with Miller, and no two of them agreed. After being convicted of murder two, Miller was judged "not guilty by reason of insanity" and sent to Atascadero. After eight years he was released a few months ago to live in the community under supervision in a 1229 outpatient program.

The last update traced Miller to Merilee Hauptner, a thirty-five-year-old checkout clerk at a Ralph's Market near the furnished room Psychiatric Social Services found for Miller when he was released four months ago. There was no information on how Miller and Hauptner met, but presumably it was in the market. A few weeks later an elated Merilee told her co-workers Miller had moved in with her. Two months later the psychologist in charge of the program went to Hauptner's apartment after Miller missed two of his weekly therapy sessions. Miller wasn't home, but Merilee Hauptner was. It was the first she knew she was living with a man who'd killed his wife and spent eight years in a mental institution. The next day her body was found in the apartment. Like Miller's wife, she'd been beaten and strangled. There was plenty of circumstantial evidence that Miller had done it, and Homicide wanted to talk to him, but Miller had dropped out of sight.

Gut instinct told Noble that Miller was the man who'd gone home with Janine Peters last night. The pattern had repeated itself. Noble didn't believe in coincidence. He looked for the name of the psychiatrist who evaluated Miller when he was first arrested for the murder of his wife. He reached for the phone.

18

The sound registered in Miller's brain a second before he recognized it. Footsteps. Quick . . . soft . . . Like hospital orderlies sneaking up to grab you if you went too close to the fence of the recreation yard.

Cursing, he dropped the wood and sprang for the door, but it slammed before he could reach it. He threw himself against it and twisted the knob, then stood back panting. The little bitch. She tricked him.

He searched his pockets for the strip of plastic he'd used to open the door before, then remembered it was still in the soggy pants he dumped in her washing machine. There was nothing at all in the pockets of the blue slacks. Mr. Eve Foxx was one of those dudes who cleaned his pockets down to the last bit of lint before he hung them away.

The garage was cold. The damp air coming through the broken window sliced through the tan sweater. Miller walked around the car, picked up the flashlight, and aimed the beam at the car. A Mercedes. Mr. Eve Foxx had bucks. It looked as spotless and empty as Foxx's pant pockets. Miller played the light inside and grunted when he saw a folded blanket on the back seat. Sure, she'd keep one handy for the kid. Kids like to take naps in the car. He opened the door, grabbed the blanket, and wrapped it around his shoulders like a poncho. It helped.

He was a little warmer, but not enough to offset the chill from the freezing cement under his stockinged feet.

The heavy pressure behind his eyes throbbed painfully. He leaned against the car, panting. The cold numbed his lungs so he had to force air in and out. Images from the past broke through the wall he kept around the memories locked in a dark corner of his mind. His mother screaming and chasing him with the broom, swinging it so furiously he couldn't dart fast enough to stay clear. His father trying to interfere, only to have her shift her abuse and rain blows on his head. The frightened child running out of the bungalow and hiding in the shadowy backyard, his bare feet icy on the rough ground where grass never survived. Shivering as he waited for his mother's rage to be spent so he could sneak back inside and crawl into bed. Whispering courageous, bold promises to himself in the dark that someday he'd run away where she'd never find him or beat him again.

After a long time the pain began to ease and he remembered where he was. Eve Foxx had locked him out of the house. He hadn't expected her to pull a stunt like this. Everything was going so well, he'd begun to trust her, to believe she wasn't like the others, like his mother.

He walked back to the door and turned the knob gently, but it was still locked. She wasn't going to open it. She didn't want him in the house. Had she gone to stay with Cindy?

Cindy. He liked the name. It was soft and cuddly, like the little blond girl herself. He wondered how serious her stomach problem was. Eve and her husband should get another opinion. It was a mistake to trust one doctor. They were supposed to be smart, but they made mistakes. They all made mistakes.

He liked Cindy, really liked her. She had such pretty golden hair, but her blue eyes were sad. He supposed it was because she was sick. He'd gotten her to smile a couple of times. Little girls were meant to smile . . . and laugh . . . and . . . He rubbed his temple.

He liked the mother, too, until she pulled this stupid stunt. His skull began to tighten again, and he breathed deeply to short-circuit the pain. Maybe he could still like her, but he couldn't trust her.

He stamped his feet to keep the circulation going, then opened the car door and released the hood latch. Putting the flashlight on the fender so he could see, he raised the hood and disconnected the distributor cap. Women were stupid about cars. She probably didn't know how to reconnect the cap, but he wasn't going to give her another chance to get lucky. She wouldn't catch him by surprise again. He let the hood down quietly and hid the rotor on a shelf behind some paint cans.

Back at the door, he listened again, but there was nothing to tell him where she was or what she was doing. She probably was back in front of the fire. He shivered and cursed softly, cold despite the blanket. He explored the garage with the light, pausing now and then when it encountered something potentially interesting. Boxes. A few tools, nothing elaborate. A small workbench. Mr. Eve Foxx wasn't much of a handyman. Firewood. Garden stuff. He edged around the car to an open cabinet of insecticides, fertilizers, and odds and ends. With a grin, he picked up a box of lawn-size trash bags.

He laid the flashlight on a shelf and pulled a plastic bag from the box. Opening it, he carefully tore the center of the bottom seam, then tested the opening over his head. It split a few inches more when he tugged on it. He took it off and made two more slits in the sides, then tried it on again. A perfect fit. Halloween. Trick or treat. A bag man. He gyrated in the beam of the flashlight so his shadow stretched across the garage, humped over the Mercedes, and climbed the wall on the other side. He laughed softly.

He took the bag off again and pulled out several more from the box. Using a ball of string he found on a shelf, he wrapped his legs and arms with plastic and tied them securely. When he finished he put on the makeshift poncho once more. Only his stockinged feet, hands, and head weren't protected by the green swaddling. He considered wrapping his feet, but it wouldn't do much good on the rough ground. The rocks and twigs would slash the thin plastic to ribbons in a minute. He'd just have to put up with cold feet for a while. He fashioned a hood from another bag, then took one more to carry the items he collected from various shelves. When he was ready he pulled the chain to release the springs on the automatic opener, then lifted the heavy door and stepped out into the wet, black night.

19

Time stopped in the dark shadows of the house, Eve's companion in terror. She stood close to the fire trying to dispel the fear that saturated her. Her teeth were chattering and violent shudders racked her. She should have stayed in the kitchen so she could hear if he started the car. Now she jumped at every nuance of the storm.

Was Miller gone or was he waiting . . . waiting for her to think he wasn't there . . . waiting to grab her if she opened the door and tried for the car? How would she know unless she unlocked the garage door to look? The idea terrified her, but she knew she had to do it if she was going to get Cindy out of here. She swallowed her rancid fear.

Cindy made a whimpering sound, and Eve went to feel her cheeks. They were burning with fever. Kneeling beside the sofa, Eve whispered, "Cindy? Cindy, honey, can you hear me?" Cindy's dark lashes fluttered but the effort of opening her eyes seemed beyond her. "Is your tummy worse, honey?" Eve asked anxiously.

Cindy's waxy eyelids opened partway. Her blue gaze was unfocused and glassy. Her lips moved, but no sound came out. Eve stroked her hot, dry skin.

"Okay, honey, just be quiet and Mommy will get something to make you feel better." Cindy's eyes closed.

Eve ran down the hall. The candle on Cindy's dresser had

burned to a stub that threw off a pale arc of light. She left the bathroom door open so she could see to fill a basin with cool water and drop a washcloth into it. On her way out she picked up the thermometer from the nightstand. She paused a moment in the hall. The candles in the dining room and kitchen cast shadows that slithered in a macabre dance across the end of the passageway. She tried to separate sounds and identify them, but there were none she could attribute to Miller. She told herself he was gone. If he intended to break down the door, he'd have done it by now. There'd be no point in staying in the cold garage if he could be near the fire. He was gone, she told herself again. He had to be gone.

Back in the den, she sat beside Cindy and coaxed her mouth open in order to put the thermometer under her tongue. Cindy lay limp. Eve had to hold her chin to keep the thermometer from slipping out. This was no psychosomatic stomachache. Cindy was really ill.

Counting impatiently to a minute, Eve read the thermometer. One hundred and one and two tenths. She couldn't wait any longer. Picking up the phone, she listened hopefully for a dial tone, but the line was still dead.

She knelt and wrung out the cloth and put it on Cindy's forehead. Cindy didn't stir. Eve gnawed her lip. She'd have to check the garage, there was no other choice. She rearranged the pillows so the cool cloth wouldn't slide from Cindy's head, then got to her feet. She had to steady herself a minute, gathering courage, before she could force herself to make her way down the hall. Cold sweat dampened her neck. If there was any sound at all in the garage, she wouldn't unlock the door. She'd think of something else. What? She couldn't do anything if Miller was still here. And if he had taken the car, there was no way for her and Cindy to get down the hill. She had cut off her own escape. The nearest neighbor was a quarter of a mile away. She had a nodding acquaintance with people she saw drive by, but she and Paul had never socialized with them. They were names on mailboxes, people who respected other people's privacy. But no one would turn her away in an emergency like this.

Could she find her way in the dark? She couldn't leave Cindy alone. She'd have to bundle her and carry her.

Eve stopped in the kitchen to catch her breath. Her pulse was pounding with the same loud cadence as the rain on the roof. The candle on the counter had gone out, and the odor of hot wax and smoking wick lingered in a thin mist. The soft clack of her loafers on the tile floor sounded like castanets, and she crouched to slip them off. The laundry-room linoleum was icy under her heavy socks, and she could feel a draft from the garage. The broken window? Or was the overhead door open? With her hands outstretched to guide her, she inched her way across the narrow room.

She stood listening, not quite touching the door, as if doing so might put her in contact with Luke Miller. Holding her breath, she concentrated on the peculiar muted sounds. The wind sounded louder, and the pounding rain on the uninsulated garage was thunderous. Somewhere water gurgled and splashed. The downspout at the front corner of the garage?

She ran her hand lightly along the doorframe until it touched the dead bolt. She gripped it with stiff fingers while she listened intently, but she couldn't detect any change in the pattern of sound. Scarcely daring to breathe, she eased the bolt slowly, ready to slam it back in place instantly at the first sign of danger. The bolt made a tiny click as it hit the end of the track. Eve pressed her ear to the door before she released the snap lock. Slowly she turned the knob and pulled the door open a crack.

Cold air swept over her. She shivered and clenched her teeth as she peered through the narrow opening. At first she couldn't see anything, but gradually her eyes adjusted and she realized the overhead door was open. She made out the shape of the Mercedes against the gray night. It was hard to keep from flinging the door open, but she cautioned herself that she had no guarantee Luke Miller was gone. Once before he'd hidden until he was ready to show himself. She stood perfectly still, scarcely breathing, and listened to the wind and rain.

The presence of the car puzzled her. Why hadn't he taken it? It didn't make sense for him to leave on foot, unless he didn't know about the valet key. Was that it? Or was he still here? Hiding . . . waiting until he was sure she couldn't lock him out again? She started to push the door shut, her stomach aching with tension, but she'd come this far, she had to go the rest of the way. Finally she opened the door wider and looked out cautiously. The sound of her own breathing was more turbulent in her ears than the storm. Nothing happened. There was only the mournful sound of the wind and a cold mistiness of rain blowing in through the open door. Weak with relief, she wiped away her frightened tears. Miller was gone. He'd opened the overhead door and left, not even taking the car. He was gone! Eve went back inside, bolting the door behind her as a precaution, and retrieved her shoes.

She'd drive directly to the hospital and have them call Dr. Provel. Cindy would need a warm coat and socks for her feet. The car would be cold at first, so she'd need the quilt too.

The candle in Cindy's room had burned out, but Eve didn't bother to get another. She knew where everything was. She moved to the closet, arms extended like antennae. Opening it, she touched dresses, skirts, blouses, and sweaters until she found the garment bag. Unzipping it, she was engulfed with the sweet aroma of cedar. She felt inside for the red princess coat trimmed with white fur that she'd gotten on sale last year and put away for Cindy to grow into. At the dresser she pawed through drawers for woolly slipper socks and leg warmers before she hurried back to the den.

Cindy had thrown off the blanket and the washcloth had slipped to the floor. The legs of her pajamas were tangled around her knees from her restless thrashing. Eve put down the things she was carrying and pulled the blanket over Cindy, then wrung out the cloth again. Putting it on her daughter's fevered brow, she held it in place a moment to see if Cindy would waken, but she only whimpered softly.

"Another few minutes, darling. Dr. Provel will make you feel better." Eve kissed the child's cheek. Then, taking a candle, she went down the hall to her bedroom. She needed a warm jacket.

Then she and Cindy would be on their way. They'd be at the hospital in a little while.

The moment she entered the room she knew something was wrong. She sensed an intangible change. Her flesh crawled and her mouth tasted metallic. Panic tightened around her like an ugly, cold snake as she glanced around the shadow-shrouded room. Her hand gripping the candlestick began to shake, making the flame waver and cast grotesque shadows that leaped back from the mirrored doors of the closet.

Luke Miller stepped out, a gleaming hammer in his hand.

20

Dorie dialed the service number again and got another busy signal. She slammed down the phone and poured herself another brandy. Turning up the volume on the television, she carried her drink to the kitchen, where she unpacked the Styrofoam containers of lasagne, linguine, and salad she'd bought on the way home. Taking plates from the cupboard, she dished out some lasagne and put it in the microwave while she readied a bowl of salad. She carried the plates to the dining room and sat where she could see the television.

She picked at the food without enjoyment, her attention divided between the news program and her irritation with Eve. Eve was a stubborn little fool. Spiteful too. Tonight wasn't the first time they'd had problems like this. Eve wasn't content taking Paul away from her. Now she was making it as difficult as possible for Dorie to see Cindy. Sometimes Dorie suspected Eve wanted to cut all the ties between them now that Paul was gone. Dorie never should have phoned Eve after the school called. She should have just picked up Cindy, brought her here, and taken the rest of the day off. She would have if Cabot hadn't been so damned insistent about his stupid meeting. She should have walked out and told him to go to hell. Cindy would be here now if she had.

She pushed salad around the bowl with her fork. The phone connection had been so terrible she didn't hear Eve's answer to

her question about taking Cindy to the doctor. Dr. Provel had
made a bloody fortune on Cindy's operation and taking care of
her since then. *He* was the one who should decide how sick she
was, not Eve. Maybe she should call him herself. Dorie shoved
her plate away. She couldn't eat. She couldn't do anything unless she was sure Cindy was all right.

She carried the plates to the kitchen and scraped the food
into the garbage disposal. She rinsed the plates and put them in
the dishwasher, then put the chicken she'd gotten for Cindy in
the refrigerator and dumped the rest of the take-out cartons
into the garbage pail. Back in the living room, she tried the
telephone again. This time she got a distinct dial tone, but Eve's
number didn't ring. From the drawer of the phone stand she
got her address book and looked up Dr. Provel's number. His
exchange answered, and Dorie left a message asking the doctor
to call her back and let her know if Eve had brought Cindy in
today.

She went back to the television and flipped stations restlessly
until she found another local news program. The gray filter of
rain made everything murky, so the storm pictures looked as if
they'd been shot in black and white. Water splashed on the
camera lens, adding authenticity. The reporter had to shout
above the cacophony of background noises. Behind him the
camera showed a dozen men and women, anonymous in oil-
skins and knee deep in swirling, muddy water, stacking sandbags across the front of a house.

". . . as neighbors and volunteers try to save other homes
along the street after Henry Sharply and his wife were taken to
the hospital. The couple's home was completely destroyed by
mud that poured down the hillside without warning. Mr. and
Mrs. Sharply were in the kitchen when the slide struck, smash-
ing windows and caving in the rear wall of the house. Although
they were badly cut by flying glass, they ran out before the
house was swept from its foundation by the force of tons of mud.

"Randy Golden, who lives next door, was also evacuating his
home because of the slide warnings. His car was loaded with
clothing and personal belongings when Randy went inside one

last time for his collection of stereo records. He described the noise he heard as 'a roar like a train going through the backyard, then a loud whooshing sound and wood splintering.' When he ran out, the Sharply house was collapsing under the wall of mud. Golden's car wasn't in the driveway anymore. It had been swept fifty yards down the street and was buried in mud and debris. You can see the sad aftermath of the slide's destructive path—twisted gas and water pipes . . . a child's tricycle which was carried down the hill. This quiet, residential neighborhood is in ruins. The wall of mud dropped over Coldwater Canyon and finally leveled off in an—"

"My God!" Dorie gasped as the camera panned the destruction. Coldwater Canyon! She snatched up the phone and dialed 911, drumming her carmine fingernails impatiently as it rang. Finally it was picked up.

"Emergency—"

"My niece and sister-in-law are up in Coldwater Canyon. I can't get through to them. I want you to send someone to make sure they're all right."

"I'm sorry, ma'am, but our men are busy—"

"Damn it, this is an emergency! I can't get them on the phone, and there's been a bad slide in Coldwater—"

"Our evacuation teams are using bullhorns to alert people."

"My niece is sick! You've got to do something!"

"What's the address?"

Dorie told him, then asked how long it would take to get back to her.

"We don't have the manpower to check individual calls," he said, "but we'll list your party's house number. If we get someone in there, we'll ask her to get in touch with you."

"That's ridiculous! It could be hours—"

"Sorry, that's the best I can do." He hung up.

Dorie slammed down the phone. Pacing, she breathed deeply to restore her sanity. Where in Coldwater Canyon had the slide been? She went back to the TV, but the news had gone on to another story. Damn! She changed stations, but couldn't find the story again. Coldwater Canyon wound from Beverly

Hills across the mountain to Sherman Oaks. The slide could have been on either side.

Mark Stein would know! His wife called this afternoon to cry about her brother's house on Mulholland Drive. The foundation was undermined by washouts, and the house had developed cracks bad enough to force them to evacuate. Dorie didn't give a damn about that, but she was sure Mark said the house was close to Coldwater. She ran back to the phone and turned pages of her directory until she found Mark's number. Ever since she'd gone to work at the studio she'd kept every staff member's number handy so she had them if Cabot wanted someone in a hurry. It wasn't unusual for him to decide at 10 P.M. that he wanted a story conference at eight the next morning. She dialed. The connection was abominable, but Mark finally answered.

"I can barely hear you, Dorie. What did you say?"

She shouted. "How close to Coldwater Canyon is your brother-in-law's house?"

"Practically on it," he shouted back. "He's on the first road going off on the city side. Why?"

"Did you see the TV news story about the mud slide in Coldwater?"

Mark Stein snorted. "Yeah. My brother-in-law is afraid his place will be next. He's sitting in front of my fireplace drinking my booze while he reads the fine print on his insurance policy."

"Where was this slide?" she demanded. "Which side of the hill?"

"The city side. Do you know where they built that big stone house on the curve last year? It's near that. Why all the questions?"

Dorie hung up and sank to the Art Deco bench with relief. The Valley side of Coldwater was still open. Eve could get down. She jumped when the phone rang and snatched it up quickly.

"Eve?"

"Miss Foxx? This is Dr. Provel's exchange. He asked me to call you back and tell you he hasn't seen Cindy today."

"Are you sure?" Dorie demanded.

The woman was curt. "That's what he said."

Dorie hung up. Just as she thought! Eve hadn't called Provel. She lifted the phone and dialed Eve's number, but the line crackled and spat without making the connection. Damn!

Surely Eve knew about the slide and the evacuation warnings. She wouldn't be stupid enough not to turn on the radio or television. But suppose the electricity was off as well as the phone? No, Paul had that powerful battery-operated radio. Surely Eve would turn it on!

Dorie was going crazy with worry. There was no telling what Eve would or wouldn't do. She was a rattlebrained actress. She was perfectly capable of not doing a damned thing but sitting and wringing her hands. The only way Dorie would have any peace of mind was to drive up and get Cindy. If Eve wanted to risk her own neck that was one thing, but she had no right to put Cindy in jeopardy. And Dorie wasn't going to let her.

She got her boots, raincoat, and a plastic hat from the closet. She sat on a chair and had one boot half on when the phone rang. She jumped up, tripping over the boot and almost knocking over Paul's picture on the table in her haste to get to the phone. She snatched it up.

"Yes?"

"Dorie, this is Farley Cunningham. Sorry to bother you. I hope I haven't caught you at a bad time."

Dorie didn't bother to disguise her annoyance. "What is it? I'm in a hurry." She hadn't seen or spoken to Farley since the day in his office when he'd informed her that she would be wasting her time and money if she tried to break her brother's will or the trust. Dorie got a bequest of $10,000. Everything else went to Eve and Cindy.

"Have you talked to Eve?" Farley asked.

"Did you hear from her?" Dorie demanded. It would be just like Eve to call Farley and not her. "I've been trying to reach her."

Farley said quickly, "Then you haven't heard from her?"

Irritated, Dorie snapped, "I talked to her about two-thirty

this afternoon. I've been calling ever since I got home to find out how Cindy is, but the one time I got through, the line was—"

"Is Cindy sick?"

"Yes, Cindy is sick!" Dorie snapped. "Eve wasn't home so the school called me. It's a good thing I took the trouble to make sure they have my phone numbers! I wish I'd gone and picked up the poor baby instead of trying to do what's right. Eve hasn't even taken her to the doctor." It gave her perverse pleasure to vent her anger.

To her astonishment, Dorie heard the line click. Furious, she slammed down the phone. Who the hell did he think he was hanging up on her? She knew what was going on. Farley Cunningham was sleeping with Eve. Well, it was about time he knew the truth about her. He'd find out that Eve wasn't a sweet, helpless bereaved widow who needed consolation. She was a cold, heartless bitch, and she was an incompetent and uncaring mother who didn't deserve a beautiful child like Cindy.

Dorie went back to the hall and picked up the boot she'd kicked aside. She yanked it on. Eve didn't deserve Cindy any more than she'd deserved Paul. Tugging on the other boot, Dorie got up and slipped on her raincoat, then stood in front of the mirror to adjust the stylish plastic hat she'd bought at Neiman-Marcus. She found her car keys in her purse before she opened the door to the attached garage of the condominium.

21

Farley tried Eve's number every ten minutes for the next two hours. When six o'clock came and went without her promised call, anxiety set in like a gnawing toothache. In desperation he finally called the one other person who might be in touch with her, her sister-in-law, Dorie Foxx. He reached her without any difficulty, though she sounded breathless and predictably bitchy when she answered. The conversation was unrewarding, and he had to hang up before his patience snapped.

The last thing he needed right now was more of Dorie's selfish complaining. Having her verify that Eve's phone was out of order wasn't very comforting. Knowing she was at the house and he couldn't reach her added to his worry. So did Dorie's statement that Cindy was sick.

He stood gazing at the downpour. He didn't like the idea of Eve being cut off in a storm like this. There were too many things that could go wrong. If Cindy was sick, as Dorie said, Eve could have more than she could handle. Had she taken Cindy to the doctor? Dorie said she hadn't, but that could easily be Dorie's paranoia. Dorie was all too willing to jump to false conclusions where Eve was concerned. Nothing would please her more than to replace the brother who'd matured and grown away from her with his young daughter. Another life to mold . . . Dorie never missed an opportunity to slash Eve with her razor tongue. And Dorie made a crisis of Cindy's stomach upsets no matter how slight they were. It was a point of considerable friction between the two women. Eve was doing her best to bring up Cindy loved but unspoiled. Given free rein, Dorie would pamper and overindulge the child into hypochondria and utter dependence on a doting aunt.

Maybe Eve was at the doctor's with Cindy right now. If she left after Dorie's call, it was conceivable that she might not be back yet. Farley picked up the phone and dialed Los Angeles information to get Dr. Provel's number. He reached an answering service, and only by telling the operator it was an emergency was promised the doctor would call him back. He paced for twenty minutes before the call came through.

Dr. Provel was surprised by his question. "No, I didn't see Cindy today."

"Did Mrs. Foxx call?" Farley wanted to know.

"No, but her sister-in-law did a little while ago asking the same thing. Do you have reason to think Cindy's having problems, Mr. Cunningham?"

"Only Dorie Foxx's word for it. Thanks, Doctor. I'm sure Eve would have called you if she thought it was serious. Not being able to get in touch with her has me worried."

"Yes, well, I'm glad to be able to put your mind at ease. If I do hear from Mrs. Foxx, I'll tell her you're trying to reach her."

Farley hung up. He should be relieved, but the nagging uneasiness wouldn't be put to rest. Eve usually waited an hour or two to see how Cindy was doing before she called the doctor. Farley had been there more than once when Eve was monitoring Cindy's temperature. But suppose Cindy *was* sick, and the phone wasn't working? He began to pace again, aware that he was magnifying his fears. He'd be as paranoid as Dorie if he kept it up. He forced himself to turn back to the television set. The storm coverage was still the main story on every news station, and the reports of flooding and slides were multiplying.

Farley glanced at his watch and realized it was almost time to leave for the banquet. How the hell could he sit through rubber chicken and more speeches when he didn't know if Eve was okay? There had been some slides in Coldwater Canyon before, but the hill behind Paul's house had come through intact. Paul had geological studies done to make sure the land was stable before he bought the place, but geological studies on dry soil were one thing; supersaturated ground was another. No hill was slideproof. And now Eve was alone up there with Cindy.

He picked up the phone and tried her number again. Dorie got through once, maybe he'd hit it lucky. He didn't. Disconnecting, he dialed his office. One of the law clerks, Lester Brandt, answered on the line the switchboard left connected after office hours. Brandt was young, ambitious, eager, and often worked late.

"I'm glad I caught you, Lester."

"How's the conference going, Mr. Cunningham?"

"Some ground that hasn't been covered a dozen times, but a lot that has. Listen, I need a personal favor."

"Sure, Mr. Cunningham."

"I've been trying to get through to Mrs. Foxx, but her phone isn't working. Will you call Captain Hazza at LAPD in North Hollywood? Use my name to get through to him. He's probably busier than a booking sergeant on Friday night, but see if he'll send someone up there to make sure Mrs. Foxx and her little girl are all right."

"I'll be glad to call, but I don't know how much good it will do. The whole city is a soggy sponge. I heard on the radio that emergency switchboards are lit up like Christmas trees. City maintenance is closing roads left and right."

"Did you hear anything about Coldwater Canyon?" The knot in Farley's stomach pulled like a hangman's noose.

"No, but I haven't listened to news since four-thirty when I went down for coffee. I'll check with North Hollywood for you. Want me to call you back?"

Farley glanced at his watch. "I'll be here another half hour. If you don't have anything by then, call me at the Miramar. I'll let the maître d' know what table I'm at so he can pull me out of the crowd."

When he hung up Farley glanced at the window. Fog had rolled in to compound the rain, and the beach and ocean were

enveloped in the solid gray mass. He wished now he hadn't
come to the seminar. He could have met Eve after her taping.
They could have picked Cindy up from school later and—

He reined his meandering thoughts. Monday-morning-quar-
terbacking wouldn't do any good. He'd registered for the seminar months ago, and Eve didn't know until last week that she'd
be shooting a commercial today. And neither knew it was going
to rain like this. He turned away from the window and finished
dressing for the banquet.

22

Rigid with terror and too numb to scream, Eve stared at Miller. The room felt icy, and she drew air into her lungs in painful little gasps. How had he gotten back into the house? Shaded by thick black brows drawn tightly together, his eyes burned in the sockets of his skull-face. His mouth was a rictus of evil as he moved toward her with the hammer raised.

Eve backed away, trying to distance herself from the rage that seemed to emanate from him. When she bumped against the wall she sidled toward the door, but Miller pounced suddenly, slamming it shut before she could slip through. He put his back against it and loomed over her.

"That wasn't nice," he said.

His voice was low and taut with anger, as if his patience had worn thin and his temper was close to the explosion point. Eve cringed under his searing gaze. Her mind reeled. He was back. Locking him in the garage had backfired. She hadn't gotten rid of him, she'd succeeded only in enraging him. Her action had brought about the thing she feared most—there was murder in his eyes now. Deep, burning hatred poured from the black pit of his madness. Her hand holding the candle was shaking so badly that Miller's shadow jumped on the wall like a menacing gargoyle. The hammer glinted dully.

Eve felt the pressure of the scissors in her pocket. Without shifting her terrified gaze from the evil mask of Miller's face, she worked her free hand into the pocket and closed it around the scissors. When Miller took a step toward her she jerked them out and stabbed desperately. Somehow Miller sensed the danger and slashed with the hammer before her blow landed. The heavy metal struck the back of her hand, and she screamed in agony as the scissors flew from her grasp. She doubled with pain. Miller snatched the candle before it fell. Unable to control her sobs, Eve pressed her bruised hand to her mouth as she tried to absorb the pain. Miller smiled. The room was hushed except for her soft whimpering.

Oh, God, why had she been such a fool to attack with that pitiful weapon? Now he was going to kill her. She closed her eyes, waiting for another blow of the hammer. When it didn't come she forced herself to open her eyes and found him watching her intently. He was playing with her terror, enjoying outwitting her. It was a game to him, and he was waiting for her next move.

Could she get him to trust her again? Somehow she had to make him believe she wouldn't do anything foolish again. She stammered as she shaped words and pushed them from her tongue.

"I—I'm sorry. You're right, it wasn't very nice. I—I was scared and worried about Cindy." In the eerie light she couldn't be sure if his expression changed. He didn't answer. She filled the ominous silence nervously. "Cindy really must go to the doctor. The medicine isn't helping. She needs—"

"How many times do I have to tell you to take better care of her? It's your fault she's sick!"

Eve shrank from his knife-edge tone. He'd never said any such thing. He told her to sit with Cindy, but the rest was his imagination.

She pleaded, "Please—her fever's going up. I have to get her to—"

"Go stay with her!" he shouted. The hammer rose in his clenched fist.

Eve swallowed bile. She nodded desperately and glanced at the door, her pulse thundering so wildly it made pinpricks of light dance before her eyes. To her astonishment, Miller stepped aside and pulled the door open.

"When she wakes up I'll make more cocoa," he said. The rage had ebbed from his voice, and he lowered the hammer slowly. Standing with his hand on the door, he motioned for Eve to pass. She had to squeeze close to him, and her head reeled as she smelled the faint odor of damp wool from Paul's sweater. She cringed when Miller's hand brushed her shoulder. Once in the hall, she ran to the den.

She sank to the sofa beside Cindy. Miller was sidetracked momentarily, but he might explode again any minute. There was no pattern to his erratic mood swings, except she knew Cindy somehow was a key to whatever sanity he had. If he was concerned enough about her, he might let them go. Eve wrung out the cloth and laid it on Cindy's head. She had to make him understand that Cindy needed a doctor. He'd been ready to kill her, Eve was sure, and the only thing that aborted his murderous rage was his concern for Cindy. He was worried because Eve left her alone even though she was sleeping. Why wouldn't he let her take Cindy to the doctor then? Because he's crazy, Eve warned herself. She couldn't afford to forget that for a minute. Cindy was the only key to Miller's weakness. How could she use it to save them?

At a soft sound she glanced around and saw Miller emerge from the dark hall. He was still carrying the hammer, which winked wickedly as it caught the firelight, but he no longer had the candle. He glanced at her, then at Cindy. The tight lines in his face eased as he gazed at the small, sleeping form. After a moment he slipped the hammer under his belt and went to the fireplace to put more logs on the burning pyre. When he closed the fire curtains Eve kept her gaze riveted on Cindy.

Miller's outburst in the bedroom was the first time he'd ordered her to take better care of Cindy or blamed her for Cindy's illness. Eve was positive of it. Years of doing commercials had sharpened her memory. Despite the nerve-racking pressure she was under, she wouldn't forget something that significant.

But the thing was, Miller *believed* he'd said those things. Had he said them to someone else at some other time?

She tried to recall details of the newspaper story that had plunged her into this nightmare. Miller murdered his wife years ago and possibly another woman a few days ago. She hadn't read the whole story. Did it mention a child? Concentrating, Eve tried to recall if she'd ever read about Luke Miller's original crime. It would have been about the time she came to Los Angeles. The newspapers were so full of crime stories, she skipped over the lurid headlines. *Daily Variety* and *The Hollywood Reporter* were more important as she found her way through the maze of a media-oriented city. She glanced at the newspaper on top of the kindling. Was page nine intact? Luke Miller's voice jarred her hopscotching thoughts.

"You can't believe everything those bastard doctors say. They make plenty of mistakes. Plenty." He hunched against the mantel and jammed his hands into the pockets of Paul's slacks. With a glance at the small wet bar Paul had installed in the corner of the room, he demanded, "Do you drink?"

She shook her head. "Sometimes a glass of wine at a party but—"

"Mothers shouldn't drink."

She let out her breath, thankful that the truth had been the right answer. Neither she nor Paul were drinkers in any sense of the word. Sometimes when Paul entertained clients or was particularly tense over some deal, he'd have a cocktail or wine. Like the night of the accident.

She turned back to Cindy but glanced sidelong nervously when Miller moved. She trembled with relief when he didn't come toward her but lifted the lid of the woodbox and looked inside. He went back to stand in front of the fire, and she felt his piercing gaze on her. She kept her head bowed, her thoughts in turmoil. She didn't want to look at him or talk to him. She felt as though she were in a maze of tall, dark hedges, where every turn led deeper to the heart of the trap instead of to freedom.

She freshened the cool cloth on Cindy's forehead. Cindy's skin was hot and dry and her eyelids waxy. From time to time her lashes fluttered and a thin line of white showed between the lids. She always slept restlessly when she was sick, as if she were searching for some reassuring glimpse of Eve. Or Paul. Eve had tried hard to explain, but it was impossible for a three-year-old to comprehend the finality of death. When Cindy had the severe gastritis attack after Paul's funeral, Dr. Provel said she was transferring her emotional pain to her delicate stomach. If she continued doing it, the psychosomatic illnesses would bring about the same result as physical ones. He cautioned Eve that she had to learn to separate the power of the child's mind from the reality of a genuine infection. It wouldn't be easy, he warned, and it would take time. Of late, Eve was sure they were both making progress, but now she'd really blown it. With this kind of weather, she never should have taken a chance that Cindy was shamming. She should have taken her to the doctor. Now they were trapped in the house with a madman, and Cindy was getting worse by the minute. Eve berated herself for doing a rotten job of separating pretense from reality.

Luke Miller was reality. He was an enigma, and Eve knew her life and Cindy's depended on defining the thin line that separated his worried-father attitude from his psychotic-killer rage. Why had the doctors ever let him out of that institution? What right did they have to release a crazy man so he could kill again? Eve tried to control the violent shivering of her body.

23

Miller watched the woman guardedly. He'd have to keep an eye on her now. She had been pretty clever locking him in the garage that way. She'd looked so innocent and acted so friendly, he never figured on her trying something like that. He got in this time by cutting a pane from the bedroom window so he could reach the bolt and crank. Afterward he taped the glass back in place so there wouldn't be a draft. She never even noticed. And just in case he needed to use it again, he could slip out the pane in a second with no one the wiser. But that wasn't going to happen. He wouldn't give her the chance to trick him again.

He studied her as she bent over the basin of water and wrung out the cloth. She looked worried. Good. Maybe it would keep her where she belonged. His anger eased as his gaze moved to the child.

"She feels better now," he said. Eve looked up with a startled expression. "Because you're with her. She needs you." He smiled to show he had forgiven her for the garage trick, but she didn't respond.

Luke turned to check the fire. Now that he'd rebuilt it, the room was pleasantly warm. There was enough wood to last awhile, but he'd have to get more eventually. Being out in the rain again had really chilled him. When he'd taken off the plastic wrappings his feet were wet and cold. Even Mr. Eve

Foxx's clean wool socks hadn't warmed them. He needed something hot in his belly. He'd forgotten his hunger for a while. Now he remembered she was supposed to bring food from the kitchen before she decided to play hide-and-seek. He walked to the sofa and looked down at her.

"You stay right here," he ordered. "I'll be back in a minute. Don't you dare leave Kristen, you hear?"

She nodded hesitantly without looking up.

"Answer me!" He didn't mean to raise his voice. It was because he was so worried about Kristen.

"Yes." She glanced up with a frightened look. "I'll stay with her. I won't go anywhere."

That was better. Miller picked up one of the new candles and tore off the cellophane. He lit it from the sputtering one on the table. It threw a wavering veil of light as he walked down the hall.

Eve listened to the storm close around the faint sound of his footsteps. She was on an emotional seesaw. He went from one extreme to another so abruptly, she didn't know what to expect. He'd called Cindy "Kristen." Instinct warned her not to correct him. Was Kristen a child of his past? His daughter?

Eve laid the wet cloth on Cindy's brow. The water in the basin wasn't cold anymore, but she didn't dare go for more. He'd ordered her to stay here, and she was too frightened to disobey. She prayed that the cold compresses were helping. It was less than a half hour since she'd taken Cindy's temperature. If she took it again and it was still going up, Eve was afraid she'd panic and set Miller off. She'd try to keep Cindy as comfortable as possible until she could devise a plan to escape.

In the kitchen Miller wedged the candle between two ceramic planters. He tiptoed back to the doorway and peered into the dining room and living room to make sure she wasn't up to any tricks. Satisfied, he pulled the small plastic flashlight, the kind women put on their key chains, he'd found in the garage from his pocket and moved to the garage door. He was out and back with an armload of wood in seconds. He dropped the wood on top of the counter. It was enough to last a couple of hours. When they ran out he'd make her go out for more.

He rummaged through the cupboards in search of food. She didn't keep a lot of canned stuff on hand. A glance inside the freezer showed it was full. They could thaw some later if they needed it. For now he settled on cans of soup, sardines, smoked oysters, and peaches, which he stuffed into the pockets of the blue slacks until they bulged. From another cupboard he took a box of crackers, then found a can opener in a drawer and a covered saucepan in a cupboard next to the stove. He took three spoons and forks from the silverware drawer. At the last minute he remembered the cocoa and milk. He had to tuck the milk carton under his arm so he could carry everything. His pockets clanked as he walked back to the den, but she didn't look up. She was stroking Kristen's hair. He was glad she was finally behaving the way a mother should. With both of them to take care of her, Kristen would get well. He set everything on the hearth and began opening the soup. He poured it into the pot and covered it before he opened the fire screen and pushed the pan against the glowing embers. While it was warming he opened the other cans. He should have brought plates. He didn't mind eating out of the cans, but it wasn't setting a good example for Kristen.

He watched her wring out the cloth again. "Is that doing any good?" he asked. His voice startled her, and she jumped.

"It should help bring down the fever."

He supposed it would. He was glad she thought of it. After a bit he said, "A little soup will be good for her."

"I don't think so."

"Chicken. It's her favorite."

She gave him a confused look and said, "Let's see how she feels when she wakes up."

He nodded and moved the coffee table so they could both reach it. He looked around for something to put under the pot so the heat wouldn't crack the glass. The rest of the newspaper he'd used to start the fire was on top of the kindling. He folded it in quarters and put it in the middle of the table, then set the opened cans of sardines, oysters, and peaches around it. He put two forks and spoons in front of her and the others on his side.

When the soup was hot he set the pan on the paper and pushed it toward her. She shook her head. "I'm not hungry."

"You have to eat."

"I— Later. You go ahead."

Shrugging, he pulled the pot to his side of the table and settled in the tweed recliner. The aroma of the hot soup made his stomach rumble, and he realized he was starved. He tore open a packet of crackers and ate ravenously. From time to time he stabbed an oyster or sardine and popped it into his mouth between spoonsful of soup. Before he knew it the pot was empty. Finally he sat back.

That was a lot better. The food warmed and relaxed him. The only thing he needed now was sleep. He hadn't slept much last night. He frowned, trying to remember the woman. He couldn't remember what she looked like, but he remembered her laughter and warm body, and how they'd run from the car to her apartment but had gotten soaked anyhow. They didn't waste any time getting into bed. She was hot and eager and made him forget about the cold in a hurry. She made him forget a lot of things.

The picture blurred, and when he tried to bring it back in focus, it wouldn't come. The next thing he remembered clearly was the pounding of the rain on the streaked windshield of the Camaro. She'd better have that wiper blade replaced. He'd have to tell her about it.

Seeing Miller in Paul's favorite chair tortured Eve. He was making himself at home as if he had every right to be here. He'd devoured the food as if he hadn't eaten for days. Now he looked settled and content, and his eyelids drooped. Eve held her breath, hoping, but Miller's head jerked up suddenly. After a few seconds he relaxed again.

Eve sat very still. Dared she try for the car if he fell asleep? She'd have to be very sure this time. But how could she be? There was no way to predict anything about him. He got in and out of the house with ease and stole about as silently as a cat. And his temper flared unexpectedly and violently, without any pattern she'd been able to discern. If she provoked him again, there was no telling what he'd do. She could make things a lot worse than they were.

She thought about the name he'd called Cindy. Kristen . . . Who was she? A little girl waiting somewhere for a daddy she might never see again? Did Miller see Kristen when he looked at Cindy? If he thought—believed—Cindy was Kristen, could Eve convince him to let "Kristen" see a doctor? It was obvious he didn't like or trust doctors, but he might do it if he was worried enough. Eve felt a stir of excitement. It was a chance, but she'd have to be very careful.

Miller was watching her somnolently. For a moment, in the flickering light, she imagined Paul sitting there the way he always had. She blinked to erase the fantasy. The man in the recliner was not Paul. He was Luke Miller, murderer. Luke Miller, capable of murdering again.

Cindy stirred and Eve turned to her quickly and stroked her cheek. Instead of being soothed, Cindy whimpered and began to cry. Miller sat up instantly. Cindy rolled onto her side and curled in a ball, pressing her arms across her stomach.

"My tummy hurts . . ." Cindy's heart-shaped face puckered and tears spilled over her lashes.

Eve bent over her. "Try to lie still, honey. Mommy will get something to make you feel better." Eve petted her, then slid to her knees and crawled to Miller's chair. Whispering, she pleaded, "She has to go to the doctor! She's worse, can't you see?"

Miller looked at the child on the sofa and his face clouded. Cindy was whimpering with little breath-catching sobs. Eve was losing the battle with her own tears. "Please, let me take her to the doctor. She needs antibiotics. He'll give her a shot—" Eve didn't realize she'd grabbed Miller's arm until she felt his muscles tighten. She pulled her hand away as if it had touched a hot stove and sank back on her heels. "Please," she begged. Still staring at Cindy, he didn't answer. Eve crawled back to the sofa and lifted Cindy into her arms. Gentling her with little rocking motions, she whispered, "Shhh, shhh, don't cry, honey. . . ." Head bent, Eve's tears fell onto the child's golden hair.

Miller pushed himself out of the comfortable chair. Eve looked up with a flicker of hope, but he went back to the fireplace and poured milk into the other pan he'd left on the hearth. Measuring with a clean spoon, he added cocoa mix. He knelt and began to warm the pan over the fire.

Eve wanted to scream. Cocoa wasn't going to help Cindy now. She needed medicine. Damn him! Cindy needed a doctor! She struggled to her feet without putting Cindy down. Miller looked around, then set the pan down and jumped up.

"Where are you going?"

"I'm taking her to the doctor."

"No you're not!" His voice shook. "I told you the bastard's a quack. He doesn't know what he's talking about. We're going to take care of her. She's going to be okay, you hear?" He punched Eve's shoulder hard enough to reel her back. She fell onto the sofa, still clutching Cindy.

Cindy wailed. Eve choked down her terror as Miller stood over them. His breath rasping, he pulled the hammer from his belt and raised it. Eve cringed and tried to shield Cindy with her body. Miller's arm started to swing downward but stopped as Cindy cried softly. It seemed an eternity until he lowered the hammer slowly to his side. Eve tried to moisten her lips but her tongue was paper-dry. Numb, she watched him go back to the fireplace and resume stirring the cocoa.

24

Dr. Grace Armand's office was in a small medical complex built like a strip shopping center. It surprised Noble, who figured all psychiatrists were millionaires with posh offices and homes in Encino or Brentwood. He was a few minutes early and had to wait, but it was pleasantly warm and the chairs in the waiting room were comfortable. Right at six the receptionist nodded toward a door and told him he could go in. He hadn't heard any signal, nor had anyone come out of the doctor's office. He thanked the girl and went in.

Wood paneling, muted colors, comfortable chairs, and a walnut desk with a phone and a few miscellaneous items on it. Noble tried to imagine himself working in such neat, comfortable surroundings. He sat across from the attractive gray-haired woman in a chic mauve suit. She looked like anything but a psychiatrist.

"What can I do for you, Sergeant Noble?" she asked with a pleasant smile.

"According to our records, you were one of the psychiatrists who examined Luke Miller eight years ago when he stood trial for his wife's murder. Do you remember the case?"

"Vividly." She gave him another smile. "I also reviewed my files when I read the story about Miller in the morning paper."

It explained how easily he'd gotten in to see her despite her busy schedule. Noble said, "What can you tell me about him?"

"Judging by this morning's paper, you think Miller may have killed again, is that right?"

"It looks more like it all the time," Noble admitted.

Dr. Armand lifted an inquisitive eyebrow. "Why?"

"There was a second murder this morning. We have a positive ID on Miller as the man last seen with the victim."

"A woman?"

Noble nodded. "The media's already having a field day with the Hauptner case. If they pick up this link between Miller and the latest victim, all hell is going to break loose." He didn't have to tell her that the medical profession would take as much heat as the police department. The doctors would be damned for letting Miller out of the hospital. The police would be double-damned for not waving some kind of magic wand and picking him up before the urge to kill came over him again.

"Can you tell me anything that will help me figure out what his next move will be? Is he apt to pick up another woman? Will he run? If so, where?"

Dr. Armand tipped her chair back slightly on its well-oiled spring. "You're asking a great deal, Sergeant. I'm not sure I can give direct answers. If I could, I'd have the solution to the questions psychiatry has been probing since Freud developed his concept of unconscious forces disrupting mental health. But I understand your position, and I'll do my best." She leaned back comfortably and regarded him with frank, gray eyes. "How familiar are you with Miller's background up to the point of his arrest?"

Noble said, "I'd like to hear your summary of it."

She nodded. "Miller had been married three years. There's not much evidence that the marriage was particularly happy. Sharon was a teenage runaway when Miller met her. Neighbors described her as quiet, mousey if you will, and afraid to stand up to Miller. But on the surface things were placid enough. They both doted on the child, a little girl named Kristen, who was born in a free clinic.

"It's doubtful that the child ever had proper medical attention. The mother never brought her back for regular checkups, and no records came to light from private physicians. When she was about two the child became ill. Like so many of these cases, the mother didn't seek medical care for some time. But eventually, when the child wasn't responding to home treatment, the mother brought her to the clinic. There were complications that were treated initially, but finally the child's problem was diagnosed as a congenital heart condition that hadn't been detected at birth. Serious deterioration and infection had set in, and there was little the doctors could do. The clinic physician recommended hospitalizing the child, but the mother refused to allow it without the father's permission.

"Miller wouldn't consider it. He insisted the two of them could take care of her. He was working an afternoon shift at the General Motors plant in the Valley and stayed up the rest of the night with the child after he got home. When he was at work he insisted that his wife be at the child's bedside every moment. Sharon begged him to let her put the child in the hospital, but according to neighbors, Miller wouldn't hear of it. To him there was no possibility that the child wouldn't respond to the loving care they were giving her. Kristen died while Miller was at work one day. What happened next is conjecture." Dr. Armand lifted a well-manicured hand, palm up.

"Neighbors heard them fighting. It was something of an event, since Sharon had never been known to raise her voice before. One might conclude from the liquor bottle the police reported finding that Sharon fortified herself with a few drinks before she had to face her husband. The coroner estimated the child died about four o'clock in the afternoon. Sharon didn't call anyone or even go to a neighbor for help. She simply waited for Miller to come home. Not unusual in the repressed personality, but the alcohol may have triggered the release of her hostilities and anguish, thus precipitating the argument the neighbors heard."

"He blamed her for the kid dying, so he beat and strangled her?" Noble asked.

Dr. Armand shrugged eloquently. "Without a doubt the child's death was a precipitating factor. Miller sat in the apartment with the two dead bodies for hours. About dawn he carried the child to the emergency room of a nearby hospital. He demanded that the intern, who happened to be female, help her. Of course, there was nothing that could be done. When the physician told Miller this, he attacked her in a maniacal rage. He had to be pulled away and restrained. He was still highly agitated and incoherent when I first saw him." Dr. Armand took a deep breath, as though telling the story pained her.

"The root of his stress was the child, of course. His mind wasn't ready to accept the fact of her death. He had no similar concern about his wife and no awareness that he'd taken her life. She ceased to exist for him. He was obsessed with the child. Over and over he demanded to be taken to her, to talk to the doctors, for specialists to be called. Even after he was sedated, his concern was exclusively for the child. The only reference he made to his wife was that she hadn't taken proper care of the little girl." Dr. Armand looked toward the window, where the office lights were reflected in the rain-spattered glass. When she looked back at Noble she said, "In my judgment, Luke Miller is a dangerous psychopath. He needs only some small quirk to trigger his killer rage. His wife discovered it accidentally when she found the courage to fight with him."

Noble registered surprise. "You're talking present tense. Are you saying this is what's happening now? He'll kill anyone who—"

The doctor's mauve shoulders hinted at a shrug. "This is strictly my opinion and off the record, Sergeant, you understand. There may be mitigating circumstances, but I believed then and still do that any direct verbal or physical attack on Miller could precipitate the same kind of violence he displayed with his wife. It could happen with anyone, but it's more likely to occur with a woman."

Noble considered the theory. It fit. If Merilee Hauptner was upset by what she learned from the social worker, she probably confronted Miller angrily. It was logical to assume that Janine Peters went crazy when she saw the picture and story in the newspaper and did the same thing. Two triggers . . . two dead women.

"Have I answered your questions, Sergeant Noble?"

"You're saying Miller can go right on killing?"

"It's quite possible, if he believes he is being threatened. Miller's case history is classic. He was an abused child. His mother was a domineering, overpowering personality without the ability to express love. His father was completely intimidated by her, as was Luke. Neither of them ever was able to please her, and she constantly lashed them with a vitriolic tongue or with any instrument that came to hand. Under pentothal Miller recounted incidents of being beaten with strap, broom, kitchen utensils, and his mother's hand. His father committed suicide when Luke was twelve. Subconsciously, Luke blamed his mother."

"Is she still alive?" Noble asked.

"She was at the time Miller was tried. She refused to testify. She died while he was in Atascadero."

"Did you see him after he was committed?"

She smiled. "No. The staff psychiatrists took over the case. My records were available to them, of course."

"In your opinion, Dr. Armand, should Miller have been released?"

She was thoughtful a moment, considering her answer carefully. "Given these latest developments, it would be easy to say no and place the burden of guilt squarely on the hospital staff. But in all fairness I have to say that I might have voted as they did if I'd been part of the mental-health team in charge of the case. There's no doubt in my mind that Miller was insane at the time he killed his wife. He was institutionalized for treatment. If, in the judgment of the people who were treating him, he had progressed from insanity to competency, they were right to release him to a community program where he'd have the chance to prove himself."

"And to kill again," Noble said bitterly.

She made the palm-up gesture again. "The examining board weighed the facts at their disposal."

"You're saying that in eight years of observation no one spotted this crazy quirk in Miller?"

"The staff at Atascadero can answer that better than I, Sergeant. As you know from the accounts of Miller's trial, mental-health experts don't always agree. Predicting violent behavior among mental patients has not, as yet, been done with any high degree of accuracy."

Noble smiled wearily. "I guess you've given me a pretty good profile of my killer, but it doesn't help find him now." Noble smiled wearily.

"I have no idea where he might head. He has no home base, no family. For the most part, Luke Miller is a very ordinary man with ordinary needs and tastes. I only hope he does not find another woman to take him in."

Noble rose and extended his hand. "Thank you, Dr. Armand. So do I."

25

Dorie tapped the steering wheel impatiently and peered through the streaming windshield. She had the defroster on high to keep the glass clear, and the steady hum of the blower irritated her. Ventura Boulevard was a crawling snake of headlights as rush-hour traffic spilled off the freeway. She hated creeping through snarled traffic. It was one of the reasons she had chosen the condominium in Toluca Lake. She was only minutes from the studio and didn't have to drive with the hordes every day. Paul laughingly called her a "city girl," but he let her choose the place she wanted. It wasn't as if she couldn't buy her own place. Paul *wanted* to do it. Even though he never spoke openly about his gratitude for all the sacrifices she'd made and the bond they shared, insisting on buying the condominium for her was an expression of it, she knew. Just as she knew that it was only infatuation he felt for Eve and that it couldn't last. Dorie hadn't expected him to stay obsessed as long as he did, but of course Cindy made the difference. Dorie had always felt Eve got pregnant deliberately for exactly that reason.

God, she missed Paul. He'd been such an essential part of her life so long, he gave meaning to her existence. At times the pain of his loss was as horrible as it had been the night she received the phone call from the hospital telling her he was dead. Dead . . . She never even had the chance to say good-bye. Eve's injuries were minor, and she was kept in the hospital only overnight. Dorie had collapsed in hysterical grief so complete she hadn't even realized Cindy was at home with a sitter. If she had, she would have rushed to be with Paul's child to try to ease some of the numbing agony.

When the light changed Dorie caught a break in the traffic and pulled into the westbound lane, blocking the intersection. She ignored the angry barrage of horns as she inched up behind a Ferrari. If Eve had done the sensible thing today and brought Cindy to her place, Dorie wouldn't be here fighting this damn traffic. Eve took perverse pleasure in antagonizing her.

It took a half hour to get to Coldwater Canyon. Dorie was fuming with frustration and irritation. She muttered a litany of curses at the storm and her sister-in-law's selfishness, but angry as she was, she wouldn't turn around until Cindy was safe in the car with her. The idea of Eve taking risks with the child's health incensed her. Eve never thought about anyone but herself. The moment she got out of the hospital she'd shuttered herself and Cindy away from everyone, ignoring Dorie's phone calls and messages, not caring that Dorie was torn apart by losing the brother she adored. Eve might at least have let her be with Cindy, but the dozens of offers to take the child so Eve could rest were spurned. Cindy was part of Paul, the only part that remained except for Dorie's memories and two albums filled with snapshots. Dorie sniffled and reached for a tissue from the box on the console.

There were only a few cars heading south on the curving, steep climb of Coldwater Canyon. Rush-hour traffic coming the other way from Beverly Hills was dwindling but still a steady flow. The intermittent glare of headlights forced her to drive at a crawl, and she concentrated on the taillights of a car she'd overtaken. She kept a safe distance but made sure she kept them in sight so she had advance warning of curves or obstacles. It was amazing that the road was still open. Water was running down the shoulders and swirling across the pavement, through, over, and around debris that had piled in miniature dams. The driveways of houses built below the street level were sandbagged to prevent the tide from coursing down. Those on the high side of the road streamed with muddy water.

The blinker of the car ahead signaled a right turn, and the wheels spewed water as it turned off. Dorie came to a stop to give the windshield wipers time to clear the glass. It was insanity to live in these damn canyons. She tried to talk Paul out of buying up here, but he was determined to have his aerie and she couldn't dissuade him. Then when he married Eve the two of them settled in like a pair of lovebirds in a nest. When Paul was alive it was one thing, but Eve didn't know a damn thing about Southern California winter storms. Maybe this would convince her to move down to civilization. There were plenty of nice homes in Studio City or Burbank. And there were excellent private schools. Cindy would have to be bused to school if they stayed here. Dorie shuddered to think of it. She decided she'd start checking schools and arm herself with facts. She'd check the real estate picture too. Cindy wouldn't be ready for school for two years, but it would probably take that long to convince Eve to move.

When Dorie finally recognized the series of curves just below Paul's driveway, she had to stop and wait until it was safe to swing out to pass some idiot who had parked on the curve. She snapped on the turn signal and crawled around the sharp turn into the driveway. Relieved to be off the winding canyon road, she shifted into low gear for the steep climb.

The woods were black walls on either side of the faint, dark ribbon of the drive in the beam of the headlights. The tires sang on the grooved concrete as the car strained through the switchbacks and up the final grade.

Stopping in front of the garage, Dorie turned off the engine. The house was dark except for a faint glow that might be candlelight. The garage door was open, and Eve had parked the Mercedes carelessly so it blocked both stalls and obviously forgotten to close the overhead door. Now that the power had gone off, it would stand open all night. Dorie found a flashlight in the glove compartment and snapped it on.

The wind had gale force in the canyon, and Dorie had to push against the car door to get it open. It was almost torn from her grasp as she struggled out. She hunched into her coat collar and ran for the shelter of the open garage. Inside, she shook her coat and wiped her spattered face. The storm sounded like a train rumbling through the canyon. Once again Dorie cursed Eve's idiocy for living up here. She tried the laundry-room door but it was locked. She knocked loudly, and when there was no answer she rummaged in her purse for the key Paul had given her when he first bought the house and she'd found him a cleaning woman. He'd forgotten she had it, Dorie was sure, and Eve never knew. It never occurred to Dorie to return the key. It was a link to Paul that Eve couldn't possibly understand.

The key turned but the door didn't budge. It was bolted. She pounded on it, but the howling storm drowned out the sound, Dorie blew out her breath irritably. She'd come too far to give up now. With no electricity here, there was absolutely no question that she had to take Cindy to her place. Hiking up her collar to meet the rain hat, she made a dash for the front door. In the wobbling beam of the flashlight, she ran right through a puddle she didn't see. Water gushed over the top of her boot and soaked her ankle. Muttering savagely, Dorie stood in the small, brick entry and focused the flashlight. She slipped the key into the lock and opened the door.

The hall was quiet and dark. She pulled off her dripping raincoat and hat and draped them over the coat rack. She sat on the hall bench to pull off her boots and rub her clammy nylons before putting her shoes back on.

The house was dark except for a sputtering candle burning in the dining room. Down the hall another faint glow indicated more candles, probably in the den. Dorie started to call out but checked herself when she heard a murmur of voices. It was faint but seemed to be coming from the family room. Eve and Cindy? No, a deeper voice . . . a man's.

Her curiosity piqued, Dorie walked quietly down the hall. She paused at the open door to Cindy's dark bedroom and cupped her hand over the flashlight. The bed was empty. Dorie listened again before she went on softly toward the den.

There was definitely a man with Eve. They were talking too quietly for Dorie to make out their words, but the conversation sounded intimate and caressing. Farley Cunningham certainly hadn't wasted any time getting here. Dorie stopped in the shadows where she could look into the room without being seen.

Eve was sitting on a quilt in front of the fireplace. A man Dorie had never seen before was sitting beside her. Dorie's face flushed, and she clenched her fists. So this was why Eve insisted on coming home!

26

Cindy tried to squirm out of her mother's arms. She rubbed her tear-streaked face and pressed a hand to her middle. "My tummy hurts," she whined.

Eve babbled soft, encouraging sounds without taking her eyes from the man kneeling by the fireplace. He wasn't going to let her and Cindy go anywhere. He flew into a rage when she mentioned the doctor. What was it he said earlier? *The bastard is a quack.* Kristen's doctor? Oh Lord, how could she find out about Kristen without setting him off again? Miller's violence had scared her out of her wits, and now he was heating cocoa as if nothing had happened.

When Miller was satisfied the cocoa was the right temperature, he filled Cindy's mug and set it on the table beside Paul's chair. He held his arms out for Cindy, and Eve recoiled, ignoring Cindy's whimpers.

"Give her to me," he ordered.

Eve tightened her hold, but Miller pried her arms loose and took Cindy. When Eve jumped up and grabbed for her daughter, Miller shoved her out of the way. Cindy wailed and tried to struggle free. Miller crossed to Paul's chair and sat with the child cradled in his lap, ignoring her screams. He tucked the blanket around her and hushed her with soft, humming sounds. Finally Cindy's lower lip quivered and she quieted. Eve sank to the sofa and watched him warily.

He spoke to Cindy gently. "No more crying now. I made you more cocoa."

"Don't want any," Cindy pouted.

"It will help your bellyache."

She whined, "Don't want it. Mama . . ." She wriggled and reached for Eve, but Miller spread the blanket over her flailing arm, trapping it so she resembled a butterfly struggling from a cocoon. When he raised the mug to her mouth Cindy compressed her lips stubbornly.

Miller was patient. "Do you know that this is magic cocoa?" he asked.

Cindy's blue gaze wavered.

"It came from Fairyland."

She sniffled and studied him curiously.

"The fairies let only good girls drink this magic cocoa because it's made from stardust and sunshine. Anyone who drinks it gets three wishes granted by the Fairy Queen." He regarded her solemnly. "Are you a good little girl?"

Cindy nodded hesitantly.

"Well, then I guess you can have some," Miller said, as though he were giving in to her begging. When he brought the cup to her lips again, Cindy sipped.

Eve watched in amazement as he continued to coax gently. Cindy's sobs ceased and the tears were drying on her face. What kind of man was this? What insanity made him ready to kill one moment and so gentle and patient the next? Somehow his persuasiveness with Cindy frightened her as much as his violence. There was an invisible aura of evil about him, something that emanated from deep in his core. Even while he had Cindy's rapt attention with his talk of fairies and magic, his eyes betrayed him. Did Cindy sense it too? There was still a puzzled expression on her cherubic face, but Miller had calmed her down, and Eve gave silent thanks.

Cindy's eyes began to droop from the combination of fever, warm cocoa, and Miller's soft droning voice. After a few minutes they closed and she was asleep. Miller's face was expressionless as he sat holding her. The room was quiet except for the

occasional spit of the fire. The irony of the pseudo-domestic
scene made Eve want to scream.

When she could stand it no longer she got up from the sofa
and walked to the cabinet Paul had built beside the fireplace.
Miller's gaze burned on her back while she rummaged in a
drawer. She found a plastic bag and began picking up the
empty food cans. Despite his invitation for her to eat, Miller had
devoured everything. Eve used a tissue from her pocket to wipe
cracker crumbs and a spot of sardine oil from the table, then
dropped it into the bag before twisting the top shut. Picking up
the two pots, she smiled nervously.

Softly, so as not to disturb the sleeping child, she said, "I'll
wash these up. I have instant coffee. Would you like some? Or
tea?" The smile felt as if it had been carved by a sharp knife.

Miller stared until she thought she would have to look away.
"Coffee," he said finally.

Eve kept the stiff smile arranged on her features as she took a
fresh candle and walked slowly from the room. She scarcely
dared breathe as she made her way down the hall. In the
kitchen she lit the candle from the stub burning on the counter,
then dripped wax into an egg cup for a makeshift holder. When
she saw the stack of logs she realized Miller had brought them in
from the garage while she was too terrified to follow him. His bit
of rational foresight heightened her terror.

She set the taper beside the sink while she ran water into the
dirty pots and let them stand. Then she got the kettle and stood
staring through the window at the storm while she filled it. The
yard was a black sea, with no demarcation between grass and
concrete. Straining, she listened for the sound of cars on the
canyon road below, but the drumming of the rain and the
hissing rattle of the wind obliterated the faint hum that was
usually audible during rush hour.

She set the kettle on the sink and opened the high cupboard
above the stove. Her hand hesitated at the shelf of prescription
bottles. Glancing over her shoulder, she picked up one and
peered at the label, put it back and took down another. *One at
bedtime as needed.* The sedative her doctor had prescribed for

the sleepless nights following Paul's death. She uncapped the bottle and shook out the contents. Three capsules. Was it enough? With shaking hands, she broke them open and dumped the powder into a blue coffee mug, praying it would dissolve and that Miller wouldn't taste it. She found the jar of instant coffee and spooned some on top of the powder, then another portion into a red mug. She got the sugar bowl. There was no cream in the refrigerator, so she poured milk into a small pitcher. Taking a tray from a bottom cupboard, she arranged the things on it. As an afterthought she filled a plate with cookies from the ceramic cookie jar shaped like a bear. Balancing the tray carefully, she carried it and the kettle back to the den.

Miller had put Cindy back on the sofa. She was sleeping quietly, her rosy cheeks smudged by drying tears. Miller took the kettle and squatted by the fire to put it on to heat. Eve set down the tray and moved closer to the fireplace.

"The house is getting cold," she said. Without answering, he glanced at Cindy. He'd tucked the cover loosely around her so she could turn without throwing it off. Eve rubbed her hands and held them toward the heat. "This is the only warm room."

"We've got plenty of wood." He gazed into the leaping flames.

Eve realized he'd added logs. She had to clear her throat before she could speak again. "I like a fire."

He glanced up but didn't answer.

She forced herself to go on. "It makes a room cozy." She had to relax his guard and get him talking. Her only hope was to learn more about him so she could find a way to convince him to let her and Cindy go. Casually she picked up the quilt Miller had thrown aside when he put the blanket on Cindy. Bending, she spread it in front of the hearth and sat down. When he glanced at her she patted a spot beside her, not trusting her voice to form the invitation. He hesitated a moment, studying her, then looked into the flames again as he moved closer, still on his haunches. After a few moments he settled back and sat, knees bent and with his feet on the hearth. His gaze was fixed straight ahead.

Eve's heart was racing. She fought the impulse to cringe. He was responding. That was what she wanted. She couldn't panic now. She clasped her knees and rested her chin on them.

"When I was a little girl my father used to build a fire on snowy winter nights. Sometimes we'd make popcorn. We had a wire basket with a long handle so you could hold it over the fire." Her voice sounded strange in the hushed room. She paused to see if he reacted. When he didn't she forced out more words. "Sometimes my mother made hot apple cider and spiced it with cloves and cinnamon." She glanced at him side-long. He was still staring into the flames, giving no clue if she was on dangerous or safe ground. Eve's mouth was dry. She stumbled on desperately. "Fireplaces and snow or rain are a perfect combination. One of the reasons I fell in love with this house was because of the fireplace. Paul said—" She clamped her lips as the name slipped out.

Miller looked at her. "Paul?"

"My husband," she said. An eternity ago she'd told him her husband would be home soon. Eons ago he may have overheard her tell Cindy daddy was in heaven.

"When's he coming home?" Miller asked.

"He—he should be here by now. I suppose the storm is delaying him." She prayed that her voice didn't betray her lie. Miller was watching her. She gazed at the fire to avoid meeting his eyes. If he questioned her about Paul, she was afraid she'd go to pieces.

"It's a tough drive from Santa Barbara in this rain," he said after a while.

Eve gave him a startled look. "Santa . . . ?" She caught herself quickly. Of course, he'd seen Farley's phone number on the pad in the bedroom. To cover her slip she said, "Yes, but he promised to get an early start, so he shouldn't be much longer." If only it were true! She thought of Farley waiting for her call. Would he try to reach her? If he did, he'd know the phone wasn't working. He might worry, but he'd assume she was all right. The seminar didn't end until tomorrow. By then . . . She concentrated on trying to get Miller to talk.

"It's taken me a long time to get used to California weather," she improvised. "I grew up in Minnesota. I've been in California nine years. Are you a Los Angeles native?"

He nodded. It was different then . . . not a big city like it was now. In a shadowed corner of his memory he heard his father's soft voice telling about the miles of orange groves that covered the Valley before World War II. Dirt roads . . . and the Big Red streetcars . . . Angel's Flight . . . He jerked around when Eve spoke again.

"Where did you live?"

"The Valley," he said. The dark veil lifted from shut-out memories. *If you made decent money, we wouldn't have to live in this dump. Look at it! Look at Luke! Your son plays in the dirt with migrant workers. Is that what you want for him? You want him to be a bean picker?* Miller shuddered, as if the broom his mother wielded had just thwacked his flesh. He shook away the hazy memory and studied the woman sitting beside him. She was prettier than his mother. Prettier than Sharon. The firelight played on her hair so it glowed like scattered sunbeams. He reached out and touched it where it lay across her shoulder.

Eve stiffened as he slipped his arm around her. This was what she'd set out to do—win his confidence, lull him. Willing herself not to pull away, she forced a tremulous smile and concentrated on the yellow tongues of flame licking at the logs.

"The city must have changed a lot over the years," she ventured.

"Yeah." *Everything is going to change. My God, couldn't he show some consideration for his wife and child! He had to be a no-good bum right to his grave!* The limp figure swayed at the end of a rope tied over the rafters in the cold garage. Luke closed his eyes to block out the image, just as he'd done that wet, cold night so long ago. To shut out the sound of his mother's screaming and the heavy blows of her hand when he sobbed in anguish for his dead father.

Eve was silent. Miller was lost in thoughts where she dared not intrude. It was impossible to keep him talking. She didn't dare come right out and ask him about Kristen for fear of unbalancing him. She gave a nervous start as a log dropped in the grate. Miller's arm tightened, and he pulled her head to his shoulder.

"It's all right," he murmured.

Eve breathed the scent of wood smoke clinging to Paul's sweater. She clenched her teeth to fight the swelling nausea. She couldn't do it—she couldn't pretend. Cindy . . . think about Cindy, she told herself. Concentrate on Cindy.

Miller stroked her hair and lifted her face. "There's nothing to worry about," he said softly.

Eve steeled herself as he bent to kiss her. His dry, hot lips burned on hers, and his hand slid to her breast. Eve's stomach churned as he caressed her possessively. She wanted to scream and pull away, but she forced herself to endure his touch.

An angry voice from the doorway made them pull apart abruptly. "Just what the hell do you call this?" Dorie strode into the room, arms akimbo.

Eve jerked away from Miller, but he pulled her back as he glared at the woman in the doorway. Dorie advanced, her face livid with rage, her finger pointed accusingly.

"I'm worrying myself sick about Cindy and trying to call you, and all the time you're having a charming little tête-à-tête with another one of your lovers! And Paul hardly cold in his grave!" Her shrill voice pierced the storm noises and reverberated in the room. On the sofa, Cindy whimpered.

Aware of the child suddenly, Dorie turned. "Cindy, darling—"

Miller jumped to his feet. "Shut up!" he ordered in a low, savage tone. "You'll wake her!" He grabbed Dorie before she could reach the sleeping child and spun her away from the sofa.

Dorie's face twisted in ugly fury. "Don't you dare tell me to shut up! Who the hell do you think you are? Get out of my way!" She tried to shove him aside, but Miller planted himself squarely in her path. "Damn it," Dorie screamed, "get out of my way!"

Miller caught her arm and flung her back. Stumbling, Dorie grabbed the doorframe. Her eyes were wild and her face flushed. "Keep your filthy hands off me, you stupid bastard!" she snarled. "Play games with your precious little Eve if you want, but don't think you can order me around!" She rubbed her arm where Miller's hand had bruised it. After the hours of worrying and the tension of driving up that goddamn canyon, her rage overflowed like the gushing storm waters outside. With Cindy sick, Eve was playing home-sweet-home with some Neanderthal! Dorie wasn't going to stand by and let Cindy be neglected so blatantly. She looked past the ape to her sister-in-law. "Why didn't you take her to the doctor?" she demanded.

Speechless, Eve shook her head as she tried to warn her sister-in-law, but Dorie wasn't paying attention. She swung around to face Miller. "I suppose you had something to do with that! Get out of my way. I'm taking Cindy." When she tried to get past, Miller spread his arms. Dorie tried to dodge under one, but he clamped it around her waist and held her. Striking with pent-up fury, she slapped him as hard as she could. He let go and stepped back. Dorie gloated. "Now get out of my way," she ordered.

Cindy began to cry. Eve crawled to her and cradled her against her body. "Shh, it's all right, honey, go back to sleep. . . ."

"Aunt Dorie? I want Aunt Dorie," Cindy whined.

Dorie drew herself up. "There! You see! Aunt Dorie's here, sweetheart," she called out. She glared at Eve. "You have no business having that child! If her father were alive—"

Miller moved like a cat, swiveling as if he intended to let Dorie pass, then spinning around to grab her by the throat. Caught off balance, Dorie stumbled back. Her arms flailed in search of the vise that had gripped her.

"No—" Eve's whimper was drowned by horrible gurgling noises as Dorie gasped for breath. Miller's huge hands tightened. One of Dorie's feet flew up and knocked the coffee tray from the table. The sugar bowl struck the hearth and smashed. Dorie's fingernails raked Miller's hands as she tried to pull him off. Her eyes bulged and her mouth worked desperately in search of air.

"Don't—oh, please don't—" Eve didn't know if she cried out the words that screamed in her head. Hugging Cindy and struggling not to be sick, she couldn't tear her gaze from the horror unfolding a few feet away. Dorie went limp like a floppy doll. Her tongue protruded and her eyes glazed. After a long time, Miller let go. Dorie fell to the carpet with a soft thump.

Cindy squirmed and tried to get out of her mother's arms. "I want Aunt Dorie. I want Aunt Dorie," she bawled.

Outside, the wind hissed through the wet leaves, and rain slapped the patio. Another log dropped in the grate as Cindy's sobs drifted into the deathly silence of the room.

27

Eve was colder than she'd ever been in her life—a deep iciness that started in her bones and pulsed through her flesh. Miller had killed Dorie. He'd snuffed out her life as if it were no more important than an insect's. *Strangled body found last week. . . . Luke Miller . . . murderer . . . insane . . .*

The room was so quiet she could hear her own heartbeat. After a long time she forced herself to look at her sister-in-law. Dorie was lying in a crumpled heap, her maroon suit and deep auburn hair like bloody splotches on the gold carpet. Even in the feeble candlelight there was no doubt she was dead. Standing over her with a vacant expression, his huge hands limp at his sides, Miller seemed hypnotized by Dorie's staring, glazed eyes. Gorge rose in Eve's throat. She compressed her lips and swallowed hard as her head began to spin.

She couldn't let Cindy see the grotesque result of a madman's fury. The horror would traumatize her beyond salvage. Her beloved Aunt Dorie . . . Eve wanted to pick up Cindy and run as fast as she could, but she was petrified with fear that Miller's murderous rage had not run its course and would be directed at her and Cindy.

Cindy whimpered, and Eve rocked her, holding her tightly to make sure Cindy couldn't turn her head. "Shhh, go back to sleep." Her voice trembled with sobs.

"I want Aunt Dorie to hold me," Cindy whined.

Eve's throat convulsed. "She—she's not here."

"I heard her," Cindy insisted crankily.

"Shhh, go back to sleep, honey. It was only a dream." Eve rocked mechanically. Cindy's hot, dry skin burned against her cheek. For a nightmarish interval Cindy's condition had been overshadowed by the horror that invaded the room, but now it returned with agonizing force. Eve remembered she'd been trying to coax Miller into conversation, searching for a way to get him to let her and Cindy leave. Had she been making progress? She tried desperately to recall what they were saying when Dorie burst in, but the memory shimmered behind a gruesome screen of panic.

Stifling a shudder, she looked at Miller. He was still staring at Dorie's body. He looked confused, as if he'd wandered into a scene he didn't understand. After a long time he pressed one hand to his head and rubbed his temple, then glanced around. When he saw Eve he scowled.

In a dazed voice he said, "I didn't know you were here, Sharon. Is Kristen feeling better?"

Numb, Eve forced out a whispered, "She's asleep." Cindy was quiet, and she prayed it was true. Miller called her "Sharon" and Cindy was once again the "Kristen" who brought such tenderness to his tone. Was the maze of his past a dangerous place to be? Or would it be more dangerous to jolt him back to the reality of being Luke Miller in this time and place? She struggled to submerge her panic as she watched him and waited.

"I told you she'd be okay," he said. He seemed to notice the body on the floor for the first time, and he rubbed his temple again. He grimaced slightly, as if there were a faint stench of garbage in the room. He glanced around, then bent over and grabbed Dorie under the arms. Her head lolled and her chin flopped to her chest. The filmed, sightless eyes stared at the floor as Miller began to drag the body from the room. One of Dorie's wine-colored, patent-leather shoes fell off and lay in the doorway like a bloody footprint.

Eve bit her lip to keep from shrieking. Miller handled the

corpse as indifferently as a load of wood. He was inhuman. The soft whisper of Dorie's body being dragged along the carpet raked Eve's tortured nerves, and she had to press a hand over her mouth to keep from vomiting. Her mind refused to think about what Miller was doing.

Eve lowered Cindy to the cushions. Sunken once more in feverish sleep, Cindy's innocence and vulnerability twisted Eve's heart. She drew the blanket over her daughter and prayed Cindy would sleep through the rest of this nightmare.

When Eve stood up the room was a maelstrom that threatened to suck her into its black core. Stumbling, she collapsed into a chair and put her head between her knees. She couldn't fall apart now. Miller's coldhearted, dispassionate act of murder made it urgent to find a way to get Cindy out of here.

Gradually the dizziness passed. Eve stood up slowly, testing her balance. She staggered to the phone. She sobbed when she heard the dial tone and quickly punched 911 while she watched the hall anxiously. Answer . . . oh God, someone answer. . . . Then, miraculously, there was a voice.

"911. Emergency."

"Help me," she whispered desperately. "He killed her—"

"Can you speak louder? I can't hear you. What is your name and address?"

"Eve Foxx. Oh please, he killed—" She heard a sound at the end of the hall. Was Miller coming back?

"Please speak up. Who . . . ?"

"Luke Miller. He's here in the house—" She heard the sound again and hung up at the unmistakable sound of Miller's footsteps approaching. Weak with terror, she knelt and began to pick up the things Dorie's foot had knocked off the table. Miraculously, the sleeping powder and coffee hadn't spilled from the blue mug. She set it on the tray. The red mug contained only a few granules. She found the spoons and the jar of instant coffee under Paul's chair. The cookies were scattered across the carpet and the milk had left a dark, wet stain on the quilt. She sponged it with a napkin, then found the plate, which had gotten badly chipped, to pile the cookies on. Turning to the fireplace, she used the hearth broom and shovel to sweep up the spilled sugar and broken bowl. She knew Miller was behind her, but he didn't speak until she dumped the litter into the wastebasket. "The kettle should be hot."

Eve clutched the desk to steady herself. Her pulse was a pounding surf competing with the storm. His voice and face were perfectly calm. It was as though Dorie had never come, never been. What had he done with her? Eve blanked out the images that crowded her mind. She couldn't think about Dorie. Not now.

She had to try twice before the words came out. "The cream and sugar spilled. I'll get some more."

"I don't need any."

Eve busied herself with the things on the table so he wouldn't see her nervousness. She spooned more coffee into the red mug and added a little more to the blue one to be on the safe side. Without sugar would the taste of the sleeping pills be easy to detect? If he was suspicious, he wouldn't drink the coffee. His calm manner would vanish in an instant if he thought she was trying to trick him again.

Seeing Cindy's pink and white quilt spread before the fireplace brought back the memory of Miller sitting beside her. He had begun to talk. The Valley . . . he said he'd lived in the Valley. Then his face took on the same expression it did after he killed Dorie—confused and far off. But it had been for only a moment. He'd relaxed and put his arm around her, kissed her. She shuddered. All the ground she gained vanished instantly when Dorie burst in. Once again the image of Dorie's twisted body superimposed itself on her thoughts, and she had to steady herself. Don't think about it. . . . You can't change it. . . . Nothing will change it. She forced her mind back to when Miller had been beside her on the quilt. He'd looked at her then as though she were someone else, the same way he looked a few minutes ago when he called her Sharon. She realized now he was different in those moments. Sharon. He sounded surprised and pleased when he spoke the name. Sharon. The wife he had murdered? She swallowed the sour taste in her mouth.

Miller was leaning against the mantel watching her. Was she Eve or Sharon to him now? He was waiting for the kettle to boil, and he looked perfectly calm. It was almost impossible to believe he was a killer behind that mask, but Eve knew she dared not lose sight of the truth for a moment.

The folded newspaper was still on the table. Would the story she hadn't finished reveal anything about Luke Miller that might help her now? She recalled reading somewhere that the worst type of psychopath was one who needed only some small quirk or physical feature to trigger his killer instinct. She felt with growing certainty that Luke Miller was that kind of psychopath. What horrible irony that Farley was at a seminar dealing with the criminally insane . . . and she was trapped with Luke Miller.

Miller wrapped a pad around the handle of the kettle and pulled it from the fire. He brought it to the table and filled the cups. When he turned back to replace the kettle Eve stirred the coffee in the blue mug, watching to see if any telltale bits of sleeping powder floated to the surface. If they did, they weren't visible in the poor light. She pushed the cup to the side of the table near the recliner. She sat in the chair close to the sofa and stirred her own coffee. She raised the red mug to her lips as Miller started for the recliner.

Before he reached it he stopped and bent to press his hand against the carpet. "It's wet," he said in a flat tone.

"The milk spilled," she said, but he wasn't listening. He patted the floor around him, following the dampness toward the patio doors. He stood up and pulled aside the drapes. Water was seeping under the glass doors, running over the metal frame and staining the carpet as it crept across the room.

Eve jumped. Hot coffee splashed down her sweater. "The pool's overflowing!"

Miller peered out into the darkness. When a flash of lightning brightened the sky he saw the flooded patio and the rain-swollen pool. Under his feet the carpet squished.

"This ever happened before?" he asked her.

"No. Paul always—my husband opens the drain valve so the water doesn't get too high."

"Do you know how to do it?"

She shook her head. "He—he takes care of it. But there are instructions somewhere. I—I can look in his desk."

Miller remembered seeing the enclosure for the pool equipment when he walked around the house. It was at least twenty feet from the patio doors. She'd like to have him out there fiddling with the drains so she could lock him out again. No way. He'd had enough soakings for one day. If she was worried about the pool, let her fix it. He pulled the drapes shut and walked to the mantel and picked up one of her husband's pipes. Prying open the tobacco can, he filled the pipe and tamped it down. He wasn't a pipe smoker, but he needed a cigarette so badly his nerves were jumpy. He took the box of long fireplace matches and went back to the chair. He sat down and got the pipe going after three tries. Finally he picked up the mug of coffee she'd fixed him. Watching her over the rim of the cup, he blew smoke contentedly between sips. The hot brew spread a warm glow through his body. He pushed the recliner back so it lifted his feet comfortably. He was warm and dry, and he was going to stay that way.

28

The aroma of Paul's pipe tobacco drifted through the room and sucked Eve into a whirlpool of memory. Paul . . . She swallowed a sob and dug her nails into her palms as she watched Miller. His peculiar half-smile was self-satisfied, as if he'd outwitted her. He wasn't going to do anything about the pool. The way the stain was creeping steadily across the carpet, the entire room would be soaked soon, but Miller didn't care. He didn't trust her. He thought it was another trick so she could lock him out. And she would if the chance came. All she needed was a few minutes to get Cindy to the car.

She watched him lift the blue mug. The pool didn't matter as long as he drank the coffee. How long would it take the sedative to act? Many times she'd tossed and turned all night, despite the pills, but she'd never taken more than one. Would three work surely and quickly?

She sipped coffee while her mind churned. The terrible feeling of being trapped in a nightmare was overwhelming. If only she'd wake, but she knew that was wishful thinking. She'd lived with the same kind of desolate fantasy after Paul died—that when she opened her eyes he wouldn't be gone. He'd be beside her. Laughing, loving Paul, with whom she had a lifetime to share. But it hadn't happened then, and it wouldn't now. Reality was the nightmare. Miller had killed Dorie. He was a madman.

Eve saw that Cindy's mouth was open and she was breathing the pathetic, feverish pant that usually accompanied her illnesses. She was so vulnerable and pale, so completely helpless, Eve's chest constricted. *She needs me. I can't let her down.* Eve blinked and stared at her murky image in the steaming coffee as she tried to ward off tears of frustration and terror.

When Miller set down his cup Eve saw he was watching her with a curious, unreadable expression. Did he suspect something was wrong with the coffee? Had he finished it? Her hands began to shake, and she clutched the red mug tightly. Should she try to get him talking again? It would be dangerous without knowing if he thought she was Sharon or Eve. He seemed totally wrapped in his own thoughts, not really seeing her even though he was looking right at her.

Miller snapped from his reverie and set the pipe in the ashtray on the table beside him. He smiled the comfortable, intimate smile of a man to a woman. A chill feathered across her flesh, and she looked away. She couldn't encourage him. No matter what she'd been willing to do earlier, she knew she'd scream if he touched her now. She could still see his thick fingers gouging into Dorie's neck. . . . She shuddered. Why didn't the sleeping pills work?

After a few minutes Miller pushed himself out of the chair. Eve's coffee mug shook so badly she had to lower it to her lap to keep the hot liquid from splashing. Her breath coiled painfully, and she couldn't let it out until he turned away and walked to the end of the sofa to inspect the water-stained carpet. His gaze circled the growing outline of moisture. Going back to the patio doors, he raised the curtain and studied the oozing water. For a moment Eve thought he was considering going out to drain the pool, but he made no move to open the door. Instead he turned away and retrieved the flashlight from the mantel, then walked toward the master bedroom. Before she could formulate any plan and put it in motion, he was back, carrying an armload of clean, folded towels from the linen closet. He bent by the patio door to arrange them along the sill, forming a neat layer, then a second one, as though it were important to have them just right. When he finished he surveyed his handiwork.

It was futile. A wall of towels wouldn't hold back the water. It would barely slow its course. The pool would keep running over until the rain stopped or some of the water was drained. But Miller seemed satisfied. He went back to the recliner and stripped off his wet socks. From the pocket of Paul's blue slacks he took another pair of hand-knit argyles and pulled them on.

Eve felt physically ill, not so much at the small, domestic gesture itself but at the ease with which Miller performed it. He knew where Paul's clothes were and laid claim to them as readily as he did everything else. He had no right. He had no right! She swallowed the painful thickness in her throat.

Miller leaned back, his eyes heavy, the faint, twisted smile still on his face. He was content. Or was he getting sleepy? Her hopes stirred. Was the sedative finally taking hold?

Miller rested his head against the back of the chair. The warmth of the fire and the hot coffee were relaxing him. It felt good to be home, he thought, out of the cold, soaking rain that had chilled him to the bone. And Sharon was here. He didn't understand why he thought she was gone. It didn't matter, as long as she was back, and as long as Kristen was getting better. He listened lazily to the sullen tattoo of the rain and the low moaning of the wind. It was a good night for holding a woman in his arms. He'd been holding Sharon close when . . . A dark cloud moved across his mind like those stupid inkblots the doctors kept showing him. Something not to remember. Something not to think about. Think about Sharon. Think about Kristen. Think about Eve. Eve. He opened his eyes with a start. It was Eve sitting across from him, not Sharon. Sharon and Kristen were gone. *You must accept that. . . . Sharon and Kristen are dead. . . .* He didn't want to accept it. Not his beautiful little Kristen. Black rings began to close in on his vision, and flashes of light speared across them. Eve, not Sharon. Cindy, not Kristen. He knew that. The doctors said it was important for him to remember that Sharon and Kristen were gone.

He was tired. He had to go to bed. Go to bed where it was

warm and comfortable and Sharon was waiting. Not Sharon
. . . Eve. He yawned and tried to clear the misty curtain
wrapped around his brain. It was like fighting fog. No matter
how hard he pushed it away, it closed in again and claimed him
in its warm embrace.

Eve set aside her coffee mug as Miller's head bobbed. The
drug was working. He was asleep . . . but how soundly? If
there had been a whole bottle of pills, she could be sure, but she
knew that drug dosages were calculated in ratio to body weight.
Miller was twice her size. Three pills might not be enough.

His head drooped, but a moment later it snapped up again
and his eyes opened. He was fighting the drowsiness. Finally his
eyes closed slowly. His mouth went slack, and he began to
breathe heavily. After a few minutes his head dropped back
against the chair in total relaxation. Eve scarcely dared breathe,
but this time he didn't waken.

Soundlessly she slid from the chair and knelt beside the sofa
to bundle Cindy into the blanket. When Cindy whimpered Eve
scooped her into her arms and pressed her close to muffle the
small, restless sounds as she shot a quick glance at Miller. He
hadn't moved. He was snoring softly. Eve struggled to her feet
and sidestepped around the coffee table. Remembering the
chill of the rest of the house and the iciness of the garage, she
reached for the warm clothes she'd gotten for Cindy but they'd
fallen to the floor and were damp from the wet carpet. She bent
and grabbed a corner of the quilt and dragged it behind her as
she hurried out and down the hall. She was shaking so hard by
the time she reached the kitchen she had to lean against the
counter to catch her breath. Shifting Cindy's weight, she spread
the quilt on the table and put Cindy on it so she could wrap her
up. Cindy fretted but didn't waken. Scooping the awkward
bundle into her arms, Eve went through the laundry room to
the garage. She gasped as the cold, damp air hit her. She pulled
the quilt over Cindy's face and stumbled toward the Mercedes.

Even with the overhead door open, the car was a hulking
shadow in the pitch-black garage. She thought about the flashlight, but there was no time to go back for it. She edged along

the side of the car, tracing the distance with her hip until the door handle hit her. Bracing Cindy, she freed a hand and stepped back to swing the door open. Her foot caught in something, and she fell back against the high cabinet Paul had built for storage. Pain jolted through her head, and she felt a warm ooze of blood under her hair. She clung to the car door until the dizziness passed and she could lay Cindy on the backseat. She tucked the quilt around the sleeping child and tented it over her face so her breath would warm the air. She closed the car door quietly.

She was so cold her teeth were chattering and her body was racked by uncontrollable spasms. She wouldn't be able to drive shaking like this. Her raincoat . . . in the laundry room . . . She dashed back for it, holding her breath while she was inside and straining to hear any sound from Miller. She pulled the coat on as she ran back to the car and got behind the wheel. In the glow of the overhead light she glanced to make sure that Cindy was all right, then opened the glove compartment and pulled out the plastic pouch of owner's manuals. The valet key was there.

The starter whined. Trying to control the panic that was so close to the surface, she tried again, but the engine didn't catch. Frantic, she twisted the key repeatedly, but the ignition ground futilely. Tears splashed down her face as she realized Miller had done something to the car.

Dorie's car!

Eve scrambled out. Peering into the darkness, she saw the dark shape of Dorie's Buick in the driveway. Ignoring the stinging rain, she raced to it and yanked open the door. As she slid behind the wheel she groped at the ignition, but the keys weren't there. Leaving the door open, she searched the seat, floor, and glove compartment. Standing in the rain, she searched the backseat. No keys. Eve pushed the wet hair from her face and leaned against the fender with the storm and the night smothering her. To be so close— Two cars, two means of escape, and she couldn't get either of them started! But surely

Dorie's car wasn't disabled. All she needed was the key. What had Dorie done with it?

Swallowing hard, Eve stared into the black cave of the garage. With sudden horrible clarity, she knew what she had stumbled over. She clutched the door handle as a spasm of nausea hit her. She breathed through her mouth rapidly until it passed. She knew what she had to do. She opened the front door of the Buick and reached in to turn on the headlights. The sudden glare cut a murky path through the gray, sheeting rain, spotlighting the garage. Eve walked back unsteadily.

She stopped beside the Mercedes and looked under the storage cabinet. In the gloomy light she saw the green plastic trash bag that her foot had tangled in. Shuddering, she crossed to it and forced herself to lift it. Dorie's crumpled body lay in a heap. The light threw grotesque shadows, and Eve struggled desperately with nausea as she crouched beside the body, avoiding looking at Dorie's distorted face. With shaking hands, she went through the pockets of her sister-in-law's suit. The keys weren't there. Eve felt under the body, trying to remember if Dorie had a purse in her hands when she'd stormed into the den. No, her hands had been empty. She wasn't wearing a coat either, yet she was dry. That could only mean she'd taken her coat off in the house.

Eve fought panic. She had to go back inside. For the first time it occurred to her to wonder how her sister-in-law had gotten into the house. Both doors were locked. The garage door was bolted too. Eve had done it when she trapped Miller outside. Miller got back in through the bedroom, but Dorie had come through the house, which meant she had a key to the front door. Her coat and purse must be in the hall. It didn't matter now where Dorie got Eve's house key as long as the car key was with her things.

Eve staggered back through the laundry room and kitchen to the front entry. Sure enough, Dorie's wet raincoat and hat were on the rack. Eve went through the pockets quickly, but there were no keys. She snatched up Dorie's purse from the bench and ran back to the kitchen, where a candle still burned. Dumping the contents of the purse on the table, she sorted through them. No keys! She fingered Dorie's wallet, card case, checkbook, and makeup as if the key might materialize from the pile. Sobbing, she finally gave up. Dorie's keys weren't there.

There was only one other possibility. Miller had them. Eve glanced through the dark living room toward the faint filter of light from the hall. Steeling herself, she walked toward the den.

29

Farley couldn't keep his attention on the conversation around the table. He kept watching the door and the maître d', who was supervising seating arrangements from a large chart. Why didn't Lester call back? A few latecomers arrived at the door and the maître d' studied his chart before signaling a waiter to escort them to the proper table.

"Farley?"

He realized Jess was talking to him. "Sorry, I didn't hear that."

"You haven't heard a word anyone's said since you sat down. Quit worrying. Lester's probably having trouble getting the call through. All the emergency lines are always backed up on days like this."

"I know, but it doesn't help." He spread an apologetic smile around at his dinner companions. The seating arrangements had been made to provide a mixed group at every table. Jeremiah Ordman was a court-appointed psychiatrist Farley knew from Los Angeles, Arnold Palombo a mental-health coordinator for an Orange County outpatient program, Hal Frazier a deputy district attorney in Ventura County. Earlier Farley had been introduced to the Santa Barbara lawyer named Drew Harrison and to Edwin Chase, a public prosecutor. The eighth chair was occupied by a plump female psychologist from San Luis Obispo who was on the staff at Atascadero. Farley hadn't caught her name. Usually he would enjoy the spirited conversation, but now he paid attention with effort.

"Of course there are incidents," Palombo was saying. "Every program has them; 1229 is no worse than others."

"You're dealing with an entirely different kind of client," Hal Frazier insisted. "They're not just criminals, they're mentally disturbed. They've already proven they don't operate under the same set of values as the rest of the community. That's where the danger—"

The woman psychologist interrupted. Farley saw her name tag said, "Landri Wexton." "But they've been treated and shown marked improvement in their behavior patterns. You forget, Mr. Mavella, they're screened carefully before they're considered for the program. They don't choose, they're chosen." Her tone had a defensive edge.

Jess said, "The county rejects nearly 15 percent of the defendants the hospitals recommend. Those who make it often are in a ratio of a hundred to one with a psychologist who sees them once a week. We're talking about mentally disordered sex offenders and criminally insane killers. Sure, some of them have adjusted, but what about the ones who are smart enough to give the right answers to the examining panel?"

"There's no way to predict behavior," Wexton said. "None of us pretends to be clairvoyant."

"In essence that's exactly what you're doing when you say they're ready to be put out in the community," Jess answered. "Releasing a defendant from custody carries with it the assumption that he's not dangerous anymore."

"They have to be given a greater degree of freedom," she insisted. "The sensible way to do it is in a controlled situation."

"How do you supervise them if they don't show up for the weekly therapy sessions? How do you control treatment if you don't know where the hell they are?" Hal Frazier asked.

"You're talking about a small minority," Palombo said. "Most patients in the outpatient programs report regularly."

"They're not patients," Jess argued. "They're defendants, convicted criminals."

"Then the question is not why we let them out, but why you put them in a mental institution in the first place," Arnold Palombo declared. " 'Not guilty by reason of insanity' is a legal invention, not a psychiatric one. When the courts say a man or woman has a mental disorder which prevents him from understanding that his behavior is criminal, and they send that person to a mental facility, he *becomes* a patient. We do our best, but our hospitals are overcrowded and understaffed—"

"The mentally ill have rights, Doctor," Landri Wexton said heatedly.

"The bottom line is financial," the Santa Barbara lawyer said. He leaned forward and drew invisible figures on the tablecloth. "The 1229 program costs around eight thousand dollars a year, per patient. It runs over twelve thousand for prison, and thirty-four or -five at a state hospital. It's not hard to understand why the program has so many fans."

"What's the cost in terms of harm done to the public when the noncustodial care doesn't work out?" Farley wanted to know. He was thinking about Luke Miller and the dead woman who'd befriended him.

"But it does work for the majority," Ordman pointed out.

Jess sat back. "Does it? I'm not blaming the psychologists who run the programs, but you have to concede they know only what they're told. They see these people four or five hours a week, sometimes less. Do you think Luke Miller discussed his feelings of hostility, or whatever the hell, with the group therapist before he disappeared, leaving a dead woman behind? His therapist made a house call to find out why he hadn't shown up for a couple of sessions. Ironic, but it's probably what set Miller off."

Ordman cut a piece of chicken with little sawing motions. "If we condemn the therapist for trying to locate his patient, should we also condemn the police for not locating their suspect before this?"

Farley wondered if there was an answer to the argument. Certainly no perfect one, except for a man's conscience. He looked up as a waiter touched his shoulder.

"Mr. Cunningham? You have a telephone call."

"Excuse me," he said, pushing out his chair and dropping his napkin beside his untouched plate. Outside, the maître d' indicated a phone bank against the wall.

"Lester?"

"Sorry it took so long," the law clerk apologized. "I tried Mrs. Foxx without any luck. The phone company says they're having trouble with lines in Coldwater Canyon. It could be days before service is fully restored. I talked to Pete Hazza, and you're out of luck about getting the department to check on Mrs. Foxx. Their switchboard is swamped. They're concentrating on evacuating danger spots and taking care of major catastrophes. They quit answering calls on noninjury accidents early this afternoon."

Farley listened with a sinking feeling. "What are the road conditions from here in?"

"The Coast Highway is closed from Point Dume to Santa Monica. They had a bad slide at Malibu that's blocking all lanes. At last report 101 is open, but there are flooded spots. Traffic is moving slowly."

"Thanks, Lester."

"Sure. Look, it's none of my business, but if you're thinking about coming back, why not wait until tomorrow? Mrs. Foxx will be all right. She's smart enough to take care of herself."

Farley wished it were that easy. Nothing would please him more than to find Eve and Cindy huddled before a warm fire. But he had to make sure. He thanked Lester, hung up, then placed another call to Dorie's apartment, but there was no answer. Without hope, he tried Eve's number as well. When he finally went back into the dining room he made his excuses to the people around the table. He told Jess he was going back to Los Angeles. Jess cautioned him about the roads, but didn't try to talk him out of going.

Thirty minutes later Farley had his bag packed and was checked out of the motel.

30

They had a positive make on Miller from Nancy Wonderland and the bartender. It took four phone calls to locate the psychologist to whom Luke Miller had been assigned as an outpatient. Dr. Quentin Yarbaroff was reluctant to talk to Noble, citing the confidentiality of the doctor-patient relationship. When Noble threatened to get a court order, Yarbaroff finally gave in, but he insisted on verifying Noble's identity first. Ten minutes later he called back and said he would meet Noble at the Threshold offices on Vineland. Sighing, Noble donned his damp raincoat and hat and drove out to the North Hollywood office. The rain had let up to a fine, misty drizzle, raising his hopes there might be a break soon, but by the time he got as far as Vanowen the deluge renewed its force and he resigned himself to another soaking.

The office of the psychological outpatient facility was in a storefront building. The sign taped to the door listed the office hours and an emergency number. A filmy drape had been drawn across the window, so everything behind it was hazy. The door was locked, but a short, slim man with a brown beard and dark eyes that looked out from under an overturned bowl of dark, curly hair let him in when he knocked.

The area had been divided into a reception room, complete with a dusty Dieffenbachia with brown-tipped leaves and several plastic upholstered chairs. A partition behind the desk was chest high. Behind it were several small cubicles and a larger area where the chairs were now pushed back against the walls but which probably was the group therapy room.

"Sergeant Noble?" Yarbaroff extended a hand and his grip was firm. Noble made it a point not to wince as his arthritis shot needles of pain. "I'm sorry to inconvenience you this way, but I find it professionally advisable to determine the authenticity of any calls about patients. Sometimes newspaper reporters use ruses to get information." Yarbaroff sat behind the desk and invited Noble to take one of the plastic chairs. Noble recognized the body language, putting a barrier between them and giving the psychologist an edge. He noticed then that Yarbaroff had a file folder in front of him. Was he boning up on Luke Miller?

Noble said he appreciated the doctor's caution, then plunged to the business at hand. "We have reason to think that Luke Miller may be connected with a case we're investigating. I'm trying to establish a pattern for his behavior if there is one."

"Does this concern the Hauptner woman's death?" Yarbaroff asked.

"That's part of it."

"Are you inferring Miller may be connected to more than one murder?"

The man was sharp. "We'd like to talk to him."

"I see. Very well, I'll answer your questions to the best of my ability. How can I aid your police hunt?"

Police hunt? The psychologist made it sound like the SWAT team was closing in on Miller. Noble let it pass. "I presume you've seen a record of Miller's file at Atascadero?"

He hedged. "An abbreviated version of it."

"Did Miller exhibit any streaks of violence while he was confined?" Noble asked.

He seemed to consider his answer a long time. "Most patients show violent tendencies at times. During the first year Miller was a patient he was highly excitable and irrational."

"Did he attack anyone physically?"

The psychologist was silent a moment, mentally reviewing Miller's file rather than opening the one in front of him. "Three separate incidents were noted, one on another patient and two on hospital personnel. He was subdued and restrained after each episode."

"Male or female?"

"I beg your pardon?"

"Did Miller attack women or men? The three incidents that were noted?"

"Oh . . . let me see. The patient was an elderly woman, the other two were female nurses."

Authority figures. "What provoked the attacks?"

"They were unprovoked. Miller was asked to do something and refused. When the nurses insisted he became violent. It took three strong orderlies to subdue him each time. He is not a small man. He's powerfully built and accustomed to manual labor. It was deemed advisable to keep him under restraints most of that first year, for the safety of the staff and patients, as well as his own."

"After the first year, what?"

"He went into a period of withdrawal. He was tractable but unable to take part in his own treatment. After he was put on medication his condition stabilized considerably."

"Exactly what does 'stabilized' mean?"

"Unchanged. He got neither better nor worse. There is little that can be done other than provide custodial care until a patient is aware that he must cooperate in working out his problem."

Noble rubbed his aching wrist. A patient was stabilized if he didn't cause trouble. Had Luke Miller been clever enough to learn not to rock the boat? "When did this picture change?"

This time Yarbaroff's memory wasn't up to the task. He consulted the file. "He began to show signs of awareness of his surroundings and condition about four years ago. It was a very gradual thing, you understand, but it was a step forward. A year later he was participating in therapy sessions and was able to see where some of his problems were rooted."

"Where was that?" Noble felt as if he were playing straight man.

"In his childhood. From a psychiatric perspective the patterns that produce the Luke Millers of the world are established early in life, probably during the first year, when the child begins to sort out his gender identity. The child fails to negotiate the first stages of development as an infant which would lead to a solid psychological structure."

Yarbaroff was talking psychological mumbo jumbo, but Noble suspected he was saying the same thing Dr. Armand had put succinctly: Miller was an abused child, thanks to his tyrannical mother and martyred father. "When was Miller first considered for release?"

"The possibility is always under consideration for every patient," Yarbaroff said in a slightly defensive tone. "Monthly reports are filed and evaluated. If you mean when the board first reviewed Miller's case, the summer of last year. He had shown remarkable progress. His file notes that he had become cooperative and confident. There were no indications of the emotional disturbances that had sent him to the institution, and no episodes of antisocial behavior. More than that, he finally accepted the fact that his wife and daughter were dead, which he'd been unable to do up until then. His freedom and privileges within the hospital were increased gradually. When he showed himself able to handle those he was considered ready for the larger experience of an outpatient program."

"Were you on the board that made the decision?"

Yarbaroff shook his head. "I run the program here, Sergeant. I've been at Atascadero numerous times, of course, but I don't usually meet patients until they're assigned to Threshold."

"Would you mind telling me a little about the program and how Luke Miller fit into it?"

The psychiatrist relaxed visibly, on familiar ground now. "Miller went to a halfway house when he was released. Most patients who have no family or friends to take them in do this. The staff here arranged the details beforehand, so he was able to move in immediately. We had no trouble finding him a job. He's an expert mechanic. There were three or four places that would have hired him."

"According to our police file, he moved in with Merilee Hauptner a month ago."

"When our clients are employed and have adjusted to the program well, they're free to live where they choose."

"Did you know about the new living arrangement?"

"Yes. We have a note of it in our records."

"Did you check out the new place?"

He hesitated only a moment. "No. There didn't seem to be any reason to do so, Sergeant. We currently have ninety-six people in the program. Time doesn't allow for investigation of every minor change that takes place. If there had been any reason to think it wasn't a good move, I would have looked into it thoroughly. You see, Miller told us he'd known the woman a long time."

"Before his hospitalization?"

"That was the inference. I believe he called her 'an old friend.' "

So Miller lied, and nobody checked out his story. It was beginning to look more and more like Dr. Armand was right. Miller didn't stand out in any crowd. He was pretty damned normal until something pushed his killer button.

"Were there any changes in Miller's behavior pattern these past few weeks?"

Yarbaroff pushed his lips in and out as he concentrated. Noble wondered if he was reviewing his actual contacts with Miller or deciding how honest to be. With nearly a hundred people to deal with every week, it wasn't likely the psychologist remembered every face and name clearly.

"Nothing comes to mind, Sergeant."

"How many sessions did Miller miss before you went to the Hauptner address?"

"Two." Yarbaroff was on certain ground again.

Noble said, "Tell me about your visit to Merilee Hauptner."

"I had several calls to make that morning. I try to check up on anyone who misses two sessions. I phoned the number Miller had given us but got no answer. I don't like to waste time trying to make house calls if people aren't home, but I was in the neighborhood, only a block away, as a matter of fact, on another call, so . . ." He left it unfinished and got back to the point. "Ms. Hauptner was astonished when I told her who I was and why I was there. Miller hadn't given her any clue to his past history. He merely said he was originally from the San Fernando Valley but had been in San Luis Obispo for the past few years. He claimed he came back because he liked L.A."

"What was her reaction after her initial surprise about his being a formal mental patient?"

"First of all, keep in mind I was under the impression she was familiar with his history. Whenever one of the people in the program makes a change—living arrangements, relationships, anything of that sort—we discuss it in the therapy sessions. Miller definitely led me and everyone else to believe he had been completely honest with his lady friend. He seemed fond of her and happy with the domestic arrangement."

"Did he say if they ever argued or fought?"

Yarbaroff shook his head. "No. When he missed the first session I made a note of it, but I wasn't overly concerned. Things come up, people forget or get busy, and Miller had been very dependable until then. He had a good job in the service department of a car agency and seemed to be adjusting well to community life."

Noble steered him back to the point. "What did Ms. Hauptner say or do?"

"She was quite upset, and fearful. I assured her he was doing very well in the program, but she was quite agitated nevertheless."

"Did you try to see Miller at the place where he worked?"

Yarbaroff ran his hand along the edge of his desk. "No, I didn't. Perhaps I should have, but as I said earlier, I had a number of calls to make. I did telephone the apartment later in the day, when Miller should have been home from work, but there was no answer."

He looked uncomfortable. No answer because Merilee Hauptner was dead and Miller gone? Noble sighed. Yarbaroff was no more accountable than a dozen other people.

"You've been very helpful, Dr. Yarbaroff. I appreciate the time you've given me." Noble closed the notebook in which he'd been writing.

"Anything I can do to cooperate."

"There is one other question. The woman patient Miller attacked during his early stay. Do you have any idea how the incident came about?"

Yarbaroff searched his memory and finally said, "I reread the hospital records after Miller's name was connected with the Hauptner murder. The woman was a manic depressive. In her manic stage she ordered other patients around imperiously. Miller was in her way and didn't move when she wanted to get by. This type of altercation is a frequent occurrence in mental facilities. When the woman tried to shove Miller aside he grabbed her by the throat. The incident took place in the day room, fortunately, so there were enough people around to pull him off before he hurt her. But you must remember, Sergeant, this was only three months after Miller arrived at Atascadero. The incidents involving the nurses were also in that first six- or eight-month period. Miller exhibited no other violent tendencies for more than seven years."

There wasn't much doubt in Noble's mind now about what triggered Miller's rages, but it didn't help if he couldn't locate him.

"At any time in your sessions or interviews with Miller, did he mention any friends or relatives, anyplace he wanted to see?"

"No."

"Was he friendly with the others in the group?"

Yarbaroff said, "If he saw any of them outside of the sessions, I wouldn't have any way of knowing it. We don't encourage close alliances. It's too easy to slip into mutual pity and excuse-making instead of bolstering and supporting each other."

Noble got to his feet and rescued his wrinkled raincoat from the chair beside him. His wrist ached miserably, but he put out his hand to the psychologist.

"Thank you, Doctor. I appreciate your help. If you think of

anything, or if you happen to hear something about Miller, give me a call."

"I will."

When he got outside the rain was coming down in torrents again. Noble wished he could go home and crawl into the sack and sleep until summer came. The radio was chirping when he unlocked the car door. He picked it up as he slid behind the wheel. The dispatcher had a message from Rothman. A call had come in to 911 from a woman who said Luke Miller was in her house. The connection was bad, and the dispatcher missed her name and address, but the technicians were working on the recording to try to decipher it.

31

Putting one foot in front of the other, Eve forced herself to walk down the dark, shadowed hall. The house that had always symbolized love and security was now a place of evil and horror. The thought of touching Miller made her shudder so violently she had to pause and catch her breath. Could she go through his pockets without waking him?

From the doorway of the den she studied the man asleep in the recliner. How often Paul had dozed in the same chair. Paul, with his gentle ways and quick smile, pretending to be asleep when Cindy tickled his feet, then leaping up to catch her in his arms and hug her tightly. The room had rung with love and laughter then. Now it was a forbidding place of evil shadows.

Miller's head lolled, and he was breathing heavily. One of his hands rested on the chair arm; the other was at his side. Eve tiptoed close, her senses keen as she listened to the soft crackle of the fire and Miller's ragged breathing. She was shaking so violently she wondered if she could go through with it.

With her gaze riveted on Miller's face, she knelt beside the chair. When there was no flicker of awareness in his slack features, she brushed her fingertips across the pockets of the navy slacks he'd taken from Paul's closet. Her touch was feathery, and Miller didn't move, but there was no telltale bulge of keys. Steadying herself, she slipped her hand between Miller's body and the chair to feel the back pockets, but he had slid down so they were hidden under his body and his weight was resting on them. It would be impossible to search the back pockets without rousing him.

She bit her lip and tried to remember what kind of key holder Dorie used. Her own house keys were on a metal ring with a fluffy yarn ball attached, and she carried her car key separately. Surely she had seen Dorie's a thousand times. An image flashed on her memory screen: Dorie carried a single, flat, no-nonsense leather case. Slipped into a back pocket, it wouldn't prod Miller if he sat on it. Praying she had missed it in her haste, she went over the side pockets of the blue slacks again. To her relief she felt the faint impression of the leather case against Miller's thigh. His arm was covering the pocket opening. Bracing herself, Eve pinched the sleeve of the alpaca sweater between her fingers and gently lifted his arm. It felt like a lead weight, and she had to steady her hand. Then when she tried to slip her fingers into the pocket opening, she realized it was impossible from where she was. She'd have to be behind him, not in front. She was so nervous that she was doing everything wrong just when time was so vital. She let down his arm, scarcely daring to breathe, but Miller didn't stir.

As she got up Eve realized that the knees of her jeans were sopping wet. She glanced at the patio doors and saw that Miller's makeshift dam of towels was saturated. The dark water stain had spread completely across the room. It didn't matter—nothing mattered but getting the keys and escaping before the sedative wore off and Miller woke. Eve shifted her position so she could reach the pocket containing the key case and leaned over Miller. As she lifted his arm again a low rumbling sound overrode the clamor of the storm. She glanced toward the patio. Under her feet the floor vibrated ominously. A thunderous noise swelled, and the house shook as if it had been struck by lightning. The drapes covering the patio doors bulged inward as the glass shattered. Water and mud spewed into the room, tearing the drapes from the rod and rocketing pieces of masonry and debris. Eve grabbed the back of the recliner to keep from being knocked over by the violent impact. She tried to shield her face with her arm as shards of glass flew through the air like bullets. A cry escaped her lips as one pierced her arm.

Miller came awake with a start and looked around in total confusion. Rain and icy air howled through the room, and a wall of mud and slime flowed across the carpet like a creeping slug. His gaze swept the empty sofa. He jumped to his feet, staggering as he tried to overcome the effects of the sedative. Still stunned by the suddenness of the destruction, it took Eve a moment to react. She wheeled and started to run, but Miller dived across the chair and grabbed her arm. His face twisted with rage, the way it had when Dorie hit him. His eyes were wild and his grip like iron. Eve fought to break away, but his fingers clawed into her flesh until she could feel them bruising her bones.

"Where's Kristen?" he screamed over the slicing wind that found passage through the broken wall. When Eve didn't answer Miller grabbed a fistful of her hair and yanked her head back. "Where is she?" he shouted. He brought up a threatening fist.

"In the car . . ." Eve wailed. She wasn't sure which frightened her more, Miller's fury or that of the storm whipping through the house. Miller shoved her aside, and she fell against the end table. It crashed to the floor. When the candle rolled onto the carpet the flame was snuffed out in the rush of wind screaming through the opening where the patio doors had been. One slithering edge of the foot-deep mud oozed into the fireplace. The hot logs sizzled and spat, and smoke belched.

The hillside had given way! The saturated ground had broken under its own weight and slid down into the already overburdened pool, which collapsed under the strain. Now a wall of mud was pushing along the path of least resistance, filling the den.

Still fighting the stupor induced by the sleeping pills, Miller rubbed his eyes and tried to clear his head. He didn't understand the destruction that was taking place as he watched. In a matter of seconds the room was reduced to rubble. He must have fallen asleep. He was groggy, and it was hard to think.

What had she done? Mud. Water. Wind. The fire erupted in sizzling, spitting sparks, then was snuffed out by the invading mud, and the room plunged into darkness. Miller shivered with the sudden cold, but it washed away some of his lethargy. In the darkness he heard a faint sound that wasn't part of the riot of noise the storm was making. Instinctively he grabbed the woman before she could get away. The bitch had her coat on. She was running away, trying to get away from him. He panted in the darkness when she yelped as his fingers dug into her arm. He held her tight while he focused his bleary thoughts.

Where was the flashlight? It had been on the table next to the candle. Miller crouched, dragging Eve down with him, and swept his hand across the floor. His breath hissed as a piece of glass pierced his palm, but he finally closed his fingers around the metal cylinder. It was wet and slimy, but the light came on when he snapped the switch. He aimed it at Eve's face.

She blinked and cringed. She was crying. Tears streaked her cheeks and her eyes were red. Her mouth was moving, but whatever she was saying was drowned by the racket of the storm. He didn't have time to deal with her now. He had to get Kristen. He shoved Eve ahead of him down the hall. If anything had happened to Kristen . . .

The candles were still burning in the dining room, but the flames leaped erratically in the draft sweeping through the house. Eve cried out with pain when Miller twisted her arm and shoved her through the kitchen and laundry room. As he pulled the door open there was another crash of breaking glass from the rear of the house. Miller thrust her ahead of him into the garage, his iron grip still clamping her wrist so she thought her arm would break. He blinked in the glare of the Buick's headlights, then let go of Eve's arm abruptly and slapped her hard.

"You stupid— You left the lights on!" he screamed above the howl of the wind. She should know better than to run the battery down that way, like she should have had the windshield wipers checked. He was sure now that she had tricked him somehow and made him fall asleep. She was going to run. She was trying to run away with his Kristen. His head ached with a dull throb and his eyes were gritty. He shivered with the cold. He couldn't stay here. He had to save Kristen before the whole hillside gave way. Another shuddering crash shook the house. The rafters of the garage groaned. He shoved Eve out into the glare of the headlights.

"If the battery's low I'm gonna break your neck!" he threatened.

Skidding and stumbling, Eve sobbed as rain pelted her bare head and streamed down her face. Miller had Dorie's car key. She'd never get it away from him. The whole hillside behind the house was giving way. It could crash down any minute and sweep the house from its foundation and toss it down the canyon like dead wood. Cindy! She wheeled and tried to dash back to the Mercedes, but Miller swung at her with the flashlight. It caught her a glancing blow on the temple, and she staggered. When Miller grabbed her she jerked away.

"Cindy's in my car! The one you fixed so it wouldn't start!" She beat at him when he held her.

Colored lights flashed across Miller's vision. Breathing hard, he grabbed her throat and closed his hand around it.

She screamed hysterically. "Kristen is in the car!" She banged her fist on the trunk of the Mercedes. Momentarily stunned, Miller's grip loosened. Eve stopped struggling and spoke hoarsely. "We have to get Kristen before we leave."

Miller's fingers relaxed, and his hand lowered. Stepping back, he flashed the light through the car window and saw the humped quilt on the backseat. How had Kristen gotten there?

"Get her," he ordered. Without waiting, he crossed the swamped driveway and got into the Buick. He turned off the lights before he tried the ignition. When the engine caught he grunted. She was lucky this time. Once the engine was idling smoothly, he put the headlights on again.

Eve scooped Cindy into her arms, stuffing the slithery quilt around her as she lifted her from the backseat. The rain pelted savagely as she ran for the Buick. Miller swung open the passenger door, and she climbed in awkwardly. The wind slammed the door against her leg, and she cried out with pain. Miller

ignored her as he leaned over the wheel. Shivering, she huddled as far from him as possible.

He released the brake, put the car in gear. He'd have to turn
around. It was too dangerous to back down the driveway. He let
the car inch close to the garage, then put it in reverse and
backed onto the wide apron. The windshield wipers slapped
rapidly but couldn't keep up with the downpour. The rain was
bouncing like hail, and he couldn't see as far as the hood orna-
ment. He cursed and rolled down his window and stuck his
head out so he could see where he was going. Even so, he had to
move carefully. He inched the car back and forth. The rear
wheels skidded when they slid off the concrete and sank in the
soggy lawn. Patiently he rocked the car until he worked it out of
the thick mud.

Cautiously he straightened the car on the driveway until it
was headed across the clearing, but as he shifted into drive a
bolt of lightning and a tremendous crash of thunder jolted the
car as if it had been struck. The car nosed down slightly. Miller
slammed on the brake. Cursing, he shoved the transmission into
reverse, backing the car suddenly so it clipped the bumper of
the Mercedes before it bounced forward and came to a stop.

A deep, black crevice snaked across the path of the headlights, widening like a film running in slow motion. Concrete
buckled and mud splattered upward like a geyser, spraying the
hood and windshield. On the hillside a thirty-foot pine leaned as
if inspecting the open pit, then dropped into it and was swallowed instantly by the dark ooze. With a crash that rocked the
car, a twenty-foot section of driveway broke away and disappeared downhill in the black night.

32

It took Farley an hour and a half to drive the thirty miles to Ventura. Following the coast, Highway 101 was usually a pleasant, scenic drive, but the storm had reduced it to a treacherous trail. The heavy rain and early darkness were compounded by dense fog rolling in from the ocean. Headlights were virtually useless; they glared against the thick screen without penetrating. From time to time fitful gusts of wind swirled across the highway and parted the thick, gray curtains, but they closed again almost instantly. People were heeding the repeated media warnings to avoid driving, and there were only a few cars on the road.

At Ventura he stopped at the Holiday Inn and got out to stretch his cramped muscles. He found a phone booth and dumped a handful of coins on the shelf before he dialed Eve's number. All he got was static and crackling noises. Knowing it was a waste of time but still hoping, he had the operator place the call. She wasn't any more successful. He tried Dorie's number then, but although it rang, there was no answer. Half the phones in the city were probably out by now.

Driving conditions improved slightly after 101 turned inland east of Ventura. The wind died considerably, so the rain wasn't driven with such force, but pockets of fog hung in low spots and reduced visibility to inches so cars had to creep along. And there was more traffic than on the coast road, and it moved sporadically. At the Camarillo grade it became a sluggish trickle. By the time he was one quarter of the way up the long, steep hill, eastbound traffic came to a complete stop. Every lane was blocked solidly with cars and trucks. All around him fuming motorists honked and finally turned off their engines to wait out the unexplained snarl. When Farley saw a man in a yellow slicker and hat walking between the lineup of cars, he rolled down his window.

"What's holding us up?"

The man veered toward him. "An eighteen wheeler with a load of canned goods jackknifed. It's blocking all four lanes. Worst goddamn mess you've ever seen."

"Any idea how long we'll be here?"

The man shrugged, and water cascaded from the wide brim of his hat. "They should have one lane open before long. People are out there picking up cans as fast as they can." The man moved on as another driver called to him.

Farley closed the window. Even when they got the lane open traffic would crawl past the accident where four lanes would have to funnel into one. It would take forever to get through the Conejo and into the San Fernando Valley, but the only other route was the state road back at Camarillo. It went into Moorpark, but he could backtrack to Thousand Oaks or Woodland Hills from there. He glanced in the rearview mirror and was dismayed when he saw an unbroken line of cars behind him. That was that. There was no way to get out of the bottleneck. He consoled himself with the knowledge that it probably wouldn't have saved him any time in the long run. On the alternate route he'd be substituting poor roads and unknown conditions for a good highway that was bound to be open soon. He resigned himself to waiting it out. Sitting back, he thought about Eve and Cindy, hoping Lester and Jess were right about there being nothing for him to worry about.

33

Eve gave a terrified scream as the car leaped back and slammed into the Mercedes. Miller jammed the gear lever to park and wiped his mouth with the back of his hand. The Buick's engine throbbed. In the murky, rain-swept splash of headlights, trickles of mud plopped from the naked hillside into the yawning pit that had been the driveway.

Eve stared through the mud-spattered windshield. If Miller hadn't reacted so quickly, they would have been killed. They would have been swept away by the slide as easily as it had taken the trees and shrubs. Trembling uncontrollably, she looked at him. He was hunched over the wheel, blinking in cadence with the slapping windshield wipers. The irony was bitter. He'd saved their lives, but now they were trapped.

Miller rubbed his eyes. He'd reversed instinctively when he felt the driveway begin to give way. His reactions behind the wheel were automatic, even though his head was still wrapped in thick wool that made it hard to think. He was having trouble staying awake. He blinked and forced his eyes open.

How had he and Sharon gotten into the car? He pressed the heel of his hand against his temple. Kristen was sick. Dying. No, he wouldn't let her die. The doctor was wrong. They were taking her home. They'd take good care of her, and she'd get well. When he looked at Sharon sitting beside him, he saw her frightened expression. She was scared about Kristen. She didn't believe him when he told her it would be all right, but it would be as soon as he could figure out what to do next.

He got out of the car. The rain soaked through his sweater and slacks in seconds, but the cold downpour cleared some of the cobwebs from his brain. He walked around to the front of the car. The wheels were only two feet from the edge of the chasm. The entire concrete apron in front of the garage was networked with cracks. In the path of the headlights he could barely make out the other side of the hole gouged by the slide. At least twenty feet across, he figured. He pushed the dripping hair from his face and wiped his eyes. One edge of the pit backed against the shorn hillside. Tree roots and rocks were exposed where the earth had fallen away. On the other side, where the terrain dropped steeply down toward Coldwater Canyon, the rushing sliding mud had cut a swath through everything in its path. It detoured around some large trees but uprooted others and tore out bushes and grass. The lush natural landscape was gone. He couldn't see an end to the path of destruction in the rainy darkness. Chances were it had gone clear down the canyon. He wouldn't be surprised if the road was blocked.

Walking cautiously to the perimeter of light, he studied the gouged hill. Around the hole the hillside was covered with a thick pad of ivy and a few scattered trees. How long would the saturated ground hold? Another slide could take the whole thing. He wiped his hand across his face.

Eve couldn't stop shivering, despite the warm air blowing from the heater. Fear had invaded every cell of her body. The storm had cut off the only escape route. The warm, safe house she loved was no longer a refuge, and the car she'd fought so hard to reach was a waiting tomb.

When Miller disappeared in the shadows she twisted to see where he'd gone. He was examining the hillside. Was he looking for a way to get around the slide? She peered at the dark, glistening foliage around the gaping hole that seemed hopeless. The secluded clearing tucked into the hillside had been a perfect hideaway for a house. Now it was a death trap. The driveway was the only approach. There were no other roads, not even a hiking trail down to Coldwater.

Miller came back. Rain and wind invaded the car as he slid behind the wheel and hunched close to the heater vent. The alpaca sweater and blue slacks clung to his body like wet leaves, and his dripping hair was plastered to his head. He wiped his hand across his face.

"The whole hill is undermined. It won't last long," he said.

Panic broke through Eve's numbness. "What are we going to do?"

He didn't answer. He stared through the mud-streaked spot the wiper and rain had cleared on the glass. After a minute he picked up the flashlight and got out again. Eve craned her neck to watch him as he went behind the car.

He walked through the garage playing the beam of light across the walls and floor. If he saw Dorie's body beside the Mercedes, he gave no sign. It was as though he had disposed of that problem totally and put it from his mind. Completing his circuit of the garage, Miller opened the door to the laundry room and vanished inside. He reappeared a minute later, still carrying the flashlight. Eve realized he was wearing shoes. Heavy work shoes. His own, unearthed from wherever they'd been hidden.

Miller flashed the light across the neatly arranged tools and supplies on pegboards Paul had installed. It stopped on a coil of heavy rope, which he lifted down and slung over his shoulder like a mountain climber. He knelt and was out of sight for a moment. When he reappeared he came out from behind the Mercedes carrying a gasoline can and a length of hose. He laid the rope and a pair of heavy work gloves on the car trunk while he uncapped the gas tank and began siphoning fuel into the can.

Cindy stirred, and Eve hushed her absently, her attention riveted on Miller. He capped the gas can and tossed the hose aside. The flashlight went off. A moment later he emerged from the garage carrying the rope and gas can. In the faint, red glow of the taillights, she saw he was wearing the heavy work gloves and had wrapped the flashlight in plastic and stuck it into the waistband of the blue slacks. Working by the light of the car headlights, he unwound one end of the rope and tied it around the trunk of a sturdy pine tree at the foot of the bank near the edge of the clearing. He snapped the rope to test the knot, then drew the other end from the coil and tied it around his chest, pulling it snug under his armpits.

Eve's fears exploded in panic. He was going to leave them here! She dumped Cindy onto the seat and jumped out of the car. She ran to Miller and grabbed his arm.

"Where are you going?" She tried to hold him, but he shoved her hand away. She grabbed him again.

"Don't leave us here!" she screamed. "We'll die! You said the hill is going—"

He whirled so fast she was hardly aware of his arm swinging. His heavy fist hit the side of her head. The blow stunned her. She rocked back, skidded, and fell. Dazed, she lay on the cold, wet grass, sobbing as she watched Miller continue his preparations.

He ran a piece of rope through the handle of the gas can and tied it around his waist. He'd have to move carefully with the weight dragging on his body, but he needed both hands free. Draping the rest of the rope over his arm, he crawled on all fours up the bank. The slick, matted ivy was an iron web. The heavy work gloves improved his grip and kept the sharp spokes of vine from puncturing his hands, but it also snagged the rope so he had to stop and untangle it every few steps. Finally he was above the level of the slide. He found a tree to wind the rope around before he began to work his way sideways.

At the lip of the hole he stopped to catch his breath while he examined the ground. The slide had begun at a small natural ledge where the rain had soaked through crevices and undermined the soil. The forty-five-degree slope above the ledge was a tangle of natural grass, cactus, and a few trees, none close enough to do him any good. He tugged at a handful of grass and it held. Miller shifted the gasoline can and spread-eagled himself on the steep slope. Gripping a handful of wet grass, he eased sideways cautiously. There were no toeholds on the weakened lip of the crater, and his feet skidded dangerously. His arms strained with tension. When he was halfway across, a hummock of grass pulled loose when he put his weight on it. He plummeted, clawing wildly and catching hold just before he slid over the edge of the crater. The gasoline can cracked against his hip, and he groaned in agony. He pressed his face to the slimy bank until the pain let up. Finally he spat mud and lifted his face to let the drenching rain clear his eyes before he crawled on, playing out the rope behind him.

After a few yards he stopped to catch his breath again and glanced back at the hazy orbs of the headlights. The damned rain was coming down harder than ever. He cursed it silently. But he'd gotten past the slide. He was on the other side. Looking down, he could make out jagged edges where the concrete had broken away. The car lights were so dim at this distance, he couldn't tell if the driveway would hold him. To be on the safe side, he kept moving until he reached a good-sized pine tree. He wrapped the rope around it before he started down at an angle. He finally reached the driveway twenty feet past the crater.

He sat down on the smooth cement, oblivious to the water and mud, his chest heaving. It was an effort to pull off the heavy gloves. His fingers were numb. He flexed his hands until they came back to life. Even so, it took a long time to get the knot undone on the rope holding the gas can, and even longer to undo the one around his waist. Finally he struggled to his feet and used the flashlight to find another sturdy tree. He tied the rope around it before he picked up the gasoline can and trudged down the hill.

The Camaro was where he left it. The windows glinted in the beam of light. He unscrewed the gas cap, then shielded the tank with his body as he transferred the gasoline. When he finished he tossed the can into the bushes and got behind the wheel. The relief of being out of the rain was overwhelming, but after a moment he began to shiver. It would be warm in Mexico. It was always warm there. If he hadn't run out of gas, he'd be in San

Diego. From there it was only a short hop across the border. He'd keep going south until the damned cold and rain were behind him forever. Forcing his stiff fingers to move, he reached into his pocket for the key he'd gotten from his sodden windbreaker when he went back for his shoes.

Start the car. Get the heater going.

The Camaro's engine sputtered until fuel got through the line, but it caught. Miller sat a moment, his head cocked, and listened. When he was satisfied the engine was running smoothly, he turned the heater on high. The sudden blast of cold air made his teeth chatter. He had to get warm. He put his head back and closed his eyes. Let the car warm up. It would take only a few minutes. He was too cold to drive. Too cold . . .

34

Choking on sobs, Eve scrambled to her knees. Her jeans were soaked, and she tasted blood on her lip where Miller had hit her. He was making his way across the slide and leaving her and Cindy behind. An hour ago she would have given anything to see him go, but now she was terrified.

She hunched on the soggy lawn and watched Miller creep across the hillside like a spider. His progress was so slow that at times she was sure he'd given up. His body was flattened against the ground, and each outpouring of effort gained him only infinitesimal progress. The gasoline can dragged like an anchor, and the rope around his waist had to be cutting into his flesh. Eve pressed her knuckles to her teeth, agonizing each move with him. If he lost his grip, the can would drag him into the morass below. The shifting, sliding mud would suffocate him before he could get free. Did she care? Was she hoping his efforts would fail? Or was she clinging to the faint, desperate hope that he might come back for them?

Miller's figure merged into the shadows beyond the haze of the light. It was worse not being able to see him, not knowing if he was still there. Miserable with the aching cold, Eve picked herself up and limped back to the Buick. She got in and hunched over the heater the way Miller had.

She was positive he was heading for the car she'd seen parked down on Coldwater. When he first stepped out of the darkness in the den—was it only hours ago?—he said his car had stalled. He'd run out of gas. That's why he had to burden himself with the can. With gasoline, he'd be on his way without another thought for her and Cindy. The police were looking for him. Instinct would make him run. She meant nothing to him. No, that wasn't true. She was a witness to Dorie's murder.

If she lived to tell . . .

In spite of the heater, she shivered violently. Rain drummed on the car roof like the rattle of bones. Miller would be better off with her dead. But he hadn't killed when he had the chance. Because of Cindy. Throughout these hours of terror, he cared about Cindy. It didn't matter if he thought she was a little girl named Kristen. He *cared*. Eve wasn't important, only Cindy. He wouldn't leave her here to die, would he? He'd come back for her. He had to. Eve realized the soft sounds were her own desperate sobs.

Eve drew the quilt away and touched Cindy's warm, sweaty cheek, her thoughts tortured. Suppose Miller didn't come back? How long would the Buick keep running? She glanced at the gauges and saw there was less than a quarter of a tank of fuel. It wasn't enough to last the night. The thought of spending the night here jolted her sharply. Miller said the hill was going to collapse. With two bad slides already, it might be only minutes. Her gaze picked at the dark ivy and deep shadows. There'd be no warning, no more than there had been when the pool burst or the driveway collapsed. At most she would have seconds to escape. To where? She glanced around helplessly. There was no place to go.

The clock on the dashboard showed only fifteen minutes had passed since Miller started his trek across the collapsed hillside. No matter how hard she strained, Eve couldn't see anything beyond the slide but the gray sheeting rain. Had he reached the canyon road? Suppose there were other slides? The thought paralyzed her. Suppose his car had been swept away or buried by mud? She bit her lip trying to ward off panic.

If the car wasn't there, would he come back? No matter what Miller was, what he'd done, she sensed his love for Kristen as

surely as she knew her own for Cindy. It was because of his
fantasy that Cindy was Kristen that they were still alive. If he
came back, it would be for Cindy.

On the rim of the washout another pine tree snapped with a
loud noise. It dropped into the crevice like a parachutist leaving
a plane, sliding across the path of the headlights and picking up
momentum as it rushed downhill. It dropped out of sight with a
crash that could be heard above the storm. The car rocked. The
sound of cracking concrete whipped through the night. Eve
clung to the dashboard as the car nosed forward and another
section of driveway broke off and fell into the sea of mud. In
panic, she grabbed the handle and unlatched the door, trying to
scoop Cindy into her arms so she could leap out. Before she
could manage, the car settled with a final shudder like a brood-
ing hen. Eve saw that the chasm in front of the car had widened.
Laying Cindy back down, she covered her eyes and prayed.

35

Jim Noble had been a cop for thirty-two years and a homicide detective for twelve. He'd been through two marriages, one live-in arrangement, and enough one-night stands that he'd lost count. He was a good cop, but he was tired. He was tired of seeing what one human being was capable of doing to another for reason or reasons unknown. He was tired of trying to figure out why killers killed and where they were going to strike next. More than anything, he was tired of the rain.

At best, police divisions weren't posh, cheerful places. The dull, rainy weather made the homicide squad room drearier than usual. Dampness seemed to hang in the building, despite the steady blast of warm air from the heating vents. The top drawer of Noble's desk held an assortment of patent medicines designed to alleviate the pain of arthritis, but none of them ever gave him the results the smiling actors on TV always got. It was probably because the commercials were filmed in nice cozy studios, under hot lights, more likely than not on sunny days. They should try doing one in this mausoleum today. Nobody would be smiling.

He sipped coffee from a ceramic cup with JIM stenciled on it in red letters. It was cold. He pushed the mug to a corner of the desk so he wouldn't forget and pick it up again. His conversations with Armand and Yarbaroff hadn't given him much to go on. Maybe he was expecting too much, wanting to establish a pattern for a man's insanity, yet he had the gut feeling there had to be at least a thread connecting it all. The phone call to 911 bothered him. The technicians had played it over a dozen times, but they hadn't gotten anything more definite than the woman's statement that Luke Miller was in her house. They were still working on it, but it might be hours before they had anything more. Noble worried that if some woman was scared enough to call Emergency, she might already be Miller's next victim. If something had set him off, he might be on a dangerous roll. Two dead women in less than a week. Maybe it was the storm. It had been raining long enough to drive anyone crazy.

Harry Rothman came in carrying a cardboard box covered with a plastic bag. He set it on a file cabinet while he took off his dripping London Fog. He pulled a handkerchief from his pocket and dried his face and hair before he brought the box to Noble's desk.

"You should wear a hat," Noble said.

Rothman looked surprised. "Why?"

"You'll wind up with aching bones like mine."

Rothman shrugged. "You wear a hat."

Noble sighed. He'd always worn one, even when he was Rothman's age. Maybe all that health food Harry ate would make a difference. They both hated the fast-food dinners that came with working late, but Harry knew a place that made veggieburgers and carob shakes.

It was the third time in a week they'd had to stay past their usual quitting time. Rothman had a wife who knew how to cook all that health stuff, and three kids who enjoyed having him home evenings. Jim Noble had a cat that scratched hell out of the furniture in his bachelor apartment when he was cooped indoors instead of out prowling. But there'd been too many complaints from neighbors about Pretty Boy terrorizing other animals, cats and dogs alike, when he was left to roam all day. When Jim was home evenings Pretty Boy was content to have a good meal and confine his tomcatting to a brief sojourn before Jim called him in for the night.

Rothman unveiled the carton of burgers, french fries, and his shake and put it on Noble's desk. "Want more coffee?" he asked, pulling up a chair.

Noble shook his head. "Miller is bugging me. Where the hell is he?"

Rothman folded back the wax paper around his veggieburger.

Noble ticked off his fingers. "In the hospital he attacked two nurses and an old lady who tried to push him around. He killed his wife when she argued with him and now two women who must have thought he was pretty normal until they found out where he'd spent the past eight years."

"Are you worried this may be a progressive thing?" Rothman asked. "You think Miller is out looking for women now?"

"I wish to hell I knew. It didn't take him long to get in out of the rain."

Rothman chewed a mouthful of burger and drank some of his shake before he said, "I wonder why he took the Peters woman's car? He didn't take Hauptner's."

Noble reached for his cheeseburger. "You think that's significant?"

Rothman shrugged. "It could mean he's on the move. Maybe he's had enough of this town and is heading out."

"He's lived in the Valley all his life."

Rothman grinned. "Reason enough to get out. Maybe we'll get lucky and he'll leave town and become someone else's problem."

"What about the woman who called 911? She said Miller was in her house."

"I wish to hell she'd coughed out her name and address clearly."

"She might have been whispering so Miller wouldn't hear."

"Maybe the whole thing was a hoax. We get more than our share of nut calls in this kind of weather."

The phone on Noble's desk rang. He lifted it, listened a moment, then quickly put down the cheeseburger. He picked up a pencil and wrote on a scratch pad.

"Yeah, okay. Thanks." He threw the pencil on the desk as he

hung up. "There goes your theory about Miller being on the move. That was Captain Hazza. A report came into Traffic a little while ago from an irate citizen. There's a car parked half-way out on the road on a dangerous curve up in Coldwater Canyon. The plates match Janine Peters's registration."

36

Miller woke with a start as lightning cut a jagged path across the sky and thunder rumbled overhead like a passing truck. For a moment his mind was blank. His mouth was dry and he felt numb. It took a few seconds to remember where he was. How long had he been asleep?

The car heater was blowing hot air directly at him. He swiveled the vent and lowered the thermostat, then switched on the lights so he could read the gas gauge. The needle was on empty, but the gallon he'd poured in the tank probably hadn't been enough to move it in the first place. There was no way to tell how much of it was left now.

When he released the emergency brake and put the Camaro in gear, the rear wheel that was on the shoulder spun and spat mud, but he gradually coaxed the car onto the blacktop. He scowled irritably at the streaks made by the faulty windshield wiper, but it wasn't important now. Kristen was. Take care of her first, then the car. Maybe that's why Sharon hadn't had it fixed. No, that was wrong. It wasn't Sharon's car. The other one. Merilee? No. Janine. Funny how he could always come up with the right name when he connected it to a car. Janine hadn't wanted him to drive the Camaro. Her car, she drove, she insisted, laughing with that throaty sound that had attracted him to her in the bar. She laughed a lot last night. He didn't remember why she'd started yelling.

The Camaro's headlights swept the hill, and he saw the steep driveway. Muddy water was pouring down it like a waterfall, splashing onto the roadway in front of him and quickly becoming part of the oozing slime and debris covering the blacktop. Beyond the driveway he could see a slide blocking the road. The big pine that he'd seen fall was wedged under the guardrail at an angle. Hunks of broken concrete, branches, and mud at least a foot deep were dammed up behind it. It wouldn't take much for the whole thing to break loose and sweep downhill again.

He nosed the car as close as he dared to the blockage, then carefully backed into the driveway. He rolled down his window and stuck his head out so he could see to climb the hill in reverse. If he had to get out in a hurry, it would be safer than backing down. The Camaro's engine missed a couple of times as it crawled up the steep driveway, but he fed it gas and kept it going. At the second switchback he stopped. He didn't want to take a chance on the driveway being safe beyond that point. From the amount of mud down in the canyon, the ground under it could be washed out twenty feet in either direction. Without support, the rest of the concrete might be ready to collapse. He crimped the wheels and set the emergency brake before he turned off the lights and ignition.

He shivered as the rain hit him like a shock wave again. He hated to leave the warm car, but the cold spurred him into moving faster. To forget how uncomfortable he was he thought about Mexico as he trudged up the hill. Kristen would like it there. She'd get well fast in the warm sun and ocean. Playing the flashlight over the dripping foliage alongside the driveway, Miller searched for the rope he'd anchored. He missed it on the first pass and had to turn back when the lip of the slide appeared in the beam of light. This time he stopped every few feet and checked every tree. In the dark they all looked alike. Confused, he tried to recall something to identify the one he'd tied the rope to, but it had just been a tree. He walked the section again slowly. This time he spotted a faint streak across the wet ground. He poked at it and found it was the rope, which was almost completely covered by leaves and mud. He shook it a couple of times, then snapped off the light, wrapped it in the plastic bag, and shoved it under his belt. Pulling on the heavy work gloves, he started up the slope, following the rope hand over hand in the darkness.

After a few minutes of climbing, he could see a faint patch of gray off to his left. The car headlights. He stopped to rest when he got to the tree he'd spooled the rope around. He wasn't far from the chasm. He had to move even slower than before. There was enough slack in the rope to let him drop dangerously if he miscalculated. This time there wouldn't be a line tied around him, only the guide rope to follow.

The hazy light wasn't enough to let him see if any more of the hill had collapsed. He'd have to take it as it came. He sucked air into his lungs, then flattened himself against the bank and put his foot out experimentally, inching forward only when he was sure it was safe.

It was easier than the first crossing because he didn't have the gasoline can banging against him, but it was slower and more dangerous. His first passage had scuffed up the soft ground, and the rain had turned it to slime. It was hard to find patches of grass to use as handholds. The ones he'd used before pulled out of the soft ground and were worthless. Half the time his feet were dangling helplessly when the ground under them slipped away at the slightest pressure. And now his body was numb with fatigue. Maybe he should go back while he still had the strength.

37

Eve jumped when the wind snapped a limb and it crashed from a tree overhead. She sat up and wiped her eyes as the branch crashed to the ground somewhere in the darkness. She couldn't sit here and wait to die. She'd come too far to quit now. She had to do something. At least try. She glanced out at the unrelenting monotony of the rain and shivered.

She couldn't take Cindy back in the house. The Buick was warm, but it was on dangerously weakened ground. She looked at the spot where Miller had vanished into the darkness. The hillside blurred like an out-of-focus photograph. She could barely see the rope he had used. His lifeline to safety. The *only* line to safety.

She braced herself to open the car door and get out. Huddling against the wind, she stumbled back across the soggy lawn to where Miller had climbed the bank. Ignoring the sharp ivy stems, she scrambled on her hands and knees up to the tree where the rope was anchored. Steadying herself, she yanked on the rope as hard as she could. It dragged like a lead weight, and as far as she could tell it was fastened on the other end. She squatted and pulled harder, but it didn't come loose. Had Miller tied it because he intended to come back or had he left it as a means of escape for her? Could she go across the way he had? Maybe alone, but she'd never make it carrying Cindy. Miller needed both hands to hang on. She would too. She'd have to strap Cindy to her back like a papoose. Slithering down the bank, she raced to the garage.

Miller had taken the heavy rope Paul had bought when he trimmed some of the trees around the house, but there was clothesline somewhere. Paul used it to fasten down their camping gear the year they went to Yosemite. She tried to remember where she'd seen it. She opened cupboards and felt blindly on the shelves, not letting herself think about Dorie's corpse at her feet. Finally her hand closed around the bundle of clothesline and she pulled it down quickly.

Back in the car, she warmed her stiff hands at the heater so she could undo the neatly tied rope. Bending over Cindy, she tried to figure the best way to fasten the quilt around her. Cindy fussed restlessly as Eve experimented with the rope. She passed it over Cindy's shoulders and around her body, but when she tugged it slid off in a tangle. The satin quilt was too slippery, but without it the lightweight blanket and Cindy would be soaked in seconds.

Cindy's yellow raincoat was in the laundry room. It wasn't all that warm, but it was waterproof. She dashed through the rain to the garage once more. She pushed at the laundry-room door but it wouldn't open. Frantic, she put her shoulder to it and shoved hard, telling herself there was no reason Miller would have locked it. When it finally opened a crack her relief was short-lived. Mud oozed through the narrow opening and poured over the sill. Eve jumped back, and the door slammed shut. Holding on to the car so she wouldn't slip, Eve backed out of the goo that spread slowly across the cement. The mud had forced its way through the whole house, spreading tentacles wherever it found open spaces. There was no way to get Cindy's coat or anything else now.

She'd give Cindy her raincoat. Unbuttoning it quickly, she shook it free of water. It was light enough so it wouldn't add bulk or weight, and she'd be able to tie the rope under Cindy's arms and legs so it wouldn't slip off. Shivering as the rain soaked her, Eve got in the backseat of the Buick so she'd have enough room to work. Lifting Cindy over the seat backs, she maneuvered her awkwardly between the headrests. Cindy began to cry.

"I'm sorry, sweetheart, please don't cry," Eve pleaded. She worked as fast as she could, but her fingers were stiff and it was difficult to get Cindy into the coat. "Don't cry, don't cry," she murmured. She fastened the buttons and buckled the belt snugly around Cindy's legs. She pulled the hood of the coat up over Cindy's head and face like a monk's cowl.

The rope was more difficult. It took several tries before she finally got it wound around Cindy's torso and legs. She left two loops to pass over her shoulders. Remembering the work gloves Miller had donned, she felt in the pocket of the raincoat for the leather gloves she'd worn this afternoon but they weren't there. There was a folded plastic rain scarf, which she put over the coat hood and tied securely under Cindy's chin.

Realizing how cold she was, Eve slapped her arms and looked out at the dark hillside. She'd be soaked and chilled in seconds, but there was no way around it. She'd have enough to think about to keep her mind off the cold. The pit definitely had widened with the second slide. The edge closest to the car came almost to the tree where Miller had started to scale the bank. The rope he'd stretched above the hole was no longer visible except in a few places where it hung down over the edge. Her life and Cindy's depended on seeing and hanging on to that rope. Once under way, there'd be no turning back. If she wasn't going to be moving blindly, she needed more light.

She got out of the car and took several cautious steps toward the hole that gaped under the headlights. The front wheels were less than a foot from the edge of the broken concrete. Did she dare pull forward so she could back up at an angle and direct the headlights at the hill? It was risky, but it might make the difference between life and death.

Teeth chattering, she got behind the wheel and released the emergency brake. She held her breath and touched the accelerator so the car inched forward, then pressed the brake in panic when she was afraid of going too far. She let her breath out slowly when the car was steady. Turning the steering wheel as far as it would go so the car would angle, she backed up until the bumper nudged the Mercedes again. Shaking, she repeated the maneuver twice more until the car was facing the most treacherous section of the slide. The hole was a yawning chasm in the veiled light. It wasn't much, but it would help, and she needed every advantage possible. Once she got out there, she couldn't let herself think about the danger. She put the transmission in park and set the hand brake. When she turned off the engine the headlights were silent beacons to her fear.

She tensed as something moved on the hillside. She leaned forward, expecting to see another section of the hill fall away. But as she stared at the spot she began to tremble with relief. Pinned in the misty glare, Luke Miller clung to the bank like a giant insect. He had come back. Eve began to cry.

38

Traffic began to move slowly after twenty minutes. The jack-knifed truck still blocked three lanes, but the spill had been cleared away. Red flares outlined the single lane that was open. It took another twenty minutes before Farley was waved through the snarl by a highway patrolman directing traffic with a powerful flashlight.

When he reached Woodland Hills traffic stalled again because a section of freeway was flooded. He followed a line of cars down the off ramp and cut over to Ventura Boulevard. Even with the car radio tuned to a station that gave frequent updates on road conditions, he couldn't avoid delays. Streets and roads were being closed faster than the news could report them, and Farley was growing more edgy by the minute.

The surface streets weren't any better than the freeway. Water was backed up at corners, overflowing curbs and creating ponds at intersections. Some spots were impassable, with water up to three feet deep, and many rush-hour drivers had underestimated the depth of the water or overestimated the power of their cars and been forced to abandon half-submerged vehicles that looked like water beetles on a dark pond.

He planned to reenter the freeway at Canoga Park, but gave up the idea and stayed on Ventura Boulevard when he heard a report that the freeway was blocked by flooding again at White Oak and that two lanes were closed at the interchange of 405

because of an accident. Farley resigned himself to crawling the
last few miles to Coldwater Canyon.

He thought about Eve and Cindy, wondering again if Dorie's
report of Cindy's illness was fact or another of her barbed attacks on Eve. Dorie had actually hoped to have Eve declared an
unfit mother and take Cindy away from her. She tried to hire a
lawyer to bring suit, but after a cursory check the attorney told
her she didn't have a case. Farley heard about it when she hired
a private detective to dig up proof that would hold up in court.
There wasn't any, and the detective abandoned the case when
Dorie tried to get him to trump up some. Afraid she might find
another detective with fewer scruples, Farley armed himself
with statements from Dr. Provel and the child psychologist,
who both agreed Eve was doing what was best for Cindy. She
had practical guidelines for telling when Cindy required medical attention. To play into the psychosomatic aspects of Cindy's
problem would make emotional cripples of both mother and
daughter. When he sent Dorie a letter and copies of the statements, she finally retreated like a wounded tigress, forfeiting
the immediate battle but not the need to continue stalking her
prey.

What Eve and Cindy needed was a man around the house.
Him. Farley had never thought much about marriage. He was
building a promising career, and he had a house in Studio City
and a happy bachelor existence he'd never considered giving
up before. He smiled at his own thoughts. Eve had finally promised to phone him on something other than business, and here
he was thinking about marriage. Maybe now that she was coming out of her shell, it wasn't such an impossible idea. He liked it.

When he finally reached Coldwater Canyon he was relieved
to see there wasn't any traffic. The significance of it didn't hit
him until he saw the flashing lights of a patrol car blocking the
road. He rolled down his window as he came to a stop. A policeman in a yellow slicker aimed a flashlight at him.

"Are you a resident, sir?"

Farley felt a twinge of panic. "What's happened, Officer?"

"Mud slide. The road's blocked. Unless you live between here and Potosi, I can't let you through."

Eve lived a good half mile beyond Potosi.

"You'll have to show some identification with your address on it," the policeman said, forestalling any inclination Farley had to lie.

"I don't live up there, but a client of mine does. Her phone is out and she's got a sick child."

"Sorry, I've got my orders. Besides, you can't get through. The slide blocked the road completely." The policeman waved the light toward a graveled turnout. "Turn around over there."

"I've got to get through," Farley insisted. He'd find a way around the slide. Walk if he had to.

"Cleanup operations haven't even started, mister," the officer said in an irritated tone. "Unless you have permission from my captain, you're out of luck. Now move on, please, you're blocking traffic." He walked toward the car that had pulled up behind Farley.

Short of running the barricade that had been placed on either end of the patrol car, Farley had no choice. He pulled into the turnout and started back down the hill. He'd see Pete Hazza and get whatever he needed to get past the barricade.

39

Drained by cold and exhaustion, Miller slid down the bank to the lawn. Pain stabbed his head, and his eyes were pressing through their sockets. With tremendous effort, he got to his feet and walked to the car. She was standing beside it. Her raincoat was gone and she looked like a drowned cat.

"Where's your coat?"

Shivering, she brushed back her wet hair. "I put it on Cindy."

He scowled, too weary to make sense of what she was saying.

"Kristen," she said quickly. "I put it on Kristen. I was going to carry her across." She pointed at the hill he'd just come down.

Miller glanced at the steep, washed-out bank, then back at her. She was crazy. "You'd never make it," he said.

"I—I had to try. I couldn't wait here and do nothing. I didn't know if you were coming back."

"I'd never leave my baby," he said angrily.

She was frightened by the wildness in his eyes. "I—I wasn't sure what you were going to do." Her tears ran into the rain streaming down her face. She was exhausted, wet, and freezing. And she was scared because her only hope to get out of here depended on a madman who walked a wavering line between concern and rage.

Miller grunted without answering. Even if he hadn't told her he was coming back, she should have known. How could he ever leave Kristen when he loved her so much? Sharon was crazy, but he wasn't going to waste time arguing with her now. The steady pounding of the rain wasn't helping that hillside. The longer he waited, the worse it would get. He pushed Sharon aside and opened the car door.

Kristen was all done up like a bedroll. Sharon had tied the long raincoat around her and made rope handles like a knapsack. Pretty clever. Maybe it was good for Sharon to be scared and worry sometimes. It made her think for herself and figure out how to do things right. Maybe he wouldn't always have to tell her how to do everything from now on. Maybe she was learning. Learning to take care of their baby better so she'd get well. Kristen wasn't going to die, no matter what that quack said. His baby wasn't going to die.

He said to Sharon, "Get in and help me lift her."

Eve crawled into the backseat and knelt beside Cindy. Miller crouched in the doorway and leaned back to pull the rope loops over his shoulders.

"Lift," he ordered.

She raised Cindy, and he tugged the loops snug. He tied the two ends of the rope together and tested the harness for slack. Biting her lip, Eve tucked the coat hood over Cindy's face and made sure the plastic scarf held it in place. Even with all the jostling, Cindy didn't open her eyes. She had sunken into deep feverish sleep again, and Eve was terrified by her pallor.

Miller settled the heavy load more securely before he eased himself out of the car carefully to be sure he didn't bang Kristen. He stood a moment, getting used to the weight. Christ, he was tired and cold. The wet sweater was rubbing his flesh raw, and he'd stopped feeling his cold, numb feet long ago. It took all his concentration to put one in front of the other as he slogged back to the hill.

He fixed his sights on the rope and took a deep breath. It looked higher than before, but he knew his perception was distorted by exhaustion. Kristen's weight threw him off balance. He crouched, grabbing handsful of ivy to pull himself forward. Once when he skidded and slipped back, Sharon reached out to steady him. He'd forgotten she was there. He grabbed more ivy and inched forward again. When he finally reached the rope he was breathing hard and had to rest a minute before he started to cross.

Eve wiped mud from her face and tried to stay clear of Miller's feet. When he slipped and fell she grabbed for Cindy, but Miller caught himself and went on without looking back. Eve struggled to keep up with him. He was going to carry Cindy across the slide. That was the important thing. When he stopped she sank into the prickly, wet ivy and tried to catch her breath. Miller was at the tree where the rope was tied, staring at the pit left by the slide as if he had to muster his strength before he could tackle it again. Could he make it with Cindy on his back? Eve saw that his two crossings had torn up a lot of the ground cover. Except for the rope, there was nothing to cling to.

Finally Miller eased himself away from the tree. Eve scrambled up behind him, but when she reached for the rope Miller kicked her away. She skidded but caught herself before she tumbled down the bank.

"Don't leave me here!" she yelled at him.

"Stay out of my way!"

Eve cringed as he kicked wet leaves and mud into her face. She sank to her knees and watched him move like a sluggish caterpillar in the misty glare of light. He pressed his body against the hillside and considered each movement before he made it. His progress was agonizingly slow, and Eve realized he was exhausted. Once, when he glanced back, his face was a pale, drawn mask with heavy-lidded eyes. He was still fighting the sleeping pills she'd given him. She prayed desperately he wouldn't succumb to them now.

Miller's shoulders were raw under the wet ropes. He couldn't feel his hands anymore. His fingers moved mechanically inside the soggy gloves: open, reach, close around the line. When he was sure he'd gone more than halfway, he glanced back and almost wept when he saw he'd covered only a few feet. He looked ahead again, determined not to think about how far he still had to go. He learned that in the hospital. If you looked back, you never got out. Shut out the past. Take one step at a time. One day, one hour, get through one incident or confrontation without losing control. He learned to turn away when other patients screamed or began fighting. Over and over he told himself it had nothing to do with him. No one was ever going to yell at him or hit him again. Not his mother, not Sharon, none of the others. No one.

He rested his head on the muddy bank. Christ, he was tired. His body ached and his limbs were numb. He was so sleepy he wondered if he'd ever feel rested again. His mind was fuzzy, and it was hard to think. Finally he forced himself to go on. For Kristen. For Kristen.

He came to a bad stretch where the slide had shorn off everything below the rope at a ninety-degree angle. A few naked tree roots poked out of the red mud that fell away to the bottom of the wash. He tugged the guideline to take up the slack, then poked his foot into the soft mud. The toe of his shoe sank and made a sucking noise when he pulled it out. He tried again but it wouldn't support his weight.

Bracing himself, he inched his hands along the rope and stepped out into the void. The sudden snap on his arms almost yanked them from their sockets. He groaned, straining to hang on. After a long time he managed to move his right hand a few inches. His body scraped along the wall, and a cascade of mud poured over him. Blinded, his hands froze on the rope. He tried to clear his eyes by rubbing his face against his shoulder, but the sweater was saturated with slime. He spat furiously and cursed as he groped for a new hold.

He had to keep going. He had to do it for Kristen. He stopped thinking and moved automatically, blindly, instinctively, ignoring the mud and rocks that pelted him in a steady spray. Get across before the whole hill goes. Get Kristen across safely. His hand touched something solid. His arms were quivering from strain, and for a moment he was numb. Then he recognized the shallower pitch of the hillside and the spikey tufts of wild grass. He'd made it. He was on the other side of the slide. With agonizing effort, he pulled himself across the lip of the hole and onto

solid ground. Exhausted, he lay panting, the guide rope still
clutched under his arm like a lifeline.

When he was finally able to breathe without racking pain, he
pulled off the gloves and wiped his eyes. Looking back, the glow
of the headlights was barely visible in the haze of rain. He
reached to touch the bundle tied across his back.

"We're safe, Kristen honey," he said aloud. "You're going to
be okay, just like Daddy promised."

It took a while before he had the strength to get up and start
down the hill toward the car.

40

Eve peered through the rain as Miller and Cindy vanished in the haze. Her teeth were chattering, and the realization that Miller wasn't coming back for her filled her with numb horror. When he got Cindy to the car he was going to drive off. She struggled to her knees in the wet ivy and reached for the rope. She couldn't let him have Cindy. She pulled herself up, then let go quickly. If Miller was still working his way across on it, she might plunge him and Cindy to their deaths by putting too much strain on the rope. But if she waited too long they'd be gone. The howling wind in the pines moaned her despair.

After a while she marshaled her energy and tested the rope again. Was it looser? Or were imagination and fear distorting her judgment? Either way, she couldn't wait another minute. She had to cross. Now. Bracing her body against the tree so she wouldn't slip, she swung her arms and stamped her feet to get her circulation going. Water and mud spattered her ankles and jeans. Trying to control her spasms of shivering, she took a deep breath and got a firm grip on the rope.

As she made the first step, lightning lit the sky and thunder crashed so close she almost let go of the rope and plunged down the hill. When she caught herself the rope burned like fire on her palms. She cried aloud, but she held on. Gasping, she flattened herself against the bank the way Miller had, her heart thundering as loudly as the storm. Cold mud oozed through her clothes and set off another fit of chills. It took all her strength to move again.

She tucked the rope under one arm and let it guide her. Every inch she moved was agony. The ten or twelve feet to the edge of the washout seemed like miles. When she finally reached it she lay trembling and gasping for breath. The image of Miller dangling over the abyss, arms straining to bear his weight, panicked her. It was at least twenty feet across. Her arms had no feeling. She'd never be able to hang on.

She had to. Her life was at stake, and unless she hurried, Cindy's would be too. If Miller drove away, she'd never catch them. Oh, God, don't let him take Cindy.

Grabbing the rope out over the yawning pit, she pushed herself off the bank. Her body slammed into the wash, setting off a spill of mud that pelted her. She ducked her face against her shoulder until it stopped, then lifted her head cautiously. Another portion of the bank had given way, exposing more tree roots and rocks. Her palms were raw, and she had to pry her fingers loose for each move. She kept her gaze on the porous mud in front of her, not daring to look down or think about the gaping crevice below her. She thought about Cindy. Get to Cindy . . .

She no longer felt the cold. She no longer felt anything but pain. Cruel, stinging pain in her hands, pain warm with her own blood. Wrenching pain in her shoulders from the unbearable strain. Pain jolting through her body to measure each inch of distance she gained. Time had no meaning in the constant and endless pain.

When she bumped against the far edge of the slide, she thought it was something blocking her way, and she began to cry until she finally realized what it was. Opening her eyes, she let the tears stream down her muddy face. She was across the slide, at the other side. Feebly she reached for a new handhold, but her hand came down on the sharp, pointed end of a stick instead of the rope. It stabbed into the pad of her thumb, and she let go with a cry. Unsupported, her body plunged and snapped, dragging torturously on the precarious grip of one hand. Mud spewed over her. She groped frantically for the rope above her. Dangling by one arm, she tried to pull herself up, but exhaustion had taken its toll. Her muscles strained and she felt her grip on the rope begin to slip.

Suddenly something clamped her wrist. She was jerked sideways, across the lip of the slide, through the mud and over rocks and branches, onto slimy but solid ground. She lay weeping helplessly, too relieved and exhausted to wonder how the miracle had been wrought until Miller's voice startled her from her daze.

"Get up!"

She blinked her eyes open, wiping away mud. Miller was holding the rope and bending over her. His face was a muddy mask except for two owlish circles around his eyes.

"Get up," he screamed. He grabbed her wrist and yanked her to her feet. She collapsed to her knees, too weak to stand. Miller shoved the rope into her hands, then turned and began to work his way through the murky gloom.

Terrified for Cindy, Eve forced herself to move. Crawling more than walking, she struggled to keep up with him. He was barely visible ahead of her. The farther they went from the slide, the darker it became. She banged into a tree and realized the rope was wound around it. She felt its direction and let herself slide as she followed it downhill. She landed with a jarring thump on the concrete driveway. Dripping and filthy, she staggered to her feet to follow Miller, who was faintly outlined by the red glow of a car's taillights.

He was already behind the wheel when she reached the car, and she got in quickly. In the faint light she saw Cindy on the backseat. The hood of the raincoat had been drawn away from her face so she could breathe, and there was a small pillow under her head. When Eve pulled the door shut warmth engulfed her. It was almost suffocating after the raw cold.

Miller had come back for her. He'd saved her life, and Cindy's too. Confusing emotions overwhelmed Eve as she was caught between renewed terror and gratitude. Miller released the brake, put the car in gear, and let it roll forward. Hunched over the steering wheel, he seemed hypnotized as he peered through the windshield. In panic, Eve realized that despite his superhuman exertion, he was still fighting the soporific effect of the sleeping pills. Her thwarted escape plan might kill them now. She studied his profile nervously in the faint glow of the dashboard lights. Was he alert enough to drive down the treacherous canyon? His face was drawn in concentration as he negotiated the hairpin turns of the driveway. Even though the car was barely moving, he touched the brake frequently and steered around debris and mud that had been deposited by the storm. He seemed confident behind the wheel, despite his obvious lethargy. How much of the narcotic was still in his system? She prayed that the rain and cold had counteracted most of it.

When they reached the lower stretch of the drive, the headlights showed a muddy cascade of water running across their path. Miller slowed and let the car roll, but before they got past the gushing water the ground suddenly trembled violently. Miller slammed the gas pedal, and Eve screamed. The car skidded and spun at a right angle before he could right it. Eve braced herself as a thunderous crash rocked the hillside and lifted the car from the ground. In the spill of the headlights, trees, mud, and concrete roared toward them. Eve screamed again.

Miller gunned the engine. The car whipped around the sharp turn to Coldwater Canyon. It slewed across the blacktop, hitting the guardrail and bouncing off as Miller struggled with the steering wheel. The car skidded sideways against the embankment on the inside of the curve and ricocheted back onto the pavement. Behind them the roar was deafening as the hill gave way and crashed down the slope.

Eve clutched the dashboard as the car rocked. Miller tightened his grip on the wheel as they took the impact of the first wave. Mud splattered and something crashed against the rear window, spiderwebbing it. He turned the wheel sharply and aimed the car at the inside bank like a bullet.

Petrified, Eve tried to grab the wheel, but Miller backhanded her a wicked blow that crashed her against the door. Stunned, she wiped blood from her mouth as the car tore through glistening oleanders and cactus before it finally shuddered to a stop. Behind them mud and debris gushed across the road, tearing out the wooden guardrail and pouring over the steep precipice to the valley below. An arm of slime snaked from the main flow and came down the road behind them, sweeping everything in its path. The car jolted as mud engulfed the wheels and splattered the windows and headlights, leaving them in a eerie, murky dimness.

41

Farley found a parking place half a block from the North Hollywood police station. He sprinted down the sidewalk, which
glistened wetly under the streetlights, jumping puddles when
he saw them in time. Even so, his slacks and shoes were soaked
when he got inside. He shook water from his coat and told the
desk officer that he had to see Captain Hazza.

The uniformed man used the phone, then said, "He's tied up.
You'll have to wait a few minutes." He indicated some chairs
along the wall and went back to his paperwork, which was
interrupted almost instantly by the phone ringing. Farley
looked up expectantly, but the man didn't signal him. The few
minutes became twenty, and Farley began to pace impatiently.
When he finally was told he could go in, he ran down the hall.

Pete Hazza gave him a distracted nod and continued talking
on the phone. When he hung up he said, "Good to see you,
Farley. I hope it's important. We're backed up into last week.
This rain—" He groaned as the phone rang again. He lifted it,
listened, then said, "The chopper pilot is standing by, but he
needs a break in the weather. Yeah. Okay." He hung up with a
weary sigh. "Like I said, we're busy."

Farley had known Hazza long enough to come right to the
point. "I need a favor," he said.

The police captain cocked his head. "Lester already called.
The answer is no."

"Let me go up. Your boys have Coldwater barricaded."

"The road's wiped out. Nobody can get through."

"I'll find a way."

"No you won't. No one's going up there until the engineers say it's safe."

Farley leaned on the desk. "A very good friend of mine is up there with a sick kid, and her phone is out. She needs help."

Pete massaged the back of his neck. "Where is her place?"

"A quarter of a mile past Clawson."

Pete shook his head. "The houses up there are cut off. There was a slide on the other side of Mulholland this afternoon and one near Potosi less than an hour ago. There's no telling what the road is like between them. Coldwater is completely blocked from both directions. You couldn't get through if I gave you permission. Are you sure she didn't come down earlier? There were evacuation warnings on radio and TV."

Farley sank into a chair. He clung to a faint, desperate hope. "I don't know, but I have to find out. Can I get across Mulholland from Laurel?"

Pete shook his head again. "Two hours ago you could have, but the road's washed out now. This is the worst storm we've had—"

"You can't just leave people up there," Farley yelled.

"We have a helicopter standing by to check the minute the rain lets up, but the chopper wouldn't have a chance in this soup." Pete leaned back in his chair. "Come on, Farley, we're doing everything we can."

Farley raked his fingers through his damp hair. "Sorry, Pete. It's been a hell of a day."

The phone rang again and Hazza picked it up. "Yeah? Sure, Jim, just a sec." He searched the papers on his desk and pulled out a sheet, then ran his finger down a list. "On the double curve a quarter of a mile below Mulholland. That's the way it was called in. Good luck."

Farley was out of the chair before Hazza cradled the phone. "What's on that curve?" he demanded.

"A stolen car. Two of our homicide men are following up a

report and trying to make a collar. They think that nut Luke Miller was driving it."

Miller— Farley had trouble breathing. "Do they have anything to tie him to it?"

"The owner of the car was found strangled in her apartment today. She was seen leaving a bar with Miller last night."

Farley sat down as icy sweat broke out on his body. Looking at him, Pete said, "What's the matter?"

"Those curves are right below Eve Foxx's driveway." Sweat trickled between Farley's shoulder blades. "Is Miller still up there?"

"We don't know, but 911 had a call from a woman who said Miller was in her house—"

Farley jumped up and leaned across the desk. "I don't care how you do it, Pete, but get me up there *now*."

Hazza looked at him for a moment, then picked up the phone.

42

The roar of the slide subsided slowly until only the sound of the rain and the low throb of the car engine broke the silence. Huddled against the door, Eve knew they were alive because Miller's quick actions and driving skill had gotten them out of the slide's direct path. While she panicked he did the one thing possible to save them. But now his mouth was a compressed thin, white line, and his eyes were glazed. The face of a killer. A vivid picture of his expression just before he choked Dorie swam before Eve's eyes. Her heartbeat echoed the storm erratically. She licked her swollen lip where he had hit her and gazed out the mud-spattered window. They were alive, but she had triggered the murderous spark that touched off his madness. He couldn't stand being screamed at or hit. Why hadn't she realized it before?

She watched him nervously. He was staring at the windshield as if mesmerized by the dirty glass. Whenever his eyes started to close, he forced them open. Eve gave thanks that the drugged stupor was dulling his rage, but it was also making him oblivious to the danger they were still in.

Looking through the filthy window, she saw the rising flow of mud around them. The steep hill kept it moving along the course of least resistance, but it had grown from a thin coating to a sluggish, lavalike mass. The shallow ditch along the shoulder, which normally let rainwater run off, was a sinkhole filled with gooey slime and silt. The car was mired in it.

Miller rubbed his eyes and yawned, then rolled down the window beside him and breathed the cold, damp air. After a minute he stuck his head out and looked in both directions. The canyon wall was close enough to reach out and touch. When he put the car in gear and pressed the gas pedal, the wheels spun. He gentled the accelerator, coaxing, but the wheels threw up a brown shower without pulling free.

He looked at her, his eyes hooded and indecipherable. "Do you know how to rock a car?" His voice slurred slightly.

She nodded.

He grunted. "Get behind the wheel. Don't give it any gas until I tell you, understand?"

She nodded again, too frightened to speak. When he tried to open his door it hit the embankment. He shoved it hard and forced it as far as it would go, then grabbed the doorframe to pull himself through the tight space. Eve slid across the seat as he edged along the car to the back. Reaching out the open window, she caught some rainwater in her palm and washed off the side mirror. The glass streaked and filmed, but at least she could see Miller. He leaned against the trunk and planted his feet in the oozing mud in search of footing.

"Okay," he yelled.

She pressed the accelerator too hard and the engine gunned. Miller swore as the spinning wheels coughed up mud that drenched him. Eve released the pedal quickly. She was so nervous, she was doing everything wrong. Miller wiped his face as he stumbled back along the side of the car. Reaching through the open window, he grabbed her hair in his filthy hand and yanked cruelly.

"You stupid broad! You said you knew how to rock it!" He slammed her head against the doorframe. Eve yelped with pain. Her vision blurred as he let go of her hair and closed his hands around her throat. Struggling for breath, she stared up at his enraged face.

"I'm sorry," she gasped. "I'm not used to this car—"

His breath blew like steam from a faulty radiator, and Eve had never seen eyes so filled with hate and rage. The pressure of his hands on her throat quivered. Miller glanced at the road, where pieces of broken concrete, uprooted shrubs, and trees that had been reduced to kindling were strewn in the ocean of mud. After what seemed an eternity, his stranglehold relaxed.

"Don't give it so much gas, and throw it in reverse as soon as it balks. You understand?" he demanded.

"Yes." It was a pitiful whisper. She sucked air greedily as Miller trudged back to his position. Rock the car so the momentum would ease it out of the mud. She'd done it a thousand times in Minnesota snow. Easy. Don't rush, don't panic. Rubbing her throat, she watched Miller in the dirty mirror and waited for his signal, concentrating, because she knew her life depended on it.

"Okay!" he shouted.

She did it right this time, giving the engine just enough gas to take advantage of the forward momentum of his push. The car moved slightly. When it strained she quickly shifted to reverse. The car rolled back. She shifted back to low, and Miller pushed again. Reverse. Low. Reverse. Low. Trembling and praying silently, she willed the car to pull free. Suddenly she felt a quick surge as the wheels found enough traction to overcome the suck of the mud. She resisted the impulse to gun the engine. Still in low, she fed gas gently. The car jerked onto the road. Eve gripped the wheel as the tires skidded on the slick pavement, but she couldn't control it. The Camaro skittered toward the guardrail and the dark void of the canyon.

Miller shouted, but the storm carried his words away. Petrified, Eve turned the steering wheel into the skid and straightened the car a moment before it would have smashed through the splintered railing and plunged down the steep embankment. The rear fender sideswiped a post with a loud crunch. The impact spun the car out of control again, back across the road. It slithered sideways, then came around miraculously when it reached the curve where it had been parked earlier. Panting, Eve realized the whole car was shaking.

She glanced in the mirror, thinking that Miller was pounding on the car in rage. But it wasn't Miller. Another avalanche was sweeping down the hillside. With a noise like a locomotive, it tore out trees like matchsticks and poured down rocks, brush, and pieces of the smashed driveway. For an instant Luke Miller froze as he watched the slide plummet toward him. Then he raced down the road only steps ahead of the cascading torrent.

43

Farley followed the detective's car up the winding canyon. The rain had dwindled from cloudburst fury to steady patter, but the two-lane blacktop was inundated with the runoff from higher levels. Signs of the storm's destructive force were everywhere: houses brooded in darkness due to power failures; trees were uprooted where supporting soil had washed away or they had been snapped off by the force of the wind; broken branches were strewn like confetti; swirling debris, natural and man-made, churned downhill in rivers of muddy water. On a sharp curve where a new house was under construction, lumber and bricks had been tossed like jetsam onto the road, and they had to get out to clear it away before they could go on.

Evidence of the big slide was visible before they reached Clawson Road. The blacktop turned ugly brown under a film of mud. Branches caught in the thick flow rose like brown, clutching fingers from the slime. Ahead of Farley the police car slowed.

Yellow blinkers had been set up, and a Caltrans maintenance truck, hazard lights flashing and motor idling, blocked both lanes. When the detectives pulled up Farley parked behind them. A man in a yellow rain suit and hard hat was standing in the beam of the truck headlights talking to two muddy workmen. He looked around as the detectives and Farley approached.

"I'm Halpern. You the guys from North Hollywood?"

"Right. Noble and Rothman." When the engineer's glance went to Farley, Noble added, "Mr. Cunningham thinks his fiancée is up there."

"Has anyone come out?" Farley asked anxiously.

"Not since this slide," Halpern said. "As near as we can estimate, it's twenty to twenty-five feet thick." He pointed to the mud, dirt, and rocks that had reclaimed the slope as if no road had ever been cut. "From the crap that's been piling up behind this, I'd be willing to bet there's another big slide above here. If this breaks loose, it will wipe out everything down there." He glanced at the steep canyon below them. It was too dark to see how many houses were in its potential path.

"How long before we can get through?" Rothman wanted to know.

The engineer shrugged. "Cleanup work is going to have to wait for daylight."

"Can anyone get in or out?"

"Not unless you can fly."

Noble squinted up at the rain silvered by the headlights of the maintenance truck. It was definitely letting up. He said to Rothman, "Call in and find out how that chopper is doing. This could be the break they've been waiting for."

Rothman went back to the car and leaned in the open doorway as he used the radio. A couple of minutes later he came back.

"It's on the way."

Farley felt the first glimmer of hope since he'd left Santa Barbara.

44

Her momentary distraction sent the car skidding into the curve. The splintered guardrail sprang into the path of the headlights. Eve wrenched the steering wheel and aimed the car toward the inside bank the way Miller had. The tires whined and spat mud, skidding dangerously, so that the car lurched back and forth between the inky black precipice and the bank.

Behind her she heard Miller's screams merge with the howling rumble of destruction. In the mirror Eve saw him a few feet behind the car, arms outstretched, reaching. Her foot went toward the brake, then pulled back as she glimpsed the horrible twisted mask of Miller's face. The distance between them widened.

Suddenly Miller stumbled as a tree branch propelled by the wind and force of the mud slide struck him across the back. His arms spread as if he were making one final grab for her as he dropped to his knees, then fell flat. A moment later the muddy water surged over him, lifting his body and swirling it like flotsam and sweeping him toward the brink of the mountainside. He vanished as mud, water, and debris carried him across the road and over the steep wall of the canyon.

The car skidded around the final sweep of the curve, and Eve struggled with the wheel to keep control. Somehow she slowed the car and managed to stay on the road even though she could barely see through the streaked windshield and her rushing tears. Darkness merged trees and road in a watery blur. She tried to follow the yellow line but it was obliterated by mud. Her terrified glance shot to the mirror when she thought she heard Luke Miller shout, but in the thundering crash of the slide it was only an echo of her conscience.

Another slide could roar down any minute. Or the dammed-up debris behind her could break loose and take the whole road with it. She glanced apprehensively at the steep slope where unseen fissures might be burgeoning that very moment.

She was gripping the wheel so tightly that pain burned her lacerated hands. Over and over she told herself it was finished. Luke Miller was dead. He couldn't have survived that fall. He was dead. She and Cindy were safe.

Sobbing, she braced herself against the shower of cold rain that came through the open window. She didn't dare take her hand off the wheel long enough to roll it up, and the heater wasn't powerful enough to override the cold air flowing in. She prayed that Cindy was warm enough. The windshield was gradually clearing, but the other windows were covered with mud and the badly cracked rear window was useless.

She drove with her foot on the brake and the transmission in low. Even so, she had to look out the open window repeatedly to make sure she didn't wander too far from the bank or close to the precipitous edge.

As she came around another sharp curve a wall of mud loomed across the road without warning. She slammed on the brake but the wheels locked and the car skidded sickeningly. Her arm shot sideways, as if Cindy were beside her needing to be protected from the impact. Eve opened her mouth to scream, and a loud buzzing sound filled the night. The Camaro slammed into the mountain of mud and threw her against the steering wheel. She slewed sideways, and her head hit the doorframe. As she fell forward against the wheel, unconscious, the horn blared.

In the backseat Cindy's relaxed body was pitched to the floor. The jolt wakened her and she began to cry.

45

A muffled sound came through the thick wall of mud separating them from the upper canyon. Noble glanced at Halpern questioningly.

"It could be anything. Sound echoes in these canyons," the Caltrans man said. He glanced down the hill and pointed to a flashing light in the distance. "That looks like your chopper." As the whir of the helicopter grew louder, Noble walked to the police car and picked up the radio to talk to the pilot, who kept the aircraft a safe distance out to avoid the steep wall of the canyon. In the reflecting glare of the searchlight two men could be seen inside the cockpit. The police radio crackled.

"O'Donnell and Shaw up here, Noble. You have a weird sense of humor. I wouldn't turn a detective out on a night like this."

"Very funny, glad you could make it," Noble said into the hand mike. "We want to know if anyone's still up there. We're looking for a blue Camaro and the man who was driving it."

The helicopter's powerful beam flashed toward the slide. Static crackled as the pilot switched on his microphone. "We'll take the easy one first, good buddy," he said. "The blue Camaro is right on the other side of your little sandpile."

"What?"

"That's right. Looks like he skidded into it. No sign of anyone, but we'll go down and have a look." The chopper flew a dozen yards up and pivoted to play the searchlight across the hill. A minute later O'Donnell said, "Someone's slumped over the wheel. Must have been knocked out by the impact. I don't think it's your man though. I'd swear it's a woman, with that long blond hair."

"Eve!" Farley said as he came up beside the homicide detective.

Noble spoke into his microphone. "No sign of the man?"

"The car's covered with mud. I can't see anything except the driver. That window's open."

If it was Eve, where was Cindy? When Noble paused to think over his next move, Farley said, "You've got to get her out of there. She may be hurt—"

Noble ignored him. "Sam, do a quick run up to the top and have a look around. See if you can find a spot to put down anywhere near the Camaro, but be careful."

"Ten-four." The helicopter moved beyond the curve, and the noise of the engine faded slowly.

"You can't just leave her there," Farley badgered.

Noble flinched as pain shot through his wrist. He eased the radio into his other hand. "Listen, Cunningham, you're here because the captain didn't leave me any choice. Sam O'Donnell is the best goddamn chopper pilot on the force. I want to know two things before I ask him to put down—can he find a safe spot, and is he sure Luke Miller isn't hiding someplace ready to jump them and hijack the chopper. If you know some better way to get the woman out of the car, be my guest. It's been a long day, and I've had it."

"Take it easy, Jim," Rothman said quietly.

"Yeah, sure." Noble tossed the radio onto the car seat and walked away. In the distance the helicopter's bullhorn boomed with a muted, hollow sound.

Rothman said to Farley, "The sergeant knows what he's doing."

Already regretting his outburst, Farley nodded. "Sorry."

Before long the helicopter came back, and Noble returned to pick up the radio.

"There's another slide up a way," the copilot reported. "At

least one house went with it, and the road's completely wiped out. From there down, the road is covered with mud."

"Any sign of residents?"

"Negative. There was no response to the horn. Everything's dark."

Noble massaged his wrist.

Ed Shaw's voice came out of the darkness. "There's no place wide enough for us to put down, but I think I can make it on the ladder, Jim."

Noble glanced up at the helicopter, and Ed Shaw waved jauntily.

"There's not much clearance for the rotor," Rothman said.

"It'll be a tight squeeze, but we can do it."

"Okay, but be careful," Noble warned.

"We always are. Ten-four."

The helicopter moved around the bend again. The steady chuck of the engine filled the silence that fell over the waiting men, who were immersed in their own thoughts. Noble thought about Merilee Hauptner and Janine Peters, who were dead because they had befriended a seemingly harmless man named Luke Miller. Rothman worried about the rotor blade hitting the canyon wall, and he steeled himself for the sound of the crash he thought was inevitable. Farley could think only about Eve. How had she gotten behind the wheel of the stolen car and, more important, was she all right, and where was Cindy? He clenched his fists and waited impatiently for word from the men in the helicopter.

Finally the radio crackled. "Jim, there's a kid—"

Farley held his breath.

"Ed's bringing her up."

"Is she all right?" Noble asked.

"She's bawling like a trooper. Here, give her to me, Ed." The muffled sound of Cindy's crying became clear over the radio. "Hey, honey, you're okay now," O'Donnell said. The radio clicked off again. When it came on five minutes later Cindy had quieted to an occasional sniffle, and Sam said, "He's bringing the woman up now." Then: "She's got some bruises and a cut on the head. She's out cold. There's no sign of anyone else near the car. I think we ought to take these two to the hospital. The kid's got a fever."

"We'll meet you there," Noble said.

"If you're finished with us for tonight, Jim, we have some more rescue missions to run while the water's turned off. We'll drop the woman and child off and be on our way."

"Ten-four." Noble hung up the radio and looked at Rothman and Farley. "If Miller's up there, he'll keep until morning. Let's get to the hospital and see what Eve Foxx can tell us about him."

Farley was already on his way to his car.

46

On the seventh day the sun rose in a sky sprinkled with puffy white clouds, silvering eucalyptus leaves that rustled in the breeze like paper fingers. It bathed a wet landscape that had greened miraculously overnight. Waterfalls splashed down hillsides and ran in gentle streams across the streets. Six days of rain had brought beauty along with awesome destruction.

It would take days to clear the slides and months to repair the giant scallops cut out of the roads. People began to salvage what they could from homes that had been ravaged by water and mud. For some there was nothing left to go home to, nothing left to save.

Eve sat at the sunny breakfast table across from Farley. She was wrapped in a soft, blue terry-cloth robe, sizes too large—his. Her bare feet were wound around the rung of the chair. She finished the scrambled eggs and bacon and pushed her plate away as Farley filled the coffee cups.

"Sergeant Noble called," Farley said.

Eve looked up expectantly, trying to read his tone.

"Good news and bad news."

She tried to laugh. "Give me the good news first."

He sat across from her and took her hand. "Luke Miller is dead. They found his body last night. Dorie's too."

Eve let out her breath. "Thank God it's over. I don't think I could live with the idea of his being alive and possibly getting out of the hospital again someday."

Farley squeezed her fingers gently. "Don't think about it."

Eve smiled ruefully. "I'll never be able to forget it. Those were the most horrible hours of my life, even worse than when Paul died. It's frightening to recognize your own violence and your weakness." When he tried to dissuade her from going on, she shook her head. "I want to talk about it. I can't keep it bottled up inside." She sipped the steaming coffee. "I would have killed him to save Cindy. That's hard for me to believe, but I know I would have if I could. I tried. I tried to stab him with a pair of scissors, but he took them away from me. If there had been more sleeping pills in the bottle, I'd have given him all of them. At first I only wanted him to go away, but after—after Dorie—I wanted him dead." Her voice broke.

Farley reached across the table and took her hand. "It was instinct. You were protecting yourself and Cindy."

"How can it be natural to want to kill? That's a lower animal instinct, not human."

"You're forgetting something. You weren't dealing with another rational human being. You were dealing with an insane killer who was acting on a primal level. He was an insane man who had some rational periods. That's different from dealing with sane people who have occasional irrational periods."

Eve sighed softly. She knew Farley was right, but it didn't make it easier to accept the violence she'd discovered in herself, or the weakness. She'd *needed* Miller. She'd welcomed him when he came back to take Cindy across the mud slide and when he kept her from falling from the rope. Insane as he was, those were acts of compassion. And she had repaid him by driving off without giving him a chance to reach the car before the hill collapsed. Miller had saved her life and Cindy's, and she had ignored his in her final dash for safety.

"Don't feel guilty," Farley said. "You did what had to be done. You saved two very important lives. If there's any blame to be placed, it has to go on a lot of shoulders. Miller's parents for being what they were and making him what he became. The psychologists and psychiatrists who didn't discover the depths of his illness. The system that let him out of the hospital. The lonely women who wanted company at any price and paid with their lives. You and Cindy were innocents caught by chance." He squeezed her hand. "It's over. Finished."

"Yes," she said with a smile. "But one thing has just begun. I discovered my own strength. I'm going to make it now, Farley. I'm through living in the past. It's time to get on with my life and Cindy's. We're both going to make it."

He smiled. "That's the best news I've heard in a long time."

She sobered. "I almost forgot, what's the bad news?"

Farley held her gaze. "The house is a total loss. A helicopter survey yesterday showed there's nothing left but a hole. Everything went in that last big slide."

She heard the news without emotion. It was a final door closing to seal off the past. This was the beginning of the future. She tried to think of words to express this to Farley, but before she found them they were interrupted.

"Mommy, I'm hungry." Cindy stood in the kitchen doorway rubbing her eyes. Her blond hair was tousled and she was wearing furry pink slippers and a long nightgown with ruffles around the neck. The doctor had released both of them from the hospital after an overnight stay. Cindy's ailment was diagnosed as a brief bout of flu. By morning her fever and stomach pains were gone. She was as good as new, despite her ordeal. Farley arrived to take them home with an armload of parcels, new clothing he'd picked out for the two of them until Eve was able to shop.

Farley scooped Cindy into his arms. "Well, how's the princess this morning?"

"I'm hungry," Cindy said, giggling as he nuzzled her cheek.

"One princess breakfast coming up." He swung her high and landed her in her mother's lap.

"Let me fix it, Farley," Eve protested.

"I enjoy doing it, let me." He busied himself pouring orange juice and readying a pan and spoon to poach an egg. "Richard Max wants to see me at eleven today," he said.

Eve looked at him. "Is he upset about your leaving the conference?"

"Office scuttlebutt says he's going to offer me a partnership." He put the glass of juice in front of Cindy.

"Farley! That's wonderful!" Eve said.

He grinned. "Yeah."

"What's a partnership?" Cindy demanded.

"It's like getting promoted in school, princess," Farley said.

" 'Cuz you're big enough?"

He laughed. "Something like that." He stirred the boiling water and slid the egg into it gently. "How about you two dropping me off at the office so you can spend the morning shopping? Pick me up at one and I'll take you both out to lunch."

Eve hesitated, then smiled. If Farley had good news, she wanted to celebrate it with him. "We'd love to, wouldn't we, Cindy?"

Cindy nodded happily and sipped her orange juice.